BITS

&

PIECES

DAWN HOSMER

3rd edition
ISBN: 978-1-7374695-1-3 paperback

First Paperback edition: November 2018
Second paperback edition: September 2019
Third paperback edition: July 2021

Cover Design: Jordan Belcher & Jason Stokes
Interior Design: Nicole Scarano

For Gabriel, Jesi, Dominic, and Krsytyna

The best bits and pieces of my life.
You add color to my world everyday.

CHAPTER 1
4 YEARS EARLIER

The heat is stifling even though it's only early June, proving the forecasters' theories that this is going to be a year of record temperatures. The humidity is so thick in the air it smothers me as I complete my five-mile run across campus, my chestnut brown hair plastered to my back. Instead of heading home as I normally do when I'm this hot, sweaty, and exhausted, I stop at The Coffee Beanery to grab an iced coffee. Nothing sounds better than something cold to chill the steam rising inside of me, seeping out of every pore. A jolt of caffeine is a necessity to give me energy to make it through showering and my counseling session, which is sure to be a treat. I wish I had an IV drip of coffee to get me through talking about my childhood issues. I'll settle for a large iced one instead.

Only one person stands in line in front of me, a man who is taking his sweet time ordering as I drip with sweat despite standing directly under the air conditioning vent. Hopefully, the blast of air isn't spreading my pungent scent throughout the restaurant. The young woman behind the counter, *Alexis* according to her name tag, is trying her hardest to be patient as the man changes his order for the third time. She gives me a slight smile with raised eyebrows as the man counts out the change from his pocket, paying the entire ten dollar and fifty-two cent bill in coins. I smile back, glad that I don't have to deal with annoying customers all day. Since I've been waiting, a line has started to form behind me. The chatter of customers fills the air, along with the scent of heaven. Coffee.

Finally, the man steps aside, dropping change on the floor in the process. I wait to step forward until he's collected it all, not even bothering to look up to see the long line that's formed thanks to his lengthy ordering and clumsiness. I finally step to the counter, my breathing now returned to its normal rate since I've had plenty of time for my racing heart to calm.

"Hi! Sorry about your wait," Alexis says with a smile and jerks her head towards the man now standing at the other end of the counter. She has a pretty smile and the loveliest green eyes. "What can I get you?"

"No worries. Large, iced coffee, heavy on the cream, no sugar," I say and grab a napkin to wipe the sweat from my forehead.

"That'll be four fifty. Please tell me you're not paying in nickels," she laughs.

"No. Pennies, actually," I joke. "Just kidding. Credit card."

Usually, I'm more careful and have my gloves on when there's a risk of touching another person, even casually. But it was so hot out this morning and I had no plans to stop anywhere after my run. Today, my hands are bare. I don't even think about it until I give my card to Alexis and my hand brushes hers.

The restaurant, the chatter of customers, my own sense of self is drowned out by a flash of yellow, giving me a glimpse of the future awaiting Alexis. Most of the time, the effect of a flash doesn't come to me instantly but this time it does. I see her face wrenched in pain; her nose bloodied. Her beautiful green eyes wide open with a dead stare. Hands encircle her throat and a hammer rests on the ground beside her.

"Miss. Are you okay?" Her question snaps me back to the present.

I can't find my voice. I am afraid if I speak, the description of the horrific scene bombarding my mind will come spilling out of my mouth. Instead of risking that, I grab my credit card and run back out the door towards home, without my coffee.

I don't take the time to process any of it until I've slumped onto my sofa, back in the safety of my home. I hate these flashes. Glimpses of events that I have no power over consume me. I have no ability to make them turn out any differently. This one ranks up there with the most disturbing of them all. I don't know the details behind the visions in my mind—not the when, or the why, or the who. All I know for sure is that I have just witnessed the murder of poor Alexis.

CHAPTER 2
NOW

Today is the perfect autumn day with the scent of fall heavy in the air. The leaves are showing their colors much earlier this year due to early frost followed by a week of warm weather. Part of the reason I chose to live here is because of fall alone. Chandlersville is the perfect small town, resting lazily in the foothills of the Blue Ridge Mountains. Only twenty thousand permanent residents live here but it bustles with life whenever the students are in session at Cardell. A lot of residents complain about the students, but for me, they're part of the charm of living here. I love their fresh energy, their ambition for life, their belief that they can change the world. It is almost electrifying—I think it would be even if I were normal. Plus, the campus is beautiful with old brick buildings and sidewalks and towering trees tucked in the shadows of the mountain range looming overhead. You can feel the history traveling on the bricked walkways, as if the knowledge gained on these grounds throughout the years is trying to seep into anyone on its paths. Whenever I can, I take my morning run across campus so that I can hear the chatter of the students covering everything from the previous night's sexual encounters, to stress about upcoming exams, to their homesickness and desires to see their families. And since I'm running, my chances of touching anyone are remote, which is imperative for me to truly relax.

My other favorite thing to do here is to drive high into the mountains, along the winding roads of the Blue Ridge Parkway, and stop at various places along the way to hike, to take in the scenery, to smell the fresh mountain air. To enjoy the peace and solitude without encountering another person for miles. The view of the fall foliage is especially beautiful from the mountaintops. It's as if God has painted an immaculate portrait in the leaves of all the colors that ravage my soul. The only time I can envision God is when I think of Him as a painter, since that's the one way I've found to relieve myself of the burdens I carry deep within.

I moved here five years ago, when I was twenty-six. I had to get away from my parents, the hustle and bustle of the city, all the memories. I needed to figure out who I was. One thing about my gift is that I've accumulated so much from others over the years that I don't know what's really mine and what's someone else's. Some things I can trace back to a flash and know who it came from; other things aren't so clear. The questions bombard my mind almost every second of every day. I place an order for a latte and wonder if I even like coffee or if I picked that up somewhere along the way. I walk down the street and am drawn to something in the window of a shop, a piece of furniture or a knick-knack and I question whether the real Tessa likes it or if the pull of the item comes from elsewhere. Each time I get dressed, I have no idea whether the clothes hanging in my closet are my style or if I inherited my choice in fashion from some stranger. I cannot do anything, make any decision, without second guessing where it came from.

Five years ago was my breaking point. I'd had enough of my family and their attempts at fixing me. I'd reached my limit with the labels, the medications, the doctors, the hospitals, feeling like a freak. My parents protested but I was too close to losing it completely, and beyond caring what they thought anymore. They have never believed me anyway, always quick to medicate me or slap a diagnosis across my forehead. I would rather be alone than always be with people who think I'm insane, crazy, needing to be locked away. Maybe I am. I'm still trying to figure that one out.

I've found one other person that actually believes me, besides my brother, Cyle. Even though I must pay her to listen, it's a relief to have someone to dump all of this on. Her name is Ophelia, and she's my therapist. She teaches courses at Cardell in addition to having her full-time counseling practice. I've seen her regularly for the past four years. From the stories she tells, she's seen and heard a lot, so very little shocks her. She is the one who pushed me to pursue painting as a way to sort out everything and help me figure out who I am, saying that in art, the real "us" tends to come to the surface. I don't know if that's true, but painting is calming and gives me a place to leave all the junk swarming around inside of me.

I am meeting with her today for our weekly Monday morning appointment. As usual, I arrive ten minutes early so that I have time to relax before our session. An instant calmness washes over me when I enter the waiting room, which I'm sure was her goal in creating this space. The walls are painted a calming shade of aqua that reminds me of the waters off the coast of the Bahamas; a memory I picked up from someone, since I've never been there myself. Photographs fill the walls, with scenery ranging from sandy shores to mountaintops. Soothing music plays through the speakers with sounds of nature filling the room—the roar of the ocean waves, birds singing their melodies, a gentle mountain spring. Instead of your typical uncomfort-able seating found in most waiting areas, there are two plush sofas and matching side chairs. There have been days I've come here so heavy with exhaustion that I manage to sink into the sofa and drift off while I wait. I could live here in this waiting room. There are no magazines, no chit chat of other patients, only the serenity of the sounds, the smell of lavender, and the comfy couches. It's the most relaxing ten minutes of my week.

The time passes too quickly and the door to Ophelia's office opens. A scruffy man, probably in his early twenties, shuffles out with down-cast eyes and quickly makes his way out the door. The look on his face shows the pain that was dredged up in his session. I'm sure I've walked out that door looking the same way countless times, afraid to make eye contact with anyone for fear that they can see straight into my battered soul.

"Tessa. Give me a couple of minutes and I'll be ready for you," Ophelia says. As usual, her curly, dirty blonde hair looks unkempt but in an attractive way. She is dressed in her typical bohemian style with a loose-fitting muted brown, tie-dyed dress with a floral print jacket and earthy shoes. The scent of vanilla and cinnamon fills the room, instantly comforting me, as she shuts the door gently behind her.

I rest my head against the back of the sofa and take in the sounds of the ocean waves filling the room. After only a few short minutes, Ophelia opens the door again. "All set, Tessa. Come in and take a seat."

Her office is as inviting, if not more so, than the waiting room. There are many seating choices, seeming to cater to whatever mood her clients are in. Today I choose the overstuffed eggplant chair in the corner, facing the windows, trees filling the view outside. I wrap my legs up in the chair with me as Ophelia brings me a cup of coffee with just the right amount of cream, in a mug that fits my hands perfectly.

"So," Ophelia says as she sits in the leather chair across from me, "how are you feeling?"

"I'm fine," I say. I know that I better clarify before Ophelia reminds me what fine stands for (*Freaked Out, Insecure, Neurotic, and Emotional*) even though all could apply to me most days. "I'm happy that it's fall but I've been having some pretty bad days."

"Glad to see you finally learned not to stick with the fine answer," Ophelia laughs and picks up her notebook and pen. "Let's talk about the last week. Have you talked to anyone besides me?"

"Well, let's see," I raise my fingers as I list off the people I've spoken to. "The cashier at The Coffee Beanery a few times, and the one at the grocery. I've talked to Cyle once on the phone. I had to call the cable company as my internet was on the fritz, so that counts as someone, right? Ummm…let me see. I think that's it."

"We've talked about this. You cannot possibly have a happy, fulfilling life if you live in complete isolation. We all need other people."

Tears instantly fill my eyes. "I know. But I'm scared."

"Of?"

"You know. All the usual. Them getting to know me and thinking I'm a freak. Touching them. I don't even know who I am, so what in the world do I have to offer anyone?"

"Will you ever know unless you take the risk to find out?" Ophelia says. I grab my first tissue, feeling like my mother as I twist it in my hands after dabbing my eyes.

"You know I've tried. I always end up right back where I started. Alone. Where it's safe."

"Any flashes this week?"

"Only one. Of course, I think it was the only person I touched all week. It was a blue one, which I actually enjoyed." I go on to tell her about the incident in the checkout line at Sweeney's, the small market on the corner near my apartment.

I had a basket of groceries and was waiting in line behind a mother and her son who looked about four years old. He was begging his mom for a piece of candy as she was trying to load her groceries into the cart.

"Charlie, I've said no a thousand times. Put that candy bar back and don't ask again," she said, without even looking back in his direction, her patience for his whining wearing thin.

He tried with his chubby, little fingers to get the candy back in the holder but instead somehow managed to knock the whole box onto the floor. He looked back to me once it fell, his lower lip sticking out, about to burst into tears.

"Oh, Charlie. Ugh..." his mother said, trying to move the cart out of the way to get back to pick up the mess.

"It's okay. We've got it, don't we Charlie?" I said, stooping down to help him pick them up. He held the box, and I placed the candy bars back in it.

We were almost finished, and his mother was thanking me, when my hand brushed against Charlie's arm. A blue flash and then the memory of being thrown into the air by a father's big strong arms, high above his head. Memories of giggling so hard that my stomach hurt and begging to do it again as those same strong arms caught me, cradling me close. That quickly, I remembered what it felt like to be loved and protected by a father. I felt the joy at being young and finding pleasure in the simplest of things. I was so thankful for those spilled candy bars and little Charlie because it gave me another place to go back to when life is too overwhelming or scary. A happy memory. A place of security where I know someone will catch me as I fall.

"That memory is so comforting. The feel of that father's arms as he catches what feels like me. But like always, remembering this and feeling it so deeply just confuses me. Did I ever feel secure like that as a kid with my father? Or are all my feelings of safety from someone else, ones I've picked up over the years?" I say and grab another tissue.

"Well, let's look at that. I want you to close your eyes and picture your father," Ophelia says as I close my eyes and his face fills my mind. "Okay. Take a couple of deep breaths and then tell me about the memories you can find with his face in them."

The memories flood in, like water spilling over a dam. "The first one that comes to mind is a family dinner. We are all there, my brothers, my mother, my father, and me. Everyone's laughing and enjoying a good meal. I'm probably six or seven. The boys are all sharing stories of different adventures they had when they were younger. They were talking about a snow day off school when they built a huge snow fort and then had snowball fights all day while hidden behind the walls of their fortresses. Everyone was talking all at once and laughing until I added my memory of the day. I was hit in the nose so hard with a snowball that blood gushed from it and Mom thought it was broken. Then, dead silence around the table. My father forcefully pushed his chair back, stood up and said that he couldn't sit there and play my pretend games. He shouted that it was Christopher who'd been hit in the nose with the snowball, not me. Then, he left the room. We ate the rest of the dinner in silence. You see, I had not even been born yet when the snowball fight occurred. This must've been a memory I got from Chris, without even knowing it."

"What do you feel when you remember that instance?" Ophelia asks.

"Rejection, embarrassment, confusion, sadness," I say as tears spill out over my still closed eyelids. "My dad always thought I was crazy or playing mind games or something. Why can't he ever just believe me?"

Silence fills the room for so long that I finally open my eyes. Ophelia sits there, pen poised above her notebook, waiting on something from me.

"Why?" I ask again.

"Why do you think?"

"Because I'm a freak. Because this kind of stuff doesn't happen to normal people. Because it's easier to just say that I'm crazy than to believe I'm some kind of anomaly with this weird, unheard of special skill or ability," I gasp for a breath in between sobs.

"I would agree with some of what you say. First, you are not a freak. Secondly, you're right that this doesn't happen to a lot of people, maybe no one else, but that doesn't mean you're not normal. It's easier for people to assign a label or diagnosis to dismiss your ability rather than try to wrap their heads around something they just can't or won't understand," Ophelia pauses. "I'm sorry that your father didn't believe you."

"Or my mother, or my brothers except Cyle, or doctors, or my friends, or anyone. Most days, I don't even know what to believe myself."

"Isn't that why you're here? You'll probably never be able to figure out why others do the things they do, say the things they say, act the way they act. What you can do is try to figure out how to accept who you are. You can also learn how to stop applying the same labels to yourself that everyone else has over the years. I thought we were making some progress there."

"Yeah, me too. Guess not," I say as I tear apart tissue number three.

"We'll come back to the memories of your father. I think it's time for a change of subject. Tell me about your painting this week."

The tension in my shoulders relaxes at the suggestion of a new topic. "I've only worked on one thing. Not really sure what it is, or what it means, but there are a lot of reds, yellows and oranges."

"Hmmm…so it sounds like a lot of pain, the future, and bad memories. Anything come to mind while you've been working on it?"

"Nothing specific. Just random things that pop into my mind. Like a wedding. Tears. Intense pain in my abdomen. A funeral. I try not to focus on any one thing for too long, like we've talked about, so that I can just let it all flow freely. I'm curious to see what surfaces after I'm finished."

"I look forward to seeing it when you're done so we can talk about it," Ophelia says as she glances at her watch. "Okay, before our time is up for today, I want to give you an assignment for next week. In addition to working on your painting, I want you to be involved and interact with more people. Find one event to attend where you're forced to connect with others. I want you to have at least five conversations with new people in the next week. More than just a thank you at a restaurant. An actual conversation."

Panic immediately rises and tightens my chest. One is a stretch, but *five*?

Ophelia senses my anxiety. "They don't have to be long conversations, but you have to reach out. You don't have to touch anyone, just talk. Wear your gloves in case there's a handshake involved. You have to do this, Tessa. Everyone needs people. You really need to make a friend," she walks to her desk and grabs a pamphlet. "Here's a list of activities going on around campus this week. Find some things that interest you and try them out. You *will* be okay."

"I can't make any promises, but I will try," I say and take the pamphlet.

"Would you like a hug?" Ophelia asks as I stand to leave.

"Not today. I just can't do it today." I've had physical contact with Ophelia several times and only occasionally gotten a flash with her. Today I can't risk it since I already feel shaken enough with the memory of my father and my impending job for the week.

"I understand. I'll see you next week," Ophelia says and then as I'm about to step through the door, "Tessa, you'll be okay."

As I walk back into the fall day that was so beautiful before my appointment, now all I see around me are the reds, yellows and oranges in the autumn leaves, taunting me.

CHAPTER 3

I was five the first time I saw the red flash. I was in pre-school at Rosedale, a private upscale daycare that was supposedly getting me prepared for kindergarten. In reality, it was more like preparation for Harvard or Yale. All of us wore uniforms of burgundy polo shirts with the *Rosedale* logo and plaid skirts for the girls, khaki pants for the boys. As if the uniforms would make us more studious. We were five-year olds—we wanted to play. Rosedale, however, was not a place for play. It was a way to corral all of us and try to train us to be good followers, something that's never been my specialty. The only enjoyable part of our day there was "outdoor play" (God forbid they call it recess like any normal school might do)—the only time we were able to act like the screaming wild banshees that we were on the inside. The only time we could use our wild imaginations and "outdoor voices".

It was a sunny, spring day and the monkey bars felt warm to the touch as Josh and I swung across them. It was part of our adventure to avoid being consumed by the lava burning below. In our game, you drop, you die. Probably because I was raised in a house with three older brothers, I was a tomboy through and through, despite my mother's efforts to sissify me with pink ruffled dresses, sparkly shoes, and flowery hair ribbons. I wasn't like the other girls at school who wanted to pretend to be a fairy princess with a magic wand or sit under the "shade tent" and do girly things during outdoor play like color or make bracelets. I wanted to have adventures and be a pirate or an explorer or a ninja. Thus, it was always me and the boys. That day, it was Josh who was my best buddy because he was one of the few kids there who actually had an imagination and knew how to use it.

That day, Josh and I were doing our best to stay on the monkey bars because we didn't want to die in the lava, and we were being chased by aliens. We were moving as quickly as we could across them. I was in the lead and almost to the other side when Josh cried out. I turned to see he had fallen into the "lava" and was laying on the ground screaming in pain. Risking my own incineration, I dropped down and ran to him, reaching him before the teacher got there.

The only words he could say were "*my arm, my arm*" as tears raced down his cheeks. I knelt to comfort him. I put my arm around his shoulders and whoosh! The red flash. It filled my eyes, my ears, my mouth…I don't know how else to explain it, other than it devoured me. It only lasted a second, but that was all it took. Then came the pain. My right arm exploded above the wrist and below the elbow. My screams matched Josh's decibel for decibel. Both of us were screaming, writhing in pain and shouting about our injured arms. Miss Jenna, our teacher, reached us and didn't know who to help first since we were both in obvious distress.

Josh was the first to speak in a gasping, wailing moan. "I fell. My arm. I hurt my arm."

She helped him to his feet as I lay screaming and thrashing on the ground.

Miss Lori, the other outdoor monitor, came rushing over to whisk Josh inside to get help. Meanwhile, Miss Jenna leaned to help me up. The pain was so intense I couldn't get words to form. All I could do was hold my arm and scream, the ear-piercing shriek that only a five-year-old girl can muster. Miss Jenna rushed me indoors, away from all the traumatized children witnessing the whole debacle.

As we walked to the Director's office, Miss Jenna spoke calmly to me. "Tessa, how did you get hurt? I didn't see you fall. I saw Josh fall, but you're okay."

Finally, I found some words. "My arm. It hurts. I want my mommy. My arm." I wailed the remainder of the walk to the office.

Once there, the director, Mrs. Mason, tried to calm the two of us, while Miss Jenna called the ambulance and our mothers. By the time the ambulance arrived, Josh's arm was starting to turn black and blue and was bent at a strange angle. Mine showed nothing. It looked normal, but it didn't feel normal. The EMT's determined that Josh had a break and recommended that his mother get him to the ER immediately. Me, nothing. They said I was fine. They had no idea why I was so inconsolable and claiming to have pain.

Josh's mother had long ago come and gone by the time my mom arrived. Despite my continued crying, I overheard Mrs. Mason telling my mom that there was nothing wrong with me. She said the teachers witnessed the whole thing and that absolutely nothing happened to me to make me cry out like I was, to give me the pain I was claiming to feel. Even so, Mrs. Mason suggested I go home for the day since I was an absolute mess and wouldn't calm down.

My mother agreed and carried me to the car as I cried, wetting her perfectly styled hair with my tears. She strapped me in and headed towards home, much to her dismay, since I interrupted her tennis match at the club.

After about five minutes in the car of listening to me carry on, my mother turned to me and said, "You are fine. Quit being so dramatic. You aren't even hurt. You need to stop all that fussing and crying and be a big girl."

"But, Mommy, my arm…it hurts so—" I started to say.

"Hush now. You're fine. I don't want to hear another word about it."

I quieted my cries the best I could for the remainder of the ride even though the pain was still unbearable. I cried myself to sleep that night, unable to stop the throbbing. My mother made it clear that it was a topic that was not to be discussed. I didn't ever mention it to her again. She doesn't know that, to this day, when the weather changes, I still feel pain in the exact same spot where Josh's arm was broken so many years ago. It's my own internal barometer, letting me know when to expect rain.

I learned that day that red equals pain.

CHAPTER 4

I give myself a last once-over in my bedroom mirror before I head out the door. I haven't been this dressed up in forever. It's been a long time since I've had a reason to dress up at all.

As part of my assignment from Ophelia, I've decided to attend the fall performance of the Cardell University symphony. I've done a good job at masking what a nervous wreck I am on the inside, feeling like a million butterflies are working their way up from my stomach into my throat. I have chosen a little black dress with black satin opera-length gloves. I figure I can count this one event as fulfilling at least two of my required five interactions for the week since I had to go to *Chauncey*'s, an upscale boutique in town, to choose an outfit for tonight. My trip there required interaction with two different saleswomen and another customer who felt the need to comment on my selections, not that her opinion was invited. One of the saleswomen—Bobbie according to her nametag—tried to convince me that gloves were out of style and didn't complement my outfit well. She went on and on, until I finally shut her down by telling her I always wear gloves, so she could either help me pick a pair that would go with the dress I'd chosen, or I'd wear the pink leather ones I had worn in the shop that day. I had only one moment of panic when Bobbie's hand brushed mine as she was handing me my bag. No flash came, though, which was a relief.

Other than the fact that I'll be around people, I'm looking forward to tonight's performance. I haven't been to a symphony since I was in my early teens and forced to go by my parents. I have come to love classical music as an adult, though, and especially enjoy the melancholy sound of the cello which seems to best reflect the general state of my life. I've always been somewhat envious of those with musical abilities, which I definitely have *not* been gifted with. I think playing an instrument would be a great way to release the sadness, fear, anxiety, confusion, and pain that well up inside. I'd much prefer to listen to the music in the comfort of my own apartment instead of in the midst of hundreds of other people. But I'm doing it regardless of how I feel. I trust that Ophelia has my best interests at heart, even though it scares the crap out of me. I purposefully reserved an aisle seat so that I can arrive at the last moment and slip in unnoticed, untouched.

With only twenty minutes until opening curtain, I rush out the door and head towards the concert hall as quickly as I can in heels. It's only six-forty but night has already consumed the world. The only downside of fall is how quickly evening comes. My body usually goes into hibernation mode this time of year and I end up in bed by ten o'clock most nights. Once spring rolls around again, my night owl ways return, and I must force myself to bed at midnight.

My plan works. I slide into seat 6A just as the lights dim without having to interact with anyone other than the usher who pointed me in the right direction. I'm anxious to sit back and let the peaceful sounds overtake me.

For the next hour, the mournful sound of the cello makes my heart ache for my family. I don't miss them often, but the music fills me for yearning for my parents, my brothers. The lively upbeat songs bring back memories of childhood and summer days spent lounging by the pool with Polly. I completely lose myself in the music and memories, some mine and some from others, until intermission is announced. *Damn!* I had forgotten about intermission. Panic instantly swells in my chest. I rise immediately in the attempt to rush out before everyone else, but others must have been planning the same because soon I am met with wall-to-wall people. Were it not for the crowd pushing me forward, I would've been immobilized by my fear.

Even though I have my gloves on, I am assaulted by flashes, so rapid fire that I almost lose my balance. Red. Blue. Purple. Yellow. Another Yellow. Orange. I sway on my feet, feeling like I'm about to pass out when a hand gently grabs my arm and steers me through the crowd, out into the foyer. After I slump back into a plush, red velvet chair, I finally get a glimpse of the man attached to the hand that saved me. He is something to look at.

"Are you okay?" He says, stooping down so that he's eye level with me.

"Umm...not really. I'm a little light-headed.," I say as I study this man's face, taken aback at how handsome he is. Dark toffee brown, wavy hair. Dark brown, almost black eyes. A goatee with a little five o'clock shadow on his cheeks. It's been a long time since I've been this close to a man, let alone one that is handsome. My heart starts to race.

"I hope I didn't scare you, but you started to sway on your feet a little back there. I thought you were going to pass out. And then, you surely would've been trampled by all these crazy symphony people," he smiles—*what a nice smile it is, too*—and extends his hand. "I'm Jonas."

Even though I usually avoid doing so at all cost, I reach my hand forward to meet his, hoping the glove does the trick. "I'm Tessa. Thank you so much for your help. I would've hated to meet my death on the floor of the symphony hall."

"Nice to meet you. Is there someone I can go get for you?" As soon as I tell him I'm alone, he continues. "Do you need some help getting back in there? Or do you want to sit here for a bit? Or, we could go to the café next door and have a cup of coffee or glass of wine."

Oh, how I want to say yes to his last offer, but intense fear paralyzes me. He must be able to see it all over my face.

He clears his throat. "I'm sorry if that was too forward. I can just leave you alone if you want. Or stay here with you. Or whatever. I'm rambling." Jonas' cheeks redden with a blush.

Before I have time to think of all the reasons why I shouldn't, I blurt out. "I'd love a glass of wine. I think it's exactly what I need."

"Alright then, let's go. Between you and me, they weren't that good anyway." He winks and holds my arm as I stand. Again, no flash. So far, so good.

Filled with fear, anxiety, hope, excitement, dread, and curiosity, we walk over to *Monticello's* for our glass of wine.

~

ONE GLASS of wine turns into two and a three-hour conversation. I don't know if it's possible to happen so quickly, but I think I'm in love. Okay, maybe not *in love*, but definitely very attracted to and intrigued by this guy.

Jonas McCafferty is his full name, and he is also thirty-one. He's an Associate Professor in the English Department at Cardell. He completed his Ph.D. here and stayed because he loves the area so much. He's originally from Tucson, Arizona and said that he had to get somewhere with a color besides brown which is one of the things he loves about this area. The conversation comes easily, with hardly a moment of silence between us. I tell him more about myself than I've told anyone, other than Ophelia, in years. He expresses interest in seeing my paintings sometime and recommends several novels he thinks I may enjoy reading. I love seeing the passion rise in him when he talks about certain books, some of his students, his desire to seek tenure here and make this his permanent home. Better yet is that we seem to share a sense of humor, dry and sarcastic.

Monticello's closes at eleven and he offers to walk me home. As much as I want to say yes, I can't. Home means possibly inviting him in. Inviting him in means getting more relaxed and removing my gloves. Removing my gloves means a greater likelihood of flashes, not that they prevented them in the theatre. I like him way too much so far to have a flash with him. I want to get to know him the good old-fashioned way—by talking. I assure him repeatedly that I'll be safe, and finally he agrees to let me go my own way. We exchange numbers and he says he'll be in touch as he hugs me good night. I feel so safe wrapped in his muscular arms. I had forgotten how good physical contact could feel and how much I've missed it.

The evening was so enjoyable, I'd forgotten about being bombarded by the flashes, until I'm home. As I sit alone in the dark on my couch, I reflect on the events of the night. As far as I can tell, there is nothing discernibly different about me so far as a result of the flashes. As always, the colors will reveal themselves when they are ready, consuming more of me than I've already lost.

As I head to bed, I choose, for the first time in a long time, to focus not on what I've potentially lost of myself, or fear what I've gained through the flashes. I choose to smile and enjoy the memories of my evening with Jonas, looking forward to the possibility of seeing him again.

CHAPTER 5

I was nine when I learned French. I don't mean I took French classes or lessons and slowly learned the language. I learned it overnight. Like, went to bed one night knowing nothing other than English and how to count to ten in Spanish, to *knowing* French. Understanding it. Speaking it. *Knowing* it.

My parents and I were on vacation as recommended by my counselor. Counselor number two, in fact—Amber Coughlin. I remember her well. She was in her mid-twenties, fresh out of college, and still overly excited to try to fix all the broken people of the world. She was intrigued by me, but at the same time I think a little scared because she didn't understand me or have the slightest clue about how to fix me. The conversation preceding the vacation was quite telling of what Miss Amber Coughlin thought about me and what my magical fix would be.

"Mr. and Mrs. Cantnor, thanks for joining us today. Tessa and I have really enjoyed our visits the last couple of months," she paused waiting for some form of acknowledgement from me. A little smile was all I could muster. Mom was already crying and tearing her tissue apart, sitting on the couch next to my father. "As Tessa and I have discussed, the things she and I talk about remain confidential unless she is a harm to herself or others, or she gives her permission. We agreed that I could discuss the things I'm going to share with you today."

At age nine, I was already cynical enough to be ready to burst out laughing at what would spill out of her mouth. I couldn't wait to hear her interpretation.

"As you know, Tessa has been having difficulties making friends, with school, with the two of you. Your chief concern when you brought her to me is that she isolates, seems depressed and that when she does come out of her shell enough to interact, she doesn't ever want to be touched. Are we on the same page?"

"She just doesn't seem like a normal nine-year-old. She always seems so sad," my mother adds while dabbing her eyes with tissue number two.

"And her stubbornness. She refuses to do anything we suggest or even demand, for that matter. She lives in her own world where she's the queen, and she doesn't think she needs to listen to anybody about anything," Dad said with a glower in my direction. Like my issues were all a big power struggle.

"We've touched on each of these things during our sessions. I'm not going to share all the details with you, rather my interpretation of them. Bottom line, Tessa is seeking attention. Specifically, your attention." I had to clamp my mouth shut to keep myself from laughing or shouting out. Did this woman not hear them, not hear *me*? The last thing I wanted or needed was attention. I got enough of that. I just wanted to be left alone to play, to read, to watch TV, to be me. Really, I would've loved to be able to stay me *and* be with other people. That's what I had hoped Miss Amber could help me figure out how to do. "Charles, you work a lot and from the sounds of it, it has become more frequent that you stay away from home for days at a time."

"I hope you're not trying to pin her behavior problem on me. Yes, I work a lot because I have an important job that requires that of me. I make a good living, one that affords Tessa a very good lifestyle," Dad said with his chest puffed out like he was prepared for a good knock-down, drag out.

"No need to get defensive, Mr. Cantnor. I'm just sharing some things I've learned and my interpretation of those details. It's what you're paying me for. I need to be able to share without worrying that I'm offending you."

"I understand. Please continue," Dad said, slumping back against the couch.

Defeated by Amber. One point for her.

"And, Catherine, you've had to pick up a lot of the slack around the home and family because Charles is often gone." The *slack* around the house—who was this woman and had she heard a word I said? Manicures, pedicures, hair appointments, tennis, wine dates with her friends, volunteering at the church. These things had nothing to do with my father being gone. She'd do the exact same thing whether he was home or not. "Tessa has to spend a lot of time alone. Even though she has three brothers, she is essentially like an only child since they are so much older and only home occasionally. And Charles, with you working all the time and Catherine, you busy taking care of the home, Tessa has learned to compensate by isolating."

Oh, I had learned to compensate by isolating. *Bingo!* She finally got something right. But I wasn't compensating for my parent's lack of attention. I was trying to stay me. Mom grabbed another tissue—number four.

"My first recommendation is that you take a family vacation…just the three of you. Go somewhere fun, laugh, spend time together, uninterrupted by work or the demands of everyday life. I think that you should all sit down together and plan it, each of you having input on the final destination." The tightness in my chest instantly crushed me. Vacation meant airplane. Airplane meant close quarters with lots of people. Lots of people meant lots of flashes. Lots of flashes meant loss of Tessa.

"But school—" I started to say, trying to squash the idea before it had a chance to fully form.

"You know, I think you're right, that's exactly what we need. Don't you think Catherine?" Dad said with a smile. A vacation he could do. That was an easy fix, something within his power to control.

"I think it would do all of us a world of good. We don't get much time together," Mom added, with no tears for once. "Even the planning sounds fun, doesn't it, Tess?"

There was no point disagreeing. They were sold on the idea; therefore, it was going to happen. Any protesting I did would just be proof of my rebellion, my attention seeking, my "issues". So, ignoring the crushing anxiety in my chest, I nodded and tried to force a smile. I'm fairly certain it came out more like a smirk.

That is how we ended up in Florida at Disney World and I learned French.

I managed to avoid touching anyone in the airport, on the plane, and for the first couple of days at Disney other than the occasional bumps into others as we waited in line. The trip was fun—it was nice to be with both of my parents and see them smile and laugh, the concerned looks on their faces gone for a while. They actually seemed younger when their faces weren't scrunched up with worry.

On our third day, it was time for us to visit Epcot, the part of the trip I was looking most forward to. I couldn't wait to visit all the mini "countries" and collect memorabilia from each. We got an early start that day to make sure we had time to make it through the entire park. Our day started in Norway where we had breakfast with the princesses. I was enamored with their beauty, even though I still wasn't into the whole princess, girly thing. Princess Jasmine was the one who "taught" me French. She was always my favorite, and I couldn't resist getting my picture taken with her. We posed for the picture, me smiling and giddy, without incident.

Afterwards, she took my hand in hers and said in a heavy accent, "You're a beautiful young princess, Tessa."

The moment our hands connected, the purple flash. I had experienced purple before and knew that it didn't cause any pain or sadness, but I wasn't quite sure what it did bring. It was later that day that I realized what "gift" came with it. It was evening, and the air had a chill. I didn't realize I was shivering until Mom asked if I was okay.

"Bien, merci. Je suis juste froid. Pouvons-nous acheter un sweatshirt?" I said. You would have thought I just told my parents to "f" off and die, the way they both looked at me, mouths gaping open.

"Wh-what did you say?" Dad asked. I had no idea why he was looking at me with his brow furrowed and stuttering over his words.

"Je suis froid. J'ai besoin d'une veste ou quelque chose." I said, puzzled as to why he didn't seem to understand what I was saying.

"Tessa, why are you speaking French? Where did you even learn French?" Mom asked.

I didn't even realize that I was speaking anything other than English. With great concentration so that I made sure I was using the correct language, I tried to explain. "It must've been Princess Jasmine. When she took my hand, I saw a purple flash. She must be French and that's how I got it. Wow! Comment cool. Je parle français."

The smiles and laughter instantly left my parents; their worry-lined faces had returned. I didn't understand why they were so concerned. Most kids must take years of a foreign language before they understand it. I got it in a second. They should be proud of me, not looking at me like I just grew two heads.

Mother announced that it was time to leave, even though we hadn't made it all the way through Epcot. I was disappointed, but excited about my newfound ability. The entire way to the car I chattered away in French, which came as easily and naturally to me as English. My parents were silent the entire ride back to the hotel, where they insisted I immediately go to bed. I heard them up talking late into the night. The next morning, they announced that our trip had been cut short and we were going home. I was devastated—we were supposed to have four more days. They wouldn't give me a clear answer as to why, only saying we needed to get home. To punish them, I purposefully spoke only French the rest of the day and pretended I couldn't understand any English. Seeing their faces cringe in embarrassment as I "couldn't understand" the flight attendant or the ticketing agent was priceless. I pretended not to understand their threats of being punished, losing privileges, never taking a trip again. Why couldn't they just ever be happy for me? What was so terrible about speaking French?

They never asked any additional questions about the incident but as soon as we got home, I was scheduled for medical testing, MRIs, bloodwork, countless doctor's visits. Just like my parents to leave it to the professionals to ask the questions. I was eventually diagnosed with a bizarre case of "Foreign Accent Syndrome", even though they could find no evidence of any physical changes in me, like a stroke or tumor.

No one seemed to hear me or believe me when I explained how it happened with Jasmine, seeing the purple flash. It was all evidence to the doctors and my parents that something had happened with me neurologically. They chalked up the flash of light I kept referring to as an indicator of ocular migraines. I was given a prescription for migraine medication to take any time I experienced flashing lights.

But what did they know? Purple flashes were awesome.

CHAPTER 6

After the fourth chime from my phone indicating texts coming through, I finally reach over and grab it off the nightstand. *Who is texting me before seven in the morning? And so incessantly, at that?*

Before I can even swipe my phone to unlock it, a craving for a cigarette hits me. *What?* I'm not a smoker. I've had one cigarette in my entire life, and it made me so sick that I've never had the desire to have another. Now, though, my entire body is screaming for one, telling me it's necessary before I do *anything*; before I can function at all.

This is ridiculous. My body is trying to convince me I'm a nicotine fiend when I *know* I'm not. Then, I remember last night's flashes. Who knows which color this one came from? I've never acquired an addiction from someone before now. But, no doubt, that's what this is, a full-blown addiction, developed in an instant.

Lucky me. Something to add to my memory box, I guess.

There are four texts from the same number, 718-5543, one with no contact name attached. It only takes me a moment to figure it out though.

The first text at six-thirty reads:

Good morning! Just wanted to say how much I enjoyed our evening. Hope we can talk soon.

Second one at six thirty-two:

This is Jonas by the way.

Third at six thirty-four:

Thought I should clarify in case you have a whole slew of men texting you about what a great time they had with you last night. LOL

Fourth at six forty-five, the one that finally woke me enough to check:

I'm really sorry. I just realized that you probably aren't even up yet. Hope I didn't wake you. I have an 8am class or I'd still be asleep myself. Sorry, sorry, sorry. Don't hold it against me. Last one, promise. If you're awake, go back to sleep, which I hope you are still asleep. I'm rambling again. Call or text later, please.

A smile works its way across my face as I read his messages. I'm touched that he thought of me first thing in the morning and obviously enjoyed our evening together as much as I did. He also must've paid enough attention to our conversation to know that I hate mornings and only get up before eight when it's absolutely necessary, which, *thank God*, isn't often. And he obviously gets a little nervous with me, enough to make him babble in a text. I figure that has to be a good sign when an English Professor, master of words, rambles with nervousness.

I text back.

Good morning back to you! Although the word 'good' doesn't really go with this time of

*morning for me. Hopefully you will get
yourself under control before class because
no one wants a babbling English Professor.
Lol*

And then I add a second one.

*And I agree, last night was wonderful. We
need to do it again soon. Call when you get
a break. I'm awake NOW so I'm off to make
coffee.*

And a third.

*A glass of wine will help me forgive you for
this early awakening.*

Now that I'm wide awake and swooning, I really do need some coffee—and a cigarette, apparently—so I throw on my robe and head to the kitchen, grabbing my box along the way. It's been a while since I've had to add anything to it and even longer since I've taken anything out to look at it in an attempt to figure it out. The last time I really examined the contents was during a session with Ophelia back when we first started meeting. She keeps pressuring me to bring it in again so that we can work through some of the things in there, but somehow, I keep "forgetting" to do so.

The things in this box scare me, that is why they're locked up. This box holds the parts of me I have acquired that I want nothing to do with, that I desperately wish I could erase. Putting things inside is one way to make sure I remember that some of the things I acquire— memories, feelings, addictions apparently—are definitely not me. In my quest to figure myself out, remembering who I am *not* helps me determine who I am. It holds the scary parts of having these flashes, the ones that make me feel out of control. That's why this craving for a cigarette needs to be written down and put in there immediately. God knows I'm enough of a mess, I really don't need to add smoking to the list of ways I'm screwed up.

I start a pot of coffee brewing and grab a piece of paper and pen. I write down today's date, October 18, 2014, and *I'm a smoker who wants a cigarette before my feet even hit the floor in the morning.* As usual, I then write a brief description of where I think this may have come from and what flash of color was associated with it. Even after replaying last night's tidal wave of flashes, I have no idea which one to trace it back to. There was a red—is this nicotine addiction pain? Well, possibly, because my body really thinks it needs some, which isn't too terribly comfortable. There were two yellow flashes so maybe someone in their future is going to become a smoker? I jot all of this down and have to walk away to grab a cup of coffee which will hopefully help clear my head. No wonder I feel half-crazy most of the time. This is impossible to figure out and it's *my* life.

A shudder works its way through me as I think of Jonas. How can I ever have a real relationship with anyone and expect them to understand any of this when it doesn't even make sense to me? I shouldn't pursue things with Jonas any further because eventually I will have a flash with him, too. I've had them with everyone close to me. If we form a relationship, at some point I will have to open up enough to share my story with him, at least the truth as I understand it. When there have only been two people in my life that accept what I'm telling them as reality, what are the chances that I'll find another? Slim to none.

My phone rings and Cyle's face and number show up.

"Good morning, my favorite brother," I say.

"Well, aren't you chipper this morning?" Cyle chuckles.

"I am chipper. Thanks for noticing."

"So, do tell. Why are you up *and* so cheerful sounding this early?"

"I'm offended. You make it seem like I'm a slacker that sleeps all day and is a grump most of the time," I respond. "Actually, the phone woke me up early this morning and apparently I'm a nicotine fiend now, so my intense cravings forced me to get out of bed."

"Tell me you're not smoking because that's the last thing you need."

"No, Daddy Cyle, I'm not smoking. Just finished writing it down and putting it in my box. But I gotta tell you, this craving for a cigarette really sucks."

"But you can't act on it. Where'd this one come from? I assume that if you had a flash that means you've been out and interacting with people."

"Actually, yes. You would be proud of me. As part of my assignment from Ophelia, I went to the symphony last night, which was great. I timed everything perfectly, so I could arrive just as the performance was starting. Too bad I forgot about the intermission rush where I was bombarded with flashes. There were so many, Cyle. I felt like I was going to pass out, and a handsome gentleman named Jonas came to my rescue. He helped me find a seat to get my bearings," a smile spreads across my face as I continue. "Then, we chatted for a while and went to the café next door for a glass of wine and to talk. We stayed for three hours, and it was wonderful. Actually, his texts are what woke me up this morning."

"Well, that explains the good mood. I'm proud of you, Tess. You haven't sounded this happy in a long time. You must like this guy," Cyle says, and I can tell he's smiling.

"I do. He's an English Professor and seems like a caring, interesting guy. I'm scared though. You know I don't like letting people in." Tears fill my eyes as I get real with him.

"I know and totally get it. You have good reasons for all the walls you have but they also keep you from ever feeling loved, accepted. Ya know?"

"Now you sound like Ophelia."

"I'm sorry, not trying to preach, but it's true. I want you to be okay, feel loved, have someone to take care of you and love you for who you are. You deserve to be happy."

There's a pause in conversation as the tears flow down my cheeks and Cyle takes a deep breath. *Why the hell do I always end up crying when I talk to Cyle and Ophelia?* Good thing they know what a mess I am.

"I love you. Thank you. Now, why are you calling so early?" I ask.

"Well, did Mom call you?" Cyle asks.

"Seriously? Does Mom ever call me?" I respond.

"Yeah well, I always hope she'll become the person she pretends to be and become a good mother to *all* her children. Wishful thinking, I know. Anyway, Dad's sick. Like, really sick."

My heart starts to race. "What's going on?"

"Apparently he collapsed last night on the way to bed and fell down almost the whole flight of stairs. Mom couldn't get him to wake up, so she called 911. It seems he's had a massive stroke and hasn't regained consciousness yet. They're not sure if he's going to make it, and if he does, what kind of shape he'll be in."

"Wow. That's awful." My mouth instantly goes dry, and my chest tightens. "How's Mom holding up? Are you heading up there?"

"I'm actually on my way now. Cory and Michelle got there last night. No one can reach Chris of course. He went to Belize for one of his trips with his buddies and either doesn't have service or is ignoring the calls. Typical Chris."

Anger overwhelms me. How could my own mother not even bother to call me herself? Or Cory for that matter? What the hell? I'm torn. Part of me wants to throw on clothes and book the next flight to New York. The other part of me says that I'm not wanted or needed, so why bother? I tell Cyle how I'm feeling.

"You need to do what you're comfortable with. I understand if you don't come but I also get why you may need to. Regardless, you need to know what's going on. I would've called last night but I guess I was hopeful that you'd hear from Mom, plus it was pretty late."

"You always keep that hope that she'll be the same Mom to me that she is to the rest of you. It's never going to happen. Anyway, I don't know what to do. I need to think about it. Will you call me when you get there, and I'll let you know what I've decided?" I pace, holding my coffee in one hand, phone in the other.

"Yeah. I'll call once I see what shape he's in. That may help you make your decision," Cyle pauses. "Okay, sis, gotta run. I love you."

"I love you, too. Be safe."

I hang up and toss the phone onto my table, feeling like I have been punched in the gut. Tension tightens my neck as my mind tries to process the fact that my dad could be dying. My dad, the man who was supposed to love me and convince me that I'm a wonderful woman, deserving of respect. The one who never showed anything for me but contempt, disgust, embarrassment, and shame. And my mom. Why the hell wouldn't she pick up the phone and call me? I know she's mad at me for leaving like I did, but this is a life and death matter, one you put aside your hurt feelings about and pick up the phone anyway. Did she tell Cory not to call, or has he been sucked into her lies so much that he doesn't consider me part of the family anymore, either? Do I even care that my dad's possibly dying because I'll miss him, or because I'll miss the idea of who he should've been to me?

I can't sort out the swarm of emotions flooding my mind, so I do the one thing I know to do. I pick up the phone and leave a message for Ophelia.

IT TAKES LESS than an hour for Ophelia to return my call. In the four years I've been seeing her, I've only used her emergency number a handful of times, so she knew to take my message seriously.

While I waited on her call, I started packing a suitcase, just in case I decided to head to New York. I weighed my options as I packed each article of clothing. I packed the black pencil skirt and decided I should go because it's the right thing to do since he's my father. I put the purple sheer button-up blouse folded neatly on top of the skirt and settled on not going because neither my mother nor father particularly care if I show up; they haven't bothered to come visit once since I moved here, nor have they made any efforts at maintaining a relationship with me beyond the monthly deposit into my bank account to pay my expenses. On that note, I decided, as I threw in five pair of underwear, I owed it to them to go, since their money keeps me fed, housed, and clothed. But then I changed my mind as I threw in several pairs of gloves. I don't owe them anything, it's their gene pools that created me and whatever weird abilities that keep me from being able to function in the real world and have a job, relationships, a normal life. They owe me every penny they've given me for the torture I've endured for years in their efforts to cure me.

By the time my cell rings, my mind is a complete and utter jumbled mess. I am no longer packing, rather just sitting on the bed next to my suitcase staring off into the distance as my thoughts assault me.

"Ophelia," my voice shakes as I answer.

"Tessa, sorry it took so long to get back to you. What's going on?"

I quickly rattle off the details as given to me by Cyle, and then start to explain my predicament.

Ophelia interrupts my tirade. "Why don't you meet me at the office in twenty minutes, so we can talk this through? It sounds like you're not thinking too clearly right now, and I don't want you to make a rash decision."

"Okay. I'll be there," I say, and my shoulders relax with relief, knowing that I can put off this decision for at least a little while longer.

As soon as the call ends a text from Jonas comes through.

How about that glass of wine tonight? Along with dinner at 7 at Sylvia's?

It sounds like the best option by far. A smile spreads across my face, breaking some of the worry that has started to settle in its creases.

Sounds fantastic. I would love to say yes but can I let you know for sure in a bit? Family emergency and I'm not sure if I'll be in town.

I no sooner hit send than my phone rings. It's Jonas.

"Hey Tess. Sorry to bug you, but is everything okay?"

His voice brings immediate comfort. The fact that he called instead of just texting touches my heart. "I'm not sure. My dad apparently had a stroke and is in the hospital in New York. I'm waiting on an update from my brother before I decide what I'm doing."

"Oh my god. I'm so sorry. How bad is he?" Worry is evident in his voice.

"I'm not really sure yet, which is why I'm kind of at a standstill on my decision about going."

"It sounds like you need to be there. Can I do anything to help?"

I don't know how to respond to this for several reasons. I don't want to dump any of my family drama, why this decision is such a hard one to make, onto him so soon after meeting each other. And, I've had very few people in my life that I can count on to help me, so his offer touches me, scares me, and amazes me all at the same time. "Well, let's just say it's all kind of complicated. Can I get back with you after I hear from my brother?"

"Of course. Let me know as soon as you hear and please let me help with whatever you need."

"Thank you. You have no idea how much your offer means," I pause as tears fill my eyes. "I'm pretty stressed and not sure what the right thing to do is, but I'll let you know once I figure it out. What sounds the best to me is that dinner and wine, but…"

"No pressure here. Just keep me posted," he says.

"Will do. We'll talk soon."

I grab my purse, throw on a coat and pair of gloves, and head across campus to meet with Ophelia. The entire walk there I replay the conversation with Jonas, which is a nice escape from thinking about my dad and right choices, wrong choices, my mother, my family. I don't even realize what a complete distraction Jonas has been until I catch Ophelia outside of her office, just unlocking the outer door as I walk up.

"Well, that's certainly not what I expected to see. A smile?" Ophelia says.

I guess I am smiling. Ophelia probably hasn't seen that on me too often. "There's a story to go with it. Trust me, there's lots of other stuff going on in this head of mine. But yes, a smile. Strange, huh?"

"Let's get in here and we can sort through some of that stuff, okay?" She says as she opens the door to her office, and I immediately head to my favorite chair. "Coffee?"

"No thanks. I won't take up too much of your time. I know you don't usually work on Saturdays."

Ophelia takes a seat in the chair opposite me. "So, your father had a stroke."

"I guess so. That's what Cyle said, anyway. He's on his way there. Cory and his wife are there, too. Chris is off gallivanting somewhere as usual. I don't know what to do. My mom didn't even call to tell me." I spill it all out without taking a breath.

"Let's take this one step at a time, okay?" Ophelia asks. "First, do you have any updates on your dad's condition? Do you know how serious it is?"

"No, I'm waiting on Cyle to call. He said he'll let me know as soon as possible."

"Okay, so it sounds like the first step should be waiting on an update before you make any decisions. Do you agree?"

I take a deep breath. Of course, this makes perfect sense. My mom has a flair for dramatics. Dad could be perfectly fine and what she called a stroke could be nothing more than a headache. "Yes."

"Let's talk through this some more, though. You said your mom didn't call you. How do you feel about that?"

"I'm pissed. How dare she? She acts like I'm not even a part of the family, like I wouldn't care that my dad is sick and in the hospital. She acts like I have done something wrong. Something to disown them, rather than the reality of them disowning me."

"We've talked a lot about how anger is a secondary emotion. What's going on beneath the anger? What feelings are there?"

"Hurt, inadequacy, rejection, sadness. You know, all the usual when it comes to my parents," I say as I try desperately to choke back the tears welling in my eyes.

"Talk more about those feelings," Ophelia says. I hate it when she makes me go deeper.

It's so much easier just being pissed.

I grab a tissue, knowing that there will be no way to keep the tears at bay once I begin. "Why doesn't she want me there? I mean, hell, she even tried to call Chris who has made it clear over the years that family is at the absolute bottom of his list of priorities. Why is Chris more accepted than I am? He's the complete opposite of everything my family represents, off exploring jungles and rainforests and fighting to save the whales. I mean, I know I'm not normal, but hell, neither is he according to my parent's standards."

I wipe the tears from my cheeks and continue as Ophelia sits, waiting. She knows once I get started, it's hard for me to stop. "I feel like she thinks I'm this horrible, awful person that wouldn't even care if my father died. That's not true. I do care. I love my dad. Yes, he's done and said lots of really hurtful, crappy, awful things to me over the years. But, he's my dad. I still remember lots of good about him, too, regardless of what our relationship is like now."

The tears flow freely now as I think back to some of my better memories with him. When I was young, and he'd take me to the park to play soccer or push me on the swings. When he'd see a good test score and tell me what a smart girl I was. When he'd help me ride the waves on beach vacations. When he'd hold me on his lap, reading my favorite book to me as I drifted off to sleep.

"What are you thinking of, Tessa?"

"Happier times with him. Times when I felt like he loved me." I'm onto tissue number two. "I wish I still felt like he did. The biggest part of me wonders if Mom didn't call me to come because my father wouldn't want me there and she knows it. He doesn't love me anymore. I have no doubt about that. But I still love him. If for nothing more than the father he used to be."

"You may never know the why behind your parents' actions. I do think this has raised a lot of things that we need to work through in future sessions. But I think today, the important thing is deciding what you want to do. Let's talk through some scenarios, okay?"

"Okay," I say, happy to change the subject away from all of these feelings.

"Let's say Cyle tells you he's stable, or things aren't as bad as they initially thought. What do you think you should do? Tell me the first thing that comes to your mind."

"In that case, stay here," I say without hesitation.

"Okay, you find out that he's not well and may not have long, then what? Remember, no thinking, just answer." Ophelia leans forward in her seat and rests her elbows on her knees.

"Then, I go." Tension instantly creeps up my neck, to my temples and a million emotions rise as I answer, but I know this is the answer I want and need to give.

"Okay. It sounds like you know what to do if you can get the emotions out of the way. I'm not saying that it's easy, but you can do whatever it is you need to, and we can deal with the emotions later," Ophelia says. "So, we have a plan then?"

"Yes. I'll wait to hear from Cyle. If Dad is stable or not so bad off, I'll stay here. If things don't look good, I'll go. Can I leave a message for you once I decide?" I say.

"Of course. And, if you do end up going and need to talk, you know how to reach me. I'll make sure to get back with you as soon as I possibly can."

Knowing this is true sends a wave of relief washing over me. "Now, before you go, tell me what that huge smile was about when you first got here," Ophelia says, leaning back with a smile.

A grin spreads across my face as I tell her all about the symphony and Jonas. "I'm so proud of you. If you don't end up going, are you going to keep that dinner date, then?"

"Of course. I'm hoping that even if I do have to go to New York, that dinner invite will come with a rain check."

"I can't wait to hear all about it on Monday if you're here. If not, as soon as you're back," Ophelia says as she opens her arms for a hug, eyebrows raised to see if I'm willing.

"What the heck?" I say and lean into her embrace. A blue flash. Oh well, blue I can do—good memories are always welcome. I can't wait to figure out what's been added to my repertoire. Only time will tell.

As I walk back to my apartment to wait on Cyle's call, the biggest thing on my mind is how badly I want a cigarette.

CHAPTER 7

Cyle is the only person in the world that I trust completely. He's the one that I can confide in about all the things I've seen and who I've become. He's seen the way the flashes have changed me throughout the years. He actually believes me and always tries to help me make sense of it all. He's helped me fill in the blanks in my early childhood, objectively, without applying labels to me like my parents and other brothers.

Two days before Christmas, the year I was twelve, Cyle came to my room to have a real heart to heart talk about what was going on with me. I, as usual, was trying to exclude myself from the festivities going on below—some over the top Christmas party my parents were throwing for their closest hundred friends and associates. The whole ordeal was torture. I stayed long enough to show my face, always making sure my hands were full of appetizers and a drink so that I didn't have to shake anyone's hand or hug them. As soon as my parents were fully occupied in their roles as entertainers, I slipped to my room. Cyle, of course, was the only one who noticed I was gone.

He came into my room and sat down on the bed next to me. I was lying there reading *The Giver* and relating so deeply that I had tears in my eyes.

"Hey sis. Why are you hiding up here?" Cyle was so handsome

with his thick dark brown hair, his deep brown eyes, muscular build and eyelashes from out of this world. He's definitely the brother that got the looks.

"You know I hate these things. Plus, I'm really into this book and just wanted to be alone."

"You shouldn't be sitting up here all by yourself during the annual Christmas party. You're twelve. You should be downstairs sneaking handfuls of cookies and candy, or sips of cocktails, and waiting for the yearly visit from Santa that Mom and Dad always plan for this shindig. He always brings good presents, at least." He paused and cleared his throat. "C'mon. What's going on with you? I've heard Mom and Dad's interpretation of it all and Cory and Chris' opinions, but I want to hear it from you. What's up?"

Tears spilled down my cheeks and the words got stuck in my throat before I could spit them out. "I hate talking about it. Nobody understands. Everybody thinks I'm a freak."

"Well, I'm not everyone else. Try me. You know I love you no matter what!" As he spoke, my mind flooded with the memory of the blue flash. I could remember him holding me with such tenderness and amazement in his eyes when I first came home as a newborn. A blue flash imprinted that memory on my brain along with feelings of absolute love and security. This was Cyle. I could talk to him.

"I don't know what's wrong with me. I've heard what Mom and Dad say, what the doctors think, but none of them are listening to me," I sobbed. "They don't believe me. They think I'm crazy or sick."

With some coaxing, I spilled it all out. The flashes and what I've determined each color means. Red is pain. Purple gives me a skill or talent. Blue is a pleasant memory from someone. Orange is a painful memory. Yellow is what I presume to be a glimpse of the future. I explained that they only come when I touch someone, and then it's only sometimes. I can go months without having a flash or I can have ten in a day. I have no control over it. Once I've had the flash though, whatever I got from it, stays with me, becomes me, changes who I am. I explained that with each flash, I am redefined. I become parts of whoever I've touched. I am still me but with bits and pieces of them woven into my soul.

I told him of my memory with the blue flash and him holding me. I described his outfit to a tee, my blanket, my clothing. The love I felt from him.

Cyle was fascinated by my stories. It was such a relief to be able to talk to someone who wasn't looking at me like I was crazy or trying to fix me. His only desire was to understand. I told him about Polly, my former best friend, and how I had the orange flash with her. The one that showed me her stepfather was molesting her. I could feel the pain in my own body, as he penetrated hers. I felt his hands groping me. His hot breath smothered my neck and the smell of alcohol seeping from his pores nauseated me. I felt my heart breaking as hers did the same. I no longer felt like a virgin at the age of ten because of what had happened to my friend. I wanted to help Polly but didn't have any idea how to do it. I told my mother that her stepfather was hurting her. Mom simply looked at me and said it was another one of my crazy, made-up stories and there was no way in the world that was happening. That he was a respectable member of the community, a good man. I don't know which was worse, feeling the pain of the abuse or my mother's dismissal of my reality.

I was able to keep my friendship with Polly for a while. Until I got the yellow flash. I saw her lifeless teenage body lying on the floor in her bedroom, her mother screaming in agony next to her. I knew she would end up taking her life, her burden too much to bear. The easiest thing to do was not hang around Polly anymore. It hurt too badly to feel her pain, to know her ending, and not be able to do anything to stop it. The whole thing had traumatized me so much that I decided being alone was much easier. Polly was my last real friend.

Cyle held me in his arms while I cried about Polly, my fear, my pain. To cheer me up, he shared some of his early memories with me, ones from when I was too young to recall. Once, when I was three, the family was sitting at the table eating dinner. I threw my spoon across the room and when Christopher handed it back to me, I grabbed his hand. I started giggling and blurted out "Chris has books with naked girls in it. Oooh, gross."

Chris' cheeks flamed red, and my parents were speechless. "Shut up, you little freak," he said and stormed away from the table. Cyle said that Mom later found his stash of nudie magazines underneath his mattress.

No wonder Chris hated me.

Cyle started laughing, barely able to get his words out. "There was also the time... you would've been about four. Cory came home from school for winter break, and he was on this big vegetarian, health-food kick. In all seriousness, you looked at him, square in the face, and said *you're still gonna be big and fat so you should just go ahead and eat candy.*"

Cyle and I both cracked up. Cory started gaining weight when he was about twenty-three and never stopped. By age twenty-eight, he weighed close to three hundred pounds.

"Guess you got a yellow flash with that one, huh?" Cyle said.

"It sounds like I've had these things my whole life. But why? What caused it? What do I do about it? Why me?" I put my hands over my face wishing I could squeeze the answers out of my brain that I so desperately wanted.

Again, Cyle wrapped his arm around me and pulled me close. "Listen, sis. I don't know what caused it, or why this is happening to you, or what you can do about it. But I do believe God gave you this gift for a reason. He knows why He made you this way."

"Well, it doesn't feel like a gift...more like a curse. I wish God would explain what to do with it. I mean, some of it's okay. The good stuff that comes with the purple, blue and sometimes the yellow flashes. But the orange and red are bad. It all changes me."

"I can't imagine. I know Mom and Dad have put you through so much with the counselors, psychiatrists, doctors, and medicines. They do love you...they just don't know how to help."

"It would help if they'd listen and stop trying to fix me."

"Well, you got me for that. I'm always just a phone call away, you know. Now, you're coming back to the party with me to see what surprises Santa has for everyone this year." He pulled me to my feet. "And don't worry, I'll stay with you and make sure no one touches you."

I trusted him to keep me safe, so I went along. On Christmas morning, Cyle handed me a present that only he and I understood the meaning of. It was a decorative box, with a lock. Inside there was a note saying *For the Bad Memories – lock them in here until you are strong enough to face them.*

CHAPTER 8

By the time I reach my apartment, I've gotten two texts from Jonas. The first one came twenty minutes ago.

Just checking in. Worried about you.

He sent the second one just four minutes ago.

I'm not trying to be a pest. Just hoping everything is okay with your dad.

Fighting the urge to text Jonas back instantly, I check my voice mail first. But, there's still no call from Cyle. I decide to give him another hour before I call him, or God forbid, my mother or Cory. Rather than keep poor Jonas waiting, I shoot back a quick text.

Thanks for checking in. Still no word from my brother. Will let you know ASAP.

With time to kill, I decide to paint. I smock up and head to my second bedroom which I've set up as a studio. It's the nicer room and the one that most people would've chosen as the master bedroom, but the lighting is perfect for painting, especially in the mornings with almost the entire east wall covered in windows.

The unfinished painting that I told Ophelia about in our last session still sits on an easel beckoning me to finish it, but my heart isn't in that one today. Instead, I set up a fresh canvas and start a new project. My painting style is abstract to say the least. I'm not one to paint bowls of fruit or nude bodies. My goal is simply to put the colors inside me, along with some of the junk that goes with those colors, onto a canvas and see what emerges. Sometimes I'm amazed with the results and the beauty that comes out of the mess. Other times, the chaos inside comes through the brush and splashes itself in a hideous fashion. Those are the pieces that usually end up in the closet. I can't ever bring myself to throw one away because each painting holds so much of me and other people's stories, it feels almost sinful to trash them. But I certainly don't want to see the ugliness inside of me displayed on the walls of my home.

Some of my better work is hanging throughout my apartment. I've given Ophelia a couple of pieces—one of which is hanging in her office, another in her home. Both of them were actually inspired by our sessions. The one in her office I titled *Deep Memories*, fitting name for a painting for my therapist. Muted pinks, whites, yellows, browns, and blacks swirl together and wisp towards the middle of the canvas, all meeting at the center. I painted this one after a particularly painful session about three years ago. The first session where I shared Polly's story with her. I was rattled physically and mentally after sharing her story. Ophelia insisted I go home and pour out myself onto the canvas. Which I did. What emerged surprised me with its beauty. Before doing the painting, I physically ached for Polly, feeling like there was a giant hole inside of me. After the painting was complete, I realized that some of the guilt, shame, and remorse I'd carried for so many years, had started to heal. Sharing my friend's tragic story with someone who simply accepted it as truth, without question, was cathartic. Talking with Ophelia had centered me as represented in the painting.

The other one I gave to Ophelia wasn't one of my favorites because it was darker and full of anger. I titled it *Unresolved* which pretty much describes my life perfectly. The lines were harsh, filled with bold colors – red, black, orange, yellow. It held no pattern, only strokes of my rage. During our session, I was unable to pinpoint where all the anger came from. Some, I'm sure was from my own life, my own experiences. But some must have come from others. As always, Ophelia had me look at the painting and say the words that came to mind. Rage. Anger. Fear. Confusion. Pain. Loss. Secrets. Loneliness. We spent the entire session delving further into each of those emotions. Afterwards, she asked if I would consider allowing her to have the painting. At first, I hesitated saying I didn't want to see that ugly side of myself each time I came for a session. She promised that she'd display it at home, rather than the office. I didn't understand why she'd want a painting that represented such an awful side of me. I still cling to the words she spoke that day during my darkest times.

"Tessa, when we care about someone, we care about *all* of them. The beauty, the pain, even the 'ugliness' as you call it. I care about you. *All* your feelings matter and are valid. Not just the comfortable, happy ones."

Of course, I gave her the painting. How could I not?

I fill my palette with paint and get to work. My phone sits on the table next to me, with the ringer turned all the way up. As usual, I turn on some music and get busy. Today's choice is Imagine Dragons. The first song that plays is *Demons* and I chuckle aloud at the irony. I quickly fall into my zone where my thoughts stop, and my hands just move. The only time my mind truly ever takes a break is while I'm working. My soul simply pours out through the brush onto the blank slate in front of me. I've never taken a formal painting class, although Ophelia has repeatedly suggested it as a way to get me out of my apartment and around other people. I do wonder where I picked up the talent or if it was one I was born with. I guess I need to add that question to the list of things to figure out about myself. But not now. Now is for creating. Now is for pouring out my essence onto this blank canvas.

I'm lost within a world of color when the phone finally rings. The sound of bells chiming pulls me back to reality where Cyle's face fills the screen of my phone. I quickly wipe my hands and pull the phone to my ear. "Hey, what's going on?"

"Hi! Sorry it took so long. The doctor just gave a report. Dad had an ischemic stroke caused by a blood clot in his carotid artery. He's stabilized right now but still not awake. They've done angioplasty to clear the blockage, so he's still out from that."

"Is he okay? Has he woken up at all?" I ask. Images of stroke victims who are paralyzed or unable to speak flood my mind.

"I guess he woke up for a while earlier today. He's having some muscle weakness on his left side and slurred speech, which is common. The doctor's main concern right now is preventing a future, more severe stroke which is why they did the angioplasty."

"Is he...is he expected to survive?" I ask, my throat tightening around the question.

"Yes. He's okay right now. Like I said, he's still out from the surgery but other than having to do some physical therapy to deal with the long-term effects of the stroke, he should be okay. He's a tough old guy, so I'm sure he'll be fine."

"So, do you think I should come?" I say and start pacing across the studio.

"That's up to you. If you need to come to see for yourself that he's okay, then do that. But I also know that's like telling you to walk into a minefield and hope you make it out alive. I assure you he's okay right now, though, and I promise to keep you posted if you decide not to come."

I clear my throat several times to try to get the lump out before I continue. "Well, I talked to Ophelia, and we decided that if he's stable, it's probably best that I don't come. Is that okay with you? Are you okay? Mom?"

"I'm fine. Cory and Michelle are here to help. I'll stick around for a bit to make sure everything's okay. And Mom is herself, ripping tissues like a mad woman."

"Did she ask if anybody let me know or bother to mention telling me at all?" I ask even though I know I don't really want the answer.

"Tess, don't go there. It doesn't matter."

"I take it that means no. As usual, I'm not important." Tears fill my eyes even though I hate myself for feeling hurt by her yet again. "I guess that my decision not to come for now is best then."

"Probably so. I'm sorry she's this way," Cyle said. "Listen, I gotta go but I promise I'll keep you posted. I'll call later tonight with an update if nothing changes before then. I love you, kiddo."

"I love you too, Cyle. Give Dad a hug for me. But don't tell him it's from me or it might kill him right then and there."

"Will do. Talk soon."

I TRY to return to my painting, but I can't get back into the groove. What I've done so far is amazing, though; one of my best pieces yet. It's unusual, but no colors stand out more than the others. Rather, there are large swirls of black, red, orange, light green, gray, purple, yellow and brown that seem to be dancing with each other across the page. The longer I study it, I decide it may just be finished. I'll come back to it later to make sure, but it looks complete the way it is.

As Ophelia has trained me to do, I try to see what the art tells me about myself, the flashes, my life. The only words that come to mind are *calm chaos*. The two words paired together seem like an oxymoron, but it's like all the colors represent the chaos within me and the way they all join together so beautifully on the canvas represents a calmness despite the varying colors. I jot this down in my painting journal with the date and the title of the painting.

I don't have to head home, where I'm not wanted or needed, apparently. That's fine. I don't need the drama there anyway. I look down at my phone and a smile spreads across my face again. My heart skips in my chest. Will Jonas' offer still be good for dinner tonight? I check the time. Four o'clock on a Friday…I doubt he has a class this late, but I don't know his teaching schedule. Just in case, I text instead of call.

Hi! Call when you have a second.

Within thirty seconds, my phone rings. I smile as I answer.

"Hey! Is everything okay with your dad?" The worry is heavy in his voice.

"He had a stroke but is stable for now. It looks like I don't need to go to New York tonight. So, does the offer of dinner still stand?"

"Wow! I'm sorry to hear about his stroke but glad he's doing okay. Are you sure about sticking around, though?"

"Absolutely sure. Let's just say things between my parents and I are a little strained. It's probably best for everyone if I don't go." I clear my throat.

"Then the offer for dinner definitely stands. There's nothing I'd enjoy more." I can hear his smile. "In fact, I think I owe you that glass of wine for your early wake-up this morning."

"Yes, yes you do." I chuckle.

"Can I pick you up at your place a little before seven?"

My heart instantly races. I've never allowed anyone into my space other than Cyle. Home is my sanctuary...the only place I have been free from flashes. I don't think I'm quite ready to allow Jonas into my life in such a huge way yet.

I must have hesitated for too long because before I answer, he says, "Or, if you prefer, we can meet at Sylvia's."

He probably will think I'm a jerk, but I say, "That sounds great. How about I meet you there at seven?"

"Looking forward to it. I'll call and get us reservations. Come hungry. I plan on ordering a little bit of everything."

"Can't wait! My stomach's rumbling now. See you soon." I swell with emotion as I hang up. Excitement about seeing him again; yet anxious about the same. Ashamed for not pouncing on the chance to have him pick me up, like a *real* date that a *normal* person would have. Guilt that I probably hurt his feelings. Disgust at my mother for not wanting me there. Sadness that I'm not really a part of my own family. Relief that I don't have to be there and put on a fake persona to make everyone think that our family is anything near functional. Worried about my father.

The bombardment of emotion is too much. The best thing for me to do is nap for an hour before I have to get ready for my date, that way I don't further offend Jonas by yawning throughout dinner. Besides, if I don't do something to escape for a while, I'll be heading to the store for a pack of cigarettes to calm my jittery hands and racing mind.

AN HOUR NAP does the trick. I wake up refreshed and much less confused, but with a serious case of butterflies about our date. I shower, then carefully apply my make-up and fix my hair. It's been a long time since I've cared about how I look, usually the drabber the better, as not to draw attention to myself. I go back and forth on selecting an outfit, not sure how formally I should dress. Sylvia's is a nice restaurant, but we're in a college town, so it's common for people to show up completely decked out in suits or college kids rolling in wearing flip flops, gym shorts and t-shirts.

After trying on several things, I finally choose a sleeveless, V-neck wrap dress with black, white, and red stripes. Paired with a three-quarter length sleeved black jacket and black heels, I feel beautiful. I've curled my hair, so it flows in ringlets down my back. My mother would be so proud at how feminine I look. I eye my gloves sitting on the dresser. They don't really flow with my ensemble, but I feel so bare without them. God, I hate that I have to wear a pair of gloves to feel safe. I slip on the red satin gloves, cursing myself for not being bold enough to go without them. I can take them off during the evening if a streak of bravery hits me. I throw my keys, credit card, driver's license and lipstick in my red wristlet and head out.

The blast of cool, fall air feels so good that I decide to walk instead of drive. It's only a couple of blocks and I have plenty of time. Besides, trying to find parking on a Friday night can be a nightmare. I arrive at the restaurant five minutes early and spot Jonas as soon as I step inside the door. The crowd takes my breath away. So many people. Everywhere. I whisper a silent prayer that he was able to get reservations. Jonas rushes to meet me. He looks amazingly handsome in his gray V-neck sweater with a black button down and black dress pants. He looks exactly like a college professor - a very handsome one at that.

He takes my arm in his and leads me towards the hostess stand. I inwardly flinch, awaiting a flash. Again, none comes. "You look stunning tonight," he says as we approach the stand. "Hi. We have reservations for seven under McCafferty."

As the hostess gathers our menus, I have a moment to speak. "You also look marvelous, Professor McCafferty." I realize I'm blushing when the heat reaches my cheeks.

The hostess leads us to a window-seat table, overlooking a pond surrounded by trees. There are spotlights scattered outside. Through the windows, we can take in some of the beautiful scenery despite the darkness settling in.

"Have you been here before?" Jonas asks as we take our seats.

"No. I've always wanted to try it. I've heard great things though."

"It's one of my favorite places in town. Do you trust me to do our ordering since I've tried just about everything here?"

"Please do. The menu is a bit overwhelming, and it all sounds delicious." I close my menu and lay it on the table. I'd rather look at him anyway.

"No allergies? Anything you can't stand?"

"Nope. Not picky here. I love food in all forms."

"That's my kind of girl," he laughs.

The waiter arrives at our table and Jonas orders enough food for about six people. He orders a bottle of Amarone after ensuring me it's the best on their wine list, followed by appetizers of lump crab cakes, bruschetta and garlic bread. For our dinners, he orders lasagna, jumbo sea scallops, and filet mignon.

As soon as the waiter walks away, I say, "Wow! You weren't kidding about coming hungry. Or, are we expecting others to join us?"

"Nope, just us. I thought you deserved a nice dinner for our first real date and because you had such a stressful day with your dad," he pauses as a smile spreads across his face. "Besides, I'm starving. I haven't eaten since breakfast."

"Ah...the truth comes out," I laugh and take my first drink of wine.

Jonas was right; the wine is deliciously rich and full-bodied. "Great wine selection."

"Thanks. It's one of my favorites. I spent a semester in Italy as a grad student and got to know quite a bit about the wines and the food...mostly the wine," he laughs, and a sparkle fills his beautiful eyes.

"So, where did you stay in Italy? What did you do there?"

"I attended the European University of Rome. I taught English courses as a teaching assistant to help cover expenses. It was a dream come true. Teach and learn during the week, travel on the weekends. Have you ever been?"

Our feast of appetizers arrives, and I take a bite before answering, "Yes, I went to Italy with my parents when I was sixteen. I would love to go back again. It was beautiful."

"Where all did you go?"

We discuss our Italian travels throughout the appetizer course. Jonas asks where else I have travelled just as our meals arrive, thankfully. This allows me time to decide how to answer the question. I have intimate knowledge of travelling many places that I've not physically been. I can describe in perfect detail the pyramids of Egypt, the Taj Mahal, even the Saharan Desert, although I've never stepped foot in any of those places. Yet, I have the memories and sensations of being there. So, do these count? Should I relay these? It is hard to know which of the memories are my own and which are from flashes when it comes to the places I've visited. Especially those from when I was younger. It's amazing how such a simple question can be so complicated to answer. Luckily, Jonas is distracted by our dinner and forgets the question he left hanging.

Even though the appetizer course would have been plenty, the food is so delicious that we devour our meals, chattering between bites. Before he has a chance to return to the earlier conversation, I ask about his family.

"My father's an Aerospace Engineer at Honeywell and is going on about twenty years with the company. My mother is a High School English teacher. Dad wanted me to follow in his footsteps and

I tried but changed my major after freshman year with a devastated GPA," Jonas pauses and takes another drink of wine. "I guess I'm more like my mom. My sister ended up following in Dad's footsteps."

"Do you only have one sibling? And she's an Engineer I take it?"

"Yep, only me and Stephanie. She's four years younger and absolutely brilliant. She's an Electrical Engineer and lives in Phoenix with her new husband, Dan, who's also an Engineer. I'm surrounded by all these brilliant, wealthy people and I choose to live the meager existence of a college professor," he laughs but some hurt peeks through his smile.

"Are you close to your sister? It must be hard with all of them in Arizona and you here. You're a world away."

"We are close. But there's always been pretty fierce competition between us. And, unfortunately, I'm always on the losing end of the deal. Six figure salary? One-point Steph. Marriage? One-point Steph. Live close to the parents, another point for her. My column is pretty blank, comparatively."

"Man, do I understand that feeling. But, from my seat, I'd say you're not giving yourself enough credit. You seem successful to me. You're following your dream, at least." And *you're gorgeous* I want to say, but don't.

"Yeah, that is something, I guess. You know how it is, though, trying to shut up the voices from the past telling you you're not measuring up? Or am I the only one that has those?" There's the sadness again, settling into the creases around his eyes despite his smile.

"Oh, gosh no. Trust me, I totally get it," I say.

"So, tell me about your family," he says. Panic bubbles in my chest.

"Well, I'm the youngest of four. I have three older brothers, Cory is sixteen years my senior, Cyle fourteen and Chris twelve. There are a lot of issues with my family. I won't bore you with all of those details, but Cyle is really the only one I'm close to," I pause, hoping he'll cut me a break and not ask any follow up questions.

"You said you were from New York. Do you get home to see your parents often?"

"I haven't been home since I left five years ago. That's a whole other conversation though."

"Wow! I'm sorry. You must miss them. I make it home at least three times a year and I get homesick sometimes. Not that I'd ever consider moving back to that barren wasteland," he laughs. He has a great smile. And amazing lips that look so kissable. The heat rises in my cheeks.

"I get homesick for the *idea* of home but then I remember what my family is really like, and I'm quite content to just stay right here."

"So, do you work besides your painting?"

I shake my head.

"Is that why you're so hungry tonight? Starving artist?"

A nervous laugh escapes me. "That must be it." I hope this will be enough of an answer. He doesn't press for more information, but the question lingers in his eyes. How do I explain that the people I can't stand and never go home to visit are the ones who pay to keep me housed, clothed, and fed? How do I make someone understand without telling the whole story? Thankfully, I don't have to tonight.

"I would love to see some of your work," Jonas says. "Did you start painting in college or before?"

I chew the inside of my cheek. How do I explain that I never graduated from college to someone who's made education their career? Feelings of failure assault me. "I'm actually self-taught."

"That's impressive. You must have a natural talent. I can't even do a paint-by-number."

"If you'll excuse me a moment, I need to run to the ladies' room." I barely have a chance to finish, and Jonas is standing behind me to pull out my chair.

My nerves are shot. All this talk about families, careers, and talent. Oh, if only he knew. He would probably run *so fast* in the other direction. As enchanting as this evening has been, and as absolutely wonderful and handsome as Jonas is, I long for the solitude of my apartment. I hate feeling like I'm only giving half-truths to this man who's handing me his life like an open book. I breathe deeply for a few moments, trying to calm my anxiety, and head back to the table with the intention of cutting the evening short.

The easy-going, relaxed man that I left at the table has been replaced by one who now has a strained smile and stress etched around his eyes. Jonas rises to pull out my chair with shaking hands.

"Is everything okay?" I ask after he's seated.

"Yeah. Sorry. I checked my phone while you were in the restroom, and I had an emergency text alert from Cardell about another missing student."

"*Another?*"

"Yeah. This is the second woman in six months. She's an eighteen-year-old freshman. Her parents just reported her missing when her roommate called them saying she hadn't shown up at a party last night, nor did she come back to the room."

"Oh my god, that's awful. And scary. Do you know her?" I ask.

"She's in my freshman comp class. Always sits in the front row and writes brilliant essays. I hope she's okay," he says, fumbling with his silverware with his still trembling hands.

"Me too. How scary." I pause, not sure that I want to know the answer to my next question. "What happened with the girl from six months ago?"

Jonas pauses a minute before responding without meeting my eyes. "They found her remains about a month after she went missing. Someone had dumped her in a field about five miles out of town."

I gasp. "That's awful. I think I remember hearing about it on the news. Was it...Amber Martin?" Images of the young, smiling girl fill my mind. Her picture was flashed across every news station for at least a month.

"Yeah. That's her," Jonas looks up, trying to keep the tears filling his eyes from falling. "Hey, I'm not trying to be rude, but do you care if we cut this short? We have a mandatory staff meeting in the morning to discuss the search efforts for Hailey. After my morning class today and all this food, I'm spent."

I'm surprised by his reaction, the shaking, the tears, cutting our evening short. How well did he know Hailey to be this upset by her disappearance? I want to ask, but instead I say, "That's fine. I'm pretty tired, too, after all of my drama today."

Jonas asks how my dad is doing as he summons the waiter, handing him his credit card without even glancing at the bill. "Last I heard, he's stable. I'll call Cyle when I get home to check in."

We make our way through the still-crowded entry of Sylvia's, back into the crisp, fall air.

"I had a great time tonight, Tessa. Sorry about cutting our evening short. I hope we can do it again soon," Jonas says as he opens his arms for a hug.

Jolts of fear sweep through me, but I want to feel his arms around me. I lean into his embrace. It feels as good as I imagined it would. He leans down and gently kisses me. His lips are warm and soft. It has been so long since I've been kissed. I could stay here forever.

A red flash penetrates me, and I break our embrace.

"I'm sorry if that was too forward," Jonas says, reaching for my hand.

"Oh, no. That was wonderful. I just had a cramp in my foot." I feel myself blushing. Why did I have to get a flash *just then*? And why did it have to be red? Thank God I've gotten so adept at thinking on my feet, coming up with excuses for my weird behavior when the flashes hit. "In fact, we can resume, if you'd like."

"There's nothing I'd like more, but I really need to get home to get some sleep. Raincheck?" He opens his arms which I promptly lean back into.

"Definitely." I don't want to leave.

"In light of tonight's news, I insist on walking you home."

I'm hesitant, but one look at him and I know he's not going to take no for an answer. He links his arm through mine, and we make our way towards my apartment. It's comforting to walk next to him, touching him. We arrive at my door far too quickly.

"You can come in if you'd like," I shock myself by saying.

Jonas pulls me in his arms and kisses me again. He finally pulls away. "As much as I would love to, I'm going to have to decline tonight. Okay?"

I want to tell him it's not okay and beg him to come in for a while so that I can linger in his embrace, continue to kiss those lips. His eyes are giving me mixed messages. They're telling me he really needs to go but that he'd love nothing more than to stay. "Raincheck number two," I say and smile, even though I want to plead with him to stay a while longer.

"I will be cashing both in soon. But tonight, sleep awaits," he says and gives my hand a squeeze.

It takes everything I have in me to turn away and walk through my front door. Jonas waits until I have locked it behind me before he leaves. I would love to stay wrapped in the warmth of his embrace with those lips on mine for hours. I wonder what pain I just inherited from him. Everything still feels fine, so it must not be a broken bone or anything. Thank God.

I call Cyle as soon as Jonas is out of view. There's no answer so I leave a message asking him to call with any changes or at least to give me an update in the morning. All the heavy Italian dishes are working their magic and I feel a food coma coming on. I change and crawl under the warmth of my covers, without bothering to wash my face or brush my teeth. As I try to drift off, I replay the evening in my mind, lingering on thoughts of the kiss. Savoring each moment, each memory.

I'm not sure how long I've been asleep when I'm jolted awake by a pain so intense that I can hardly breathe, with sobs wracking my body. It is the pain of a broken heart, one shattered beyond repair. I have no doubts that it is from the red flash with Jonas. Along with the pain, I have the memory of a young, beautiful brunette in a pink and white casket. I feel her cold, lifeless hand in my own. I feel the certainty of knowing my life is completely different than what it's supposed to be because of the death of this woman whose name I don't even know.

CHAPTER 9

My phone rouses me from sleep at ten. I was up until five mourning the loss of this woman I don't know. I even broke down and bought a pack of cigarettes. I smoked three, which surprisingly helped calm me, and put the rest of the pack in my memory box. I tried to convince my breaking heart that I didn't know her, but it wouldn't listen. It was as futile as my mom trying to tell me my arm didn't hurt when I was in preschool. The pain was real and intense. It is now a part of me, my own broken heart. I had to fight the urge to call Jonas to find out who the woman is, where this feeling of loss comes from. There was no way to ask the question, though, without explaining.

"Hello," I say without even checking to see who it is.

"Did I wake you? You're going to hate me. Two days in a row." It's Jonas.

"I had trouble sleeping last night or I'd already be up. And I don't hate you." I cover the phone as I yawn.

"I just got done with my meeting and thought maybe you'd like to meet for breakfast. If not, though, you can just call when you're awake."

"If you can give me a few minutes to pull myself together, I'd love to." I stretch and stifle another yawn.

"Great. I'll grab us a table at *Monticello's*. Take your time. I'll load up on coffee."

"See you in a few," I say as I kick off my comforter.

I catch the first glimpse of myself as I'm brushing my teeth and realize that agreeing to meet was a mistake. How am I going to explain the puffy eyes and reddened, splotchy cheeks?

It looks like I've been up crying all night—which I have, but what reason do I give? Because he will surely ask. *Oh, yeah. I was up crying all night because my heart is broken over the death of some woman I don't even know. Someone I think is important to you. Shoulder-length brown hair? Buried in a pink and white casket? Wearing a mauve dress? Shattered your heart and your future? Ring any bells?* God, I hate the flashes. I hate the lies I must tell. I hate losing yet another part of me to a memory that's not even mine.

I don't know if I'll be able to look at Jonas anymore without seeing both of our broken hearts. Maybe I should just text him and say I can't meet right now. But his arms, his kiss… I'll come up with something. *Sick dad.* That's it. I'm sure I can weave some story around that. I detest liars, which is one reason it's easier for me to have no one in my life to lie to. I should just cut this off now before either one of us gets hurt. But those arms. Those lips. Those eyes. *Ugh.*

The battle in my mind rages on as I get dressed and pull my hair into a ponytail. My desire to see him again wins this internal war. The short walk gives me the time I need to come up with an acceptable story for my current condition regarding Dad, childhood issues triggered, blah, blah, blah. With one look at Jonas, though, I realize I probably won't need to explain a thing. He looks worse than I do. If I look like I've been up crying all night, he's been crying for a week. He appears to have aged about five years overnight, weariness filling every pore on his face.

He stands and pulls me into a hug as I approach the table. Part of me cringes, dreading another flash. The bigger part of me instantly relaxes into his embrace. We both sit after he kisses me on the cheek.

"I ordered croissants and coffee, is that okay?" He points to the spread in front of us.

This man has quite an appetite.

"Looks great. Thanks." I start buttering a warm croissant.

"I'm really sorry about last night and cutting things short. I've just been having a rough time lately with a couple of things and desperately needed some sleep. Which, unfortunately, I didn't get much of." He runs his hand through his hair.

"Are you okay? Anything you need to talk about?" These are the words that come out of my mouth when what I really want to ask is if the way he looks has anything to do with the woman in the pink and white casket.

"I'm alright. Just a rough night," he pauses and takes a bite of his jellied croissant. "Anyway, how are you? How's your dad?"

I pause a moment not sure whether to proceed with my "story" as I rehearsed on my walk here, or to just tell the truth. I look into his kind eyes and the truth prevails. "I'm okay. I kind of had a rough night myself. I haven't gotten any updates on Dad, but hopefully Cyle will call this morning. How was your meeting?"

"Depressing. Still nothing about Hailey, which isn't good. I guess she texted her friends around midnight saying she was on her way to meet them at a party across campus. She never showed, though. Several video cameras around town have captured her movements and the police are trying to piece together some kind of timeline. Her last text was at twelve-thirty to her mother, and it just said *I love you.* Several people said she had been drinking, so there's the normal concerns of whether she fell, hit her head and is lying hurt somewhere. Or, whether someone abducted her. Either scenario is pretty scary." Another pass of his hand through his hair, followed by a bite of his croissant.

"Oh my god. That's awful. Her poor family must be worried sick."

"They are. They're coming into town from Boston today." Jonas looks away as tears fill his eyes. "We've been cautioned against comparing this to the Amber Martin case, but it sure feels like the same story to me."

"It sounds pretty similar. What's going on in our charming little town?" As I ask the question, I sense the irony. This place has always been *my* safe haven, yet it isn't seeming so safe anymore.

"I don't know," he says and glances out the window for a moment. He clears his throat and returns his gaze to me. "Anyway, if Hailey doesn't surface sometime today, the University and Police Department are coordinating a search effort tomorrow. Would you want to help with that?"

"Definitely. Anything I can do to help," I say without hesitation, surprising myself.

"Great. I'll keep you posted throughout the day as I get details. I can't stay long this morning as I have major grading to do if I'm going to spend tomorrow helping with the search, but I wanted to at least apologize for last night and see your beautiful face."

The heat floods my cheeks and I know I'm bright red. Somehow, I manage to maintain eye contact and be bold in return. "No need to apologize. Any excuse to see you again works for me. Did I mention how nice that kiss was?" *I can't believe myself. This is not me speaking.*

"That kiss *was* spectacular. We'll have to try another today, just to make sure we don't forget." He takes my hand, without a glove, since I removed them to eat my breakfast.

Another red flash instantly consumes me. *Damn! Can't I get any other color from him? Is he full of pain, or what?* I wait for a feeling of physical pain to be associated with the flash, but again, nothing comes immediately. I put the flash out of my mind. Right now, I want to focus on him the last few minutes we have together. I'll deal with whatever pain there is later. Right now, I'm enjoying his fingers caressing mine.

I finish my croissant and coffee as quickly as I can because I'm actually looking forward to our goodbye. Jonas has the remaining eight croissants boxed up—*did he really think we'd eat them all?*—and sends half with me, despite my protests. As soon as we're outside, he pulls me close and kisses me. Tenderly at first, but then it quickly becomes more urgent and heated. There's a need in the kiss beyond anything sexual, although that's there as well. I press myself closer, wanting to feel every inch of his body against mine. His hands work their way down my back, finally reaching the bare skin above my waistband. The warmth of his hands spreads desire tingling throughout my body. *God, I want to bring him home with me. I never want this to end.* Beyond our physical want and need for each other, something else is happening between us. Both of our broken hearts are trying to heal in the exchange.

He has a strength I do not and pulls away. He takes my face in his hands and looks into my eyes. "Tessa, you are beautiful. I'm so thankful to have met you." I'm melting as he puts his lips to mine again. All too quickly, the kiss ends "Okay, I've gotta go. Grading awaits. If I don't go now, I may just follow you home."

"That would be okay with me." *Did I really just say that?*

"Probably not the best idea right now. You'd have mobs of angry freshmen hunting you down come Monday when I don't have their papers returned to them." He bends for one last quick kiss. "We'll talk or text later. Let me know if you hear anything about your dad and I'll give you details on tomorrow."

"Okay," I say as we head off in our separate directions. I stop and watch him. "Jonas?"

He turns to look at me, handsome as ever despite the rough night he had. "Yeah?"

"Thank you."

"For?" He asks with raised eyebrows.

"For everything. For dinner, breakfast, the kiss, being you."

"My pleasure - all of it." He blows a kiss and turns away.

Is it possible to be in love so quickly? I have no idea. I don't think I've ever been in love before. Of course, I know what it feels like, and my brain thinks I have, but there's never been another person that I could reach out and wrap my arms around that I've loved. If it's not love now, it's destined to be, I'm sure. This thought should scare the crap out of me, but for some reason, it doesn't. I want to know everything there is to know about him, even if it comes in flashes. And for the first time in my life, I actually *want* to share everything about myself with him. Not the flashes...*yet*. Maybe someday. I want to enjoy more of him before I scare him away.

~

ONCE I'M HOME, the inspiration to paint hits me. I head to the studio, smock up and study the painting I worked on yesterday to see if anything needs to be added. Today I realize that it reminds me of Jonas and my feelings for him. The lust, the desire, the need. All the colors melt together perfectly, even though they aren't necessarily ones I would usually pair. So many parts of me are represented—darkness, pain, joy, good memories, fear, the future, and Jonas. He's the thread that pulls it all together in such a beautiful fashion, making something lovely out of what would otherwise be a mess. This one, *Calm Chaos*, is complete. It's my favorite piece I've done thus far. I plan on hanging this one above my sofa.

I have other paintings I've started and should finish but I'm drawn to a blank canvas. I need a fresh place to dump all my new emotions. I grab my palette just as a text from Cyle comes through.

Dad's awake. Feisty as ever. Doing okay but probably good you didn't come. I'll call later with details. He's keeping everyone busy. Love you!

I text back and tell him I love him, too. I laugh as I imagine Dad barking orders at everyone around him, expecting treatment like he's staying in a five-star hotel. He's used to everyone catering to his every demand. I didn't even realize how stressed this whole thing with my dad was making me until now, when I feel my neck and shoulders relax with the revelation that I don't have to go home. Thank God, I don't have to go since I'm not always the best at biting my tongue around my parents.

I enter my painting trance and completely lose myself. I realize I've been working all day when the room darkens and instead of relying on natural light, I have to flip on my overhead. It's almost five o'clock. Now that I'm aware of the time, I feel my stomach rumbling, letting me loudly know it doesn't appreciate being starved all day. I'm thankful that Jonas sent home a boatload of croissants.

I walk into my kitchen, butter one of the flaky pastries, and grab a water bottle. I text Jonas as I eat.

Just wanted you to know I am thinking about you and hope your grading is going well.

He responds quickly which makes me smile.

Grading stinks. Some of these students should NOT be allowed to set foot on a college campus let alone earn a degree lol. Halfway done. Call you later?

I can only imagine some of the idiotic ramblings he has to read through. Just overhearing some of the conversations across campus tells me that there are some immature, senseless students wandering around.

Of course. Counting the minutes until I hear your voice.

When did I become so bold? It's normally hard for me to go somewhere that I may encounter another person. Now I'm practically throwing myself at Jonas' feet. This must be love, or lust, or something I've not experienced before.

And I yours. It seems like days since I've seen you, but it's only been hours. Talk soon.

I feel like a teenager and totally giddy at realizing he's feeling the same about me, as I am about him. Yet, fear descends on me like a dark cloud moving in before a storm. We're both falling, fast and hard. I have no idea how to do this whole relationship, falling in love *thing*. How do I ever get real enough with Jonas to let him past these walls I've built to protect me from the flashes? To protect me from the ways I've changed? To protect me from others? And how do I heal a broken heart if I don't even know why I have it? I want to be able to show Jonas all of me but how do I do that when I don't even know who the hell I am?

I finish eating and fight the urge to break open my box to have a cigarette. Instead, I go back to the studio to finish my painting. As usual, I get so lost in my work, that I rarely stand back to examine a painting until I'm at a stopping point. My hunger kept me from doing so before, so I'm just now looking at my latest masterpiece.

I'm stunned because it's the first time I've ever painted a person. Then it hits me. I'm breathless and collapse into tears as my brain wraps around what, rather *who*, I just painted.

It's her...the woman from my dream. Even though she is painted in shades of blues, yellows, purples, reds and greens, there is no doubt that it is her. It reverberates in my shattered heart. Memories swarm me — kissing those lips, caressing that cheek, gazing into those eyes, running my fingers through her long hair. Memories — of her smile, her tender lips on mine, her arms around me—crush me. More devastating than feeling all these emotions, is the realization of the depths of Jonas' love for her. This woman, who is dead. Is there any hope of him ever loving me when his feelings for her were so strong?

I know her name now as it echoes in my soul. *Mallory*. The love of Jonas' life.

CHAPTER 10

I cried myself to sleep for the second night in a row. This heartbreak thing is something I could live without. My dreams were plagued with memories of "my" time with Mallory. Making love to her. Laughing with her. Holding her in my arms. Loving her with my whole being. I tried to jolt myself awake to stop the onslaught of Jonas' memories, but I couldn't until now. It's six- thirty and the sun is just starting to peek out from behind the mountains. Before I get out of bed, I grab my phone realizing I didn't hear back from Jonas or Cyle before I drifted off.

I have three missed calls from Cyle, two from Jonas, two voice-mails, and a text. Cyle's message simply says that Dad is doing better, and we can talk today. Jonas' text says he left me a voice mail and gives details for today's search, asking if I'm still on to help. The search party is setting up on the College Green and working out from there at nine.

I text Jonas back to apologize and tell him I'll meet him there. I listen to the voicemail.

"Hey, Tessa. Jonas here. I just wanted to call to hear your voice. Missing it and you. See you soon but not soon enough." A smile spreads across my face. By the time I finish listening to his message, he's texted back.

Great! See you about eight forty-five?

I start to text back saying that I can't wait, but then decide this might not be an appropriate response to participating in a search for the missing girl. Instead, I say yes, that I'll see him soon.

Since I have plenty of time before we meet, I enjoy several cups of coffee (and a cigarette) before getting in the shower. It's there that my thoughts run rampant with questions about Mallory. Jonas called her Mal. All I know for sure is that Jonas loved her deeply and that their relationship was serious. I know that she's dead. I can fill in bits of their story—which is now my story, too—from other memories. But I want the whole story. I want to know what happened to her. I want to know *everything* about their relationship. When they met. How long they knew each other. How serious things were between them. If he still misses her. If he will ever be able to move on. I've tried to explain to Ophelia that this is exactly why it is so much easier for me to be alone, isolated from the world. She refuses to buy my excuses, though. I plan on giving her an earful at our Monday session. Perhaps I should call her and ask her to reserve a two-hour slot.

I'm out the door by eight-twenty so that I don't have to rush across campus. I have on a sweater, turtleneck, jeans, boots, coat, and gloves to help protect me from the chilly day. The air is crisp and fresh. The sound of leaves crunching beneath my feet soothes my nerves and calms my mind. Everything is quiet this time of day since students are sleeping off their hangovers, or just getting to bed after partying all night. It stays quiet until I reach the back of the buildings on the perimeter of College Green. I can't see around the buildings, but from the shouts, murmurs, and voices I hear, a lot of people have shown up to help with the search.

Damn! I was so quick to agree to help so that I could spend more time with Jonas that I forgot that search equals crowds of people in close proximity.

What was I thinking? I wasn't thinking, I was swooning. I could kick myself. Or I could turn around and go back home. But I feel like I should stay. This is someone Jonas cares about, and I told him I would come. Plus, if someone I loved was missing, I would want as many people as possible searching. This town is my home; thus, I have a vested interest in making sure that it stays safe. I just need to suck it up, deal with my anxiety and face whatever lies on the other side of these buildings. *Ophelia will be so proud.*

I round the corner and see hundreds of people gathered on the lawn swarming around in mass chaos. I force myself forward instead of running in the other direction like I want to do. A quiet, serene drive up the mountains sounds much more appealing than this. I pull out my phone and send Jonas a text asking where he is. He tells me to stay at the east edge of the crowd and he'll find me in a few minutes. I lean against a large maple tree while I wait, observing the herd of people in front of me. The sea of faces is an eclectic mixture. The majority are college students sprinkled with groups of older people, some obviously affiliated with the school, some townspeople. There are student groups huddled into assemblies around the periphery, some holding signs and chanting. ENOUGH IS ENOUGH. HOW MANY WOMEN HAVE TO DIE? TIME TO END THE SILENCE. CARDELL= COVERUP. SAVE OUR GIRLS. END THE VIOLENCE. IS THIS NUMBER 4?

Reading the signs, I realize there must be much more to the story than what Jonas shared. Number four what? *Women missing?* Are they all Cardell students? Why haven't I heard of any of these missing women besides Amber Martin? I thought her murder was just a fluke, so to speak. A random act of violence.

I nearly jump out of my skin when someone touches my arm.

"Sorry. I didn't mean to startle you," Jonas says.

"Crap. I was taking all of this in and not paying attention," I say spreading out my hand towards the people. "Quite a crowd."

We peruse the sea of faces. "It always is," Jonas says with a faraway look. "Anyway, let's go get signed in." He stands on tiptoe and points. "The tent is over there. Past this mob."

Of course, it is. Nothing sounds less appealing than trying to fight our way through this crowd.

"There's got to be a line. Let's walk around the edge til we can find the end," he suggests which sounds like a great idea to me. He grabs my hand, and we head towards the front of the crowd.

As we walk, a sobbing woman runs towards us. "Professor McCafferty, wait up!" We stop and she quickly reaches us. "Have you heard anything? I can't believe this is happening again. And to Hailey. Where could she be? Do you think someone hurt her? I'm worried sick," She cries out with no pause for a breath.

Jonas puts his arm lightly around her shoulders. "I know, Madison. I hope she's okay. This must be awful for you."

"It is. I can't stop crying. I can't sleep. All I can do is think about where she could be, wonder if she's okay. Pray she hasn't been hurt… or worse." She wipes her nose with a tissue. "I see her things lying all over the room, her unmade bed. I keep thinking she's going to walk in the door any minute. The police took her laptop and tablet and have searched through her things."

She stops again to wipe her nose. "What if someone's killed her, too? Oh my god! I can't take it!"

Jonas stays composed throughout and stands to face her, putting a hand on each arm. "Madison, look at me," he says, and she complies. "You need to take a deep breath and don't let your mind get the best of you. Are you participating in the search today?"

"Yeah, a whole group of us from Dabney are. We can't just sit and wait."

"You've got to focus on doing what you can to help. Right now, that means calming down and helping with the search. If you're so upset, you can't search too well, now can you?" Madison shakes her head and takes another deep breath. I'm impressed at how well Jonas is handling this hysterical young woman with such authority and calmness. "Where are your friends?" She points to a group of sobbing girls in the midst of the crowd. "Someone needs to be strong and help reign in everyone's emotions. For Hailey. So you guys can be helpful today. Can you do that?"

Madison visibly calms as Jonas talks to her. She continues breathing deeply as he coaches her in how to best help her friends, giving her the words to say to help quiet their raging emotions and fears. "You're allowed to cry, scream, kick, be afraid, and let your thoughts run as wild as you want after the search, but for now, you're all needed. Hailey needs you to be calm and find something that may help us find her."

Madison leans in and gives Jonas a shallow hug. "Thanks for this. You're right. I've got to get us all under control. I needed this dose of reality."

"You're welcome. Now get back over there." Madison runs off, no longer crying, to rally in her friends.

Jonas turns to me. "Sorry about that."

"No problem. You did great. Are you that close to all of your students?" I take hold of his hand.

"I tend to build connections with them pretty easily because of the nature of my job. They all have to share parts of themselves with me in their writing, or in their conversations about books we read, that other professors aren't privy to. I'm sure I have to share more about myself than, oh, a calculus professor."

"Plus, it doesn't hurt that you're young and good looking," I say and wink at him. "I bet a lot of the girls have a crush on you."

He laughs. "I've had my share of those, too. I've become a master at shutting that down though."

"I bet you have. Anyway, you did great with her. I'm totally impressed."

"That's all that matters," he says with a wink. "Now, let's go get registered." He squeezes my hand, and we head off to the mile-long line curving out from the tent.

WE ARE SPLIT into twenty groups with twenty people in each. Each group is assigned a designated area of town to search over the next four hours. Then when we return, new groups will be sent out. Each group has a "captain" with a walkie-talkie, crowbar (in case anything heavy needs to be pried), and a map. The searchers all get bright yellow vests, work gloves (yay me!), a flashlight, water, a bag of trail mix, and a metal poker stick. Jonas is the captain of our group, and our search zone is a wooded area just outside of town. Cardell buses line up waiting for those groups, like ours, who are searching areas outside of the immediate campus. Half of our group are students. The others seem to be paired off in groups of two almost like they're friends going to brunch, or a couple going on a date. There is one older gentleman by himself. Since Jonas must navigate and report in, I decide to offer to be this man's partner in the search. We were given strict instructions not to wander off alone and that if we spot something, to have "our buddy" also take notice before the captain calls it in.

The area we are given is heavily wooded and the leaf cover on the ground makes it an extremely tedious area to search. It is at least ten degrees cooler under the canopy of trees and a chill quickly settles into my bones. My partner is Carl, a seventy-three-year-old retired fire-fighter who has lived in the Chandlersville area his entire life. His wife of fifty years passed away three years ago, and he said he does what-ever he can to keep himself busy and moving. As we trek across our grid of the terrain, Carl proves his agility and fitness. I run out of breath and need to stop for breaks more often than he does. Since Carl's participated in countless searches over the years, he is thorough and a good person to have as a partner. He points out places to look that I might normally miss, like a hole at the base of a tree big enough that someone could stash a weapon or a piece of clothing. Everything we find, whether we think it is important or not, must be marked with a small orange triangle marker, indicated on the map and reported when we return to the sign-in tent. So far, Carl and I have found a red sock, that looks like it belongs to a child, a black scarf hanging on a tree limb, a size seven brown woman's shoe, various items of trash—beer bottle, condom wrapper, empty pack of cigarettes, fast food bags. Most of the items have obviously been here for a while as they are buried under layers of leaves or have weeds growing through them. Or they are trash, discarded out someone's car window. But still they must be marked.

How will the police ever sort through and decide what is important and what isn't when just the two of us have found so many items and there are four hundred people searching in this round alone? Chills race up my spine at the realization that perhaps these findings will only be important if a searcher finds what we're really out here looking for, Hailey's body. As much as I want to be helpful and assist however I can in locating this poor girl, the thought of stumbling across her body sickens me. I don't think I could handle it.

I breathe a sigh of relief when Jonas announces to our group that the bus is waiting for us on the main road and that it is time to head back. I feel like I have been half-holding my breath for the entire four hours, dreading finding a body or, worse yet, *a body part*. Carl must have been able to sense my tension as many times throughout the search, he'd try to make light-hearted conversation to help the time pass. He talked a lot about his family—two sons and two daughters, eight grandchildren, three great grand-children—and some of the humorous stories from his career.

He was easy to talk to and I found myself opening up about my family a bit, of course not mentioning all of the drama. I told him about my father's recent stroke after he shared that his wife had died of a stroke at the age of seventy, six years younger than my father. *Maybe I should go visit my dad after all.* Or maybe spending the afternoon with a father figure who spoke so highly of his children gave me false hopes that my dad thinks of me the same way. The boys maybe, but not me. Maybe I should get Carl's information and visit him instead.

I was able to sit with Jonas on the bus ride back. "So, how are you holding up, Captain?" I ask.

"I'm drained. I'm signed up for the next round, too. Wish I would've thought that one through when they passed around the sheet at the staff meeting," he pauses. "Unless, of course, they've found something that would warrant stopping the search." By something, I know he means Hailey.

"I couldn't do it. I'm beat. This rough terrain about did me in," I say. "That's very nice of you to do it, though."

"Anything I can do to help. I know how hard this is on her family and friends. They just need some answers. Any part I can play in helping get them, I will do." Now I feel like a wimpy and selfish slacker.

"You're a very good man, Professor McCafferty."

"I don't know about that. Doing the best I can, but thanks."

"So, I noticed a lot of the signs the students were holding back there said things that indicated this has happened before. I mean, other than Amber and Hailey."

"Yeah, unfortunately, it has. She's the fourth girl to go missing in four years, all Cardell students. All murdered," Jonas looks out the window.

"Why have I not heard about this? I mean, I heard a lot about Amber, but I don't think I heard anything about the others."

"That's part of the problem. A lot of the students and other community groups think Cardell has tried to cover-up a lot of this by keeping the news media quiet so as not to scare off potential students or donors. That's probably why you heard so much about Amber. People are sick of the silence and think it's only allowing the problem to continue, more girls to go missing. A lot of these organizations made sure to blast social media, news stations, papers, anything they could when Amber went missing, hoping they'd figure out who was behind all of this and stop the cover-up."

"Do they suspect it's the same person behind all of the murders?"

"According to the authorities at Cardell, there's no link. Of course, a link could mean a potential serial killer running loose on the streets of their beautiful university, so they're going to be very unlikely to find one. You should look this up on the internet to see all the theories going on out there. Makes you wonder, Jonas says and raises a hand to rub his shoulder.

"Here, let me help," I say and begin massaging his shoulders and neck. "Did you know any of the other women?"

Jonas clears his throat and doesn't respond right away. When he answers, he speaks so quietly I can barely hear him. "Yeah," he looks out the window for a moment before continuing. "Hey, listen, can you hold this end of the map for me while I scope out the next area I'm assigned to? Get a lay of the land before I have a group of people out there."

"Sure," I say picking up on his cue that it's time for the end of his massage and a change of subject.

As we study the map the rest of the way back to campus, I realize what a huge task this will be for the police. There are so many places that someone familiar with the area could leave a body. Rivers, valleys, mountains, fields, ditches, abandoned properties... Places one could be dumped and never found.

When we get back to campus, the number of people on College Green seems to have tripled. Jonas grabs my hand as we make our way through the crowd back to the sign-in table so that I can return my supplies. Student groups continue their chants. NO MORE VIOLENCE. STOP THE COVER UP. SAVE OUR GIRLS. Signs are everywhere. The crowd seems infuriated, their tension and frustration filling the air. Media outlets surround the outskirts of the group, filming the returning searchers, the students gathering, the chaos unfolding. An NBC and CNN truck are parked next to the Green, so it appears the students are getting their voices heard by a national audience.

As we make our way through the thickest part of the group, the crowd presses against us. It is impossible to squeeze through without touching anyone. I still have Jonas' hand but there are people on every side, bumping, pushing, grazing into us.

Suddenly, I am paralyzed by a flash unlike any I've ever experienced before. A lightning bolt rips through me, slicing apart my very essence. A blinding light robs me of my vision. Buzzing louder than any noise I've ever heard pierces my ears, penetrates my brain. As the bolt works its way through my body, images and feelings bombard my mind. Women's faces with wide, dead eyes look up at me, my hands around their throats. Their screams fill my mind. Hailey's face, wrenched in pain. Amber's face, screaming in agony. A woman with short blond hair pleading with me to stop. A woman with auburn hair splayed out on the ground, her legs bloodied and spread. And the last face, the one that has been plaguing my dreams, the one I just painted yesterday. *Mallory*. Mallory, taking her last breath, my hands around her throat. Mallory looking into my eyes as tears roll down her cut and bloodied cheeks.

The crowd parts around me as my screams fill the air. Jonas catches me as I start to fall. I cannot breathe. I need to get out of here. I need to get away from everyone, including Jonas. Someone here, in this group, killed these women. Someone who just touched me. That someone *could be* Jonas.

CHAPTER 11

I pull free from Jonas and start to push my way through the crowd, trying to memorize all the faces before me, knowing that one of them is *the one*. The one who pierced me with lightning. With these images.

There are too many. It is a sea of black, white, Asian, short, tall, man, woman... I can't distinguish any one face from the others. I cannot focus on the present. I keep going back and forth between the real, live people in front of me and the dead eyes of the murdered women in my mind. The ones I have memories of killing.

"Tessa, stop! Wait!" Jonas calls out.

I fight my way through the crowd faster, trying to get away. He grabs my arm. "Tessa, are you okay?"

In a voice I don't even recognize as my own, I yell so loudly that it quiets the crowd around us. "Stop. Leave me alone!" All eyes turn to us. His chin trembles and I know he's wounded, but I don't care. He could be the one that gave me these awful memories...a rapist, a murderer.

He drops his hand and I run through the crowd, finally breaking free. As each foot hits the pavement, a different thought pounds in my head.

Hailey's skin beneath my hands.

Jonas' concern for Hailey at the restaurant.

The black mini-skirt Amber was wearing.

The closeness Jonas shares with his students.

The cries of a woman with short-blond hair, pleading for her life, saying her mom is dying of cancer...to please let her live.

Jonas immersing himself in the search, as killers are known to do.

Penetrating the woman with the auburn hair. Hurting her. Making her bleed.

Jonas knew Mallory, loved her even.

Hiding Mallory in high weeds to conceal her body.

The power surging through me as I raped each one.

The feeling of wholeness as each woman took their last breath.

The intensity with which Jonas pursued me. Was I to be the next victim?

I can't breathe. My chest is being crushed. My head is going to explode. My identity is being lost. I am becoming someone else. Someone I can't run from because they are now a part of me. Through it all, my heart is breaking with the memories of losing Mallory.

Once I make it in my apartment, I head straight to the medicine cabinet, rifling through pill bottles. I've got to make this stop. My mind is going to crack, split open if I don't. I am teetering on the edge of insanity. I find the bottle I'm looking for and take four Xanax, praying they'll work. I rush to grab my memory box and get my cigarettes, hoping they will calm me until the pills kick in. My hands shake so badly, it's hard to get a cigarette out.

My cell phone rings. It's Cyle. I can't answer right now. I cannot find my voice. I smoke a cigarette. My racing heart still hasn't calmed. The assault on my mind hasn't slowed. My entire body trembles. The phone rings again. Jonas. I throw my phone against the wall to stop the ringing.

Sobs wrack my body. Tears waterfall down my cheeks. Anxiety quivers deep in my muscles, spasming. Fear shudders through me. I can't catch my breath. I smoke another cigarette. *Waiting.* Waiting for the pills to kick in so I can breathe. Waiting for my mind to calm. Waiting for these thoughts to stop.

The women's dead eyes stare at me, peering into my soul. They see me. Pleasure courses through my body at this thought. The thought of being seen. I run to the bathroom and vomit, trying to rid myself of the truth.

I am now a killer.

I collapse under the weight of this realization onto the bathroom floor, an inhuman wail echoes off the walls around me.

I VOMIT until there is nothing left but dry heaves and, even then, my body won't stop trying to expel my new truth. I stumble to the medicine cabinet and pop a couple more Xanax. And finally. Finally, I fall asleep, curled into a ball on the living room floor. I'm disoriented when I wake up in the darkened room, confused about where I am and what time it is. My mind is fuzzy and I'm light-headed as I pull myself up off the floor and head towards the kitchen for a drink. My throat is raw from crying and vomiting. My vision is blurry from crying and sleep. It's eight o'clock. I have lost the entire day.

I chug a glass of water, trying to rid my mouth of the foul taste. My head throbs and I'm starving. I search the refrigerator for something but there's only milk, an expired yogurt, a cheese stick, and some stale bread. The leftover croissants from Jonas sit on the counter, but I can't bear to eat them. My plan was to go to the grocery store after the search today. Since that didn't happen, I'm left with the choice of not eating or forcing myself to go out and grab something. My rumbling stomach forces my decision.

I pull my hair into a ponytail, brush my teeth, and splash water on my face. I avoid looking at my reflection because I know I look terrible. Plus, I am afraid to look into my eyes not knowing if a different person will now look back at me. My thoughts start to race filled with images from the flash. I start counting to give me something to focus on besides the memories.

One…two…three…four…five…six…

Hailey's scream pierces me, slicing through me like a sword.

Seven...eight...nine...ten...

The smell of damp earth assaults me as I carefully place Mallory's body amongst the weeds.

I make it to forty and out the door of my apartment. I breathe deeply for the first time in hours. The cool air fills my lungs and calms my thoughts enough to keep me moving forward. Instead of counting, I focus on the brick sidewalk. The wind rustling in the trees, singing to the moon hanging low in the sky. I go to Lenny's Bagels because it's closest, just around the block from my apartment. I place my order for an Everything bagel with cream cheese, a bag of chips, a fruit cup, and an iced tea to go. I say the names of each of the bagels in my head as I wait, trying to keep my focus on the present. *Asiago, Cinnamon, Garlic, Sourdough, Pretzel, Everything...*

A woman's voice placing her order interrupts my thoughts. A young woman, probably about nineteen, with shoulder-length dirty blond hair. Alone. Placing a to-go order.

The cashier hands me my bag and I move to fill my iced tea. I take my time, putting the right amount of ice in the cup. De-seeding my lemon. Filling the cup with tea. Slowly snapping the lid on. Unwrapping the straw. Sliding the straw in the cup. All the while, aware of the woman at the counter, waiting on her order.

She finally leaves and I follow. I walk a few steps behind her in the direction opposite my apartment. My mind is battling a raging war with itself.

Turn around. Go home.

She's alone.

I am NOT a killer.

I want to feel her skin.

No. Stop!

Hear her screams.

TURN AROUND!!!

See the fear in her eyes.

This is not who I am.

Feel my hands around her throat.

The woman stops, stooping down to tie her shoe. She's right in front of me, within my reach. I could have her. She turns to look at me, realizing I am close.

"Hey!" She says as our eyes connect, not knowing the danger she's in. "Sorry for blocking the path."

Grab her.

My mind automatically notes the dark alleyway within feet of where we're standing. My body trembles with excitement over the possibility and fear over the new me winning this battle.

No! I will not do this. I will not do this. I will not do this.

It takes all my strength and will to turn around and run back towards home, the war in my mind raging on. A strong, strange force in me is trying to draw me back to the woman. I push myself forward, clawing to reach the safety of home. I'm panting by the time I reach my door. I get inside as quickly as I can, and again, must run to the bathroom to throw up, sick with the anxiety, the fear, the excitement.

I'm no longer hungry for the food I bought. My appetites are different now. I take two more pills and head to the studio, hoping to dump this onto a canvas, to rid myself of it. I lose the next several hours painting what's inside of me, lost in my world of color and desire. I stand back to examine my work when my heart tells me it's complete.

I gasp in horror. Five sets of eyes stare back at me. Eyes with no life left in them. Lives gone—I remember taking them.

CHAPTER 12

I do not sleep longer than a few minutes. My peace is gone. My only comfort is in painting. My days and nights are filled with going back and forth between my computer and the studio. Computer to research about the missing girls from Cardell. Studio to paint what's swelling inside of me. I'm functioning on pure adrenalin; the *fear* of this new me fuels me. I have no need for food, so I don't eat. I occasionally remember to drink water and keep my pill bottle close at hand so that if the anxiety turns to desperation, I can try to quell it with Xanax. The medicine only takes the edge off, it doesn't stop the raging storm within me. I need to know who the killer is…who I am becoming. I need to know if it is Jonas. I don't want it to be Jonas. But I need to know. But I don't want to know. Back and forth my mind goes. Wanting and needing. Needing and wanting. Burning desire propels me forward, trying to piece together the truth.

The internet research on Hailey uncovers a lot of information since her missing person's case is so fresh. The media outlets are plastering her face all over the news, hoping someone can offer a clue to her whereabouts. She's a beautiful young woman with blue eyes and straight, long brown hair. She's from Boston and is a freshman studying Biomedical Engineering. According to her professors, she's brilliant and has aced all of her assignments and tests thus far. She's outgoing and seems to have a wide circle of friends, or at least it appears so on her Facebook page. The pictures posted of her on social media show that she's made the most of her college experience so far by attending sporting events, playing intramural tennis, attending weekend parties and, of course, celebrating her freedom from her parents' scrutiny by drinking on the weekends.

The news reports don't state it, but Hailey was a virgin. I know this because I remember the blood and the screams of pain as I penetrated her. I cry as I remember the agony she felt.

I take out my notebook and make a list of what the police know thus far based on my research:

- *Was supposed to go to a party across campus a little after midnight. Never showed.*
- *Texted Mom at twelve thirty and said, "I love you." Her mom didn't see the text until the next morning.*
- *Party in her dorm, Dabney Hall, earlier that evening. Had been drinking heavily.*
- *Police searched her online accounts and computer. Nothing found that would lead them to any suspects.*
- *They are asking anyone to come forward that saw Hailey at any point that night, to hopefully offer some insight.*
- *They recovered her cell phone in the search, a mile away, in the trash can at Starfire Gas Station.*

Several video cameras caught footage of her at different places across campus between eleven and midnight. Much of the video footage has been posted online in hopes that someone will recognize something that could be helpful to the police. I view them, one by one, and note the time and details in my notebook. The first camera caught sight of her as she was heading out of her dorm at eleven fifteen wearing tight black pants, high heels, and a red crop top with her belly exposed. *I remember removing those pants and hiding them in the bottom of my closet later, keeping them close so I could hold them near and smell her scent.*

Another camera catches view of her at eleven thirty walking down McCutcheon Street, obviously intoxicated as she stumbles several times. *Jonas lives on McCutcheon Street.* At eleven thirty-eight, also on McCutcheon Street, she can be seen looking behind her and then running, seemingly in a hurry to get somewhere, or get away from someone. No one else appears in the footage, though. In the third video recording, she appears uptown where shops and bars are frequented by college students. She's seen there at eleven fifty-two, still stumbling a bit as she walks, but stopping at one point to talk to a group of people. Several of the businesses uptown have security cameras that monitor the area directly in front of their establishments, so her steps are easy to trace for the next fifteen minutes.

She stops and sits down at the outdoor seating area at Sweeney's, a popular bar for townsfolk and students alike, at eleven fifty-five. She sits for a couple of minutes by herself and looks around. Then she's seen outside of Pelaski Jewelers walking by herself, a group of men following closely behind her. One of them can be seen gesturing in her direction and saying something. The last video footage of her is at five past midnight where she is seen from the Bank of Chandlersville's recording, standing across the street with her back to the camera, talking to someone standing in the shadows. She stands there for several minutes, seemingly talking to this person, then the camera shows the person in the shadows link hands with her and they walk off together down the alley across the street from the bank. The person was never in clear view of the camera, as if he knew it was there and was intentionally avoiding it. All you can see of him is his lower arm and hand where it links with Hailey's.

It looks like someone she knew. She didn't seem afraid. She wasn't trying to pull away. It looks like she walked off with him willingly. Would she have been this comfortable walking off with Jonas? He indicated that a lot of his students have crushes on him. Was Hailey one of them? She certainly would have felt comfortable being alone with her professor. I try to zoom in on their hands, searching for something that would indicate it is him. The image is too fuzzy, and they move quickly out of sight. I can't tell if it's a male or female, black or white. I try to force myself to remember that moment, but it must not have been one that transferred to me in the flash, because nothing comes to me.

A video is also posted of the press conference held late Sunday afternoon with her parents. Hailey's mother and father stand before the cameras, leaning into one another, like it's the only way they can remain standing. Her mother's hands tremble as tears flow down her cheeks. Her father's hands curl into fists as he talks and his voice chokes with emotion. They look as though they haven't slept since they got the news of their daughter's disappearance, their faces gaunt, their cheeks hollowed, and their eyes dulled. Hailey's mother wears a button with a picture of a smiling Hailey. Her father holds up a family picture of them taken only three short months ago, all of them (she, her parents, and her younger brother) bronzed from the sun, standing on a beach, the wind blowing their hair. Huge smiles spread across their faces.

Her mother remains silent while her father pleads for Hailey's life, for help finding his precious daughter. I can tell by studying the mother's face that if she even attempts to speak, she will crumple to the floor, her pain and fear shredding her into a million tiny pieces. The speech is brief, but I can't make it through the entire thing without breaking down into sobs. My brain keeps switching back and forth between the smiling Hailey in the pictures on my computer screen and Hailey's face as I remember it, pain in every crease, panic in each utterance, fear trembling throughout her body. I slam my laptop shut and start to pace.

Try to remember something about the killer, I scream at myself. *Can I see his hands as they close around her throat? No. Can I see any part of his clothing? No. Can I see where they were?* I pace back and forth, back and forth, back and forth. There's an image there, but I can't bring it into focus. It's muddled with all the information, her parent's faces, their family picture, Hailey's pain. Back and forth, back and forth, back and forth. Maybe if I sit for a moment and close my eyes, something will come to me. I lie back on the couch and wait for the images to form.

They come in bursts. A car. I'm in the driver's seat. Hailey asks if I'm lost. I can't hear the answer given. Hailey starts to cry. She realizes that we're headed away from the party I was supposed to be delivering her to. A voice spits at her to shut up. Hailey screams. A punch hard enough to quiet her. Then...nothing. Blank.

I sit a few minutes longer but nothing more...nothing more. I flee to my studio.

I paint. I lose myself in the colors for hours. I have no need to keep track of time since eating and sleeping elude me. I don't stop until it's complete. Once I look at it; one more piece of the puzzle. As I examine the portrait, it all comes rushing back. After strangling her, I picked her up and carried her. The high from watching her die, from seeing her dead eyes staring at me, from knowing that I was the last face she would ever see, still courses through my body. I walked with her slung over my shoulder for about ten minutes until I found the perfect spot. Water. With all my strength, I throw her as far out as I can. I watch her sink away, her hair swirling out around her like a lion's mane. The water drinks her slowly, pulling her into its embrace, letting her fall into the darkness.

If I were a stranger looking at the work I'd just completed, I would be in awe, enraptured with its beauty. It looks like a woman peacefully drifting away without a care in the world. But, I know the brutality she had to face to finally gain the freedom that the water offered. The only peace she got was from her death. It gave her an escape from the pain and fear. The pain and fear that I inflicted upon her.

My memories of that night stop when she is no longer visible. The flash doesn't take me any further, no matter how hard I will it to. I fall to the floor, sobbing. *I do not want this. I don't want to know this stuff. I don't want to remember these things. I do not want to feel this way.* I do not want to crave the feel of a woman's body lying under mine. I don't want to need the gaze of a dead woman's eyes upon me to feel alive. I don't want to feel pleasure at the memories of her torture. But, I do. For all of it, I do.

The sun is starting to rise, and I have no tears left. It's morning, but

I have no idea which morning, how much time has passed since the flash. I've lived several lifetimes since that moment.

I head back to the computer, this time to search for information on Amber. I remember—as me—when she initially went missing, and the horror I felt for her family and friends. Amber was taken on April 16, 2014…exactly six months prior to Hailey's disappearance. She, too, was an Engineering student—I make note of this. Could the link be a professor since she and Hailey would have to take similar courses for their major? Even though Amber was a sophomore, that doesn't mean their courses didn't overlap. It's normal for students to not be able to fit all their classes in their freshman year. Amber is also a pretty girl. Same as Hailey, she has blue eyes and long dirty blond hair. Her blue eyes pleaded with me for mercy even after her death. I showed her none.

I shake my head trying to clear it of the memories. *Focus, focus, focus*…I chant to myself until I'm able to read again.

I make a list for Amber, too.

- *Lived off campus in Chesterfield Apartments with three female roommates.*
- *From Gray, Tennessee.*
- *Was supposed to go to a friend's house at 8 pm, who lived several blocks away, to study for a Physics exam. Never showed.*
- *The friend started trying to call her cell phone at 8:30 because it was unusual for her to be late. Phone went straight to voice mail. Texts went unread.*
- *Cell phone found the next day, smashed in a lot behind Ridgeway Gas Station. (I circle this as Hailey's was also found at a gas station).*
- *Volunteer searches held four times over the course of the month she was missing, exploring even the most remote areas. Police searches conducted daily.*
- *Skeleton remains found approximately four and a half weeks later in a field off of*

Bantam Road by a hunter's dog. Dog carried part of Amber's arm to its owner.

I pull up images of the area. Bantam Road is one that I travel often on my drives to the foothills for hiking. It is a creepy place, even in the daylight. The road is completely tree covered, blocking out most of the sun even on the brightest of days. Ramshackle houses can be spotted every mile or two. I can't remember ever seeing a field in the area. Looking at an aerial map now, I see why. There is a thick forest of trees almost the entire length of the road that extends back about a quarter of a mile. In several places in the area, the trees have been cleared out to make room for fields. There are four or five discernable fields that I see on the map. I need to see if there are any bodies of water nearby. If so, maybe the killer took Hailey's body to the same location. I don't see any on the map large enough to match the image in my mind. Creeks and rivers, but no lakes or ponds. The water where Hailey lies was deep enough for her to sink, and large enough that I can recall seeing nothing but water.

I study the photos of Amber. Laughing with her friends. Holding her much younger brother in her arms, both smiling jubilantly. Hugging her mother. I watch all of the interviews and video clips I can find about her. I join the Facebook page entitled *Help Find Amber Martin*. There are dozens more pictures there that I study closely.

Again, I am assaulted with memories from the flash. I chase Amber through the forest. She trips, falls, cuts her cheek, the blood oozes down her white shirt. I laugh as she struggles to get up. I kick her back down each time she manages to rise. I rape her the first time on the forest floor, cutting off her black miniskirt with my pocketknife. I run my knife up the insides of both of her legs, just enough to draw blood. Tear off her white shirt. Force her to walk naked and barefoot after I finish. Rape her a second time once we reach the field.

Pleasure ripples through me as she screams in agony. I strangle her and watch her die as I explode inside of her. Her blue eyes stare straight through me the entire time. I smear clumps of mud all over her body. Over everything but her eyes. I want them to see. The most intense high of my life floods me as I walk away.

This time when I vomit, I don't make it to the bathroom. There's nothing in me to come out except for the ugliness of who I've become.

Again, I paint, trying to dump the hideousness somewhere. Thoughts of Jonas invade me. The comfort and safety I felt in his arms...*did the other women feel that with him right before he slaughtered them?* His lips on mine...*did that same mouth rake these women's bodies in hatred and anger as he raped them?* Feeling lost in his eyes. *Eyes, eyes, eyes.* Those dead eyes staring up at me. *Did he get lost in the eyes of the dead?*

This flash is so different. I've gotten so many memories from it. *Why? Why? Why? Why?* Tears stream down my cheeks as I paint. My mind shouts a mantra of two things over and over, both of them questions, as I work until the painting is complete. *Why? Jonas? Why? Jonas? Why? Jonas?*

The room darkens around me as I work. That which is inside of me needs to get out, though, so I don't stop. Vision isn't necessary to let it escape onto the page. It flows through my fingertips, like the mud that covered Amber's body. When I'm ready to see what has emerged, I turn on the light and look. Splatterings of color splay across the canvas to form the outline of a woman's hair and face; blue eyes prominently look off in the distance, fear etched in their corners. She's trying to find a place to run, to escape. Her hair is wisps of paint. Red, blue, brown. Coming from her eye is a single tear, the color of blood. I weep for her pain.

I'm unaware of the passing of time. I don't know if I've slept or not. A loud knock on my apartment door rouses me from the fetal position I'm lying in on the studio floor, underneath the painting of the woman crying blood. I'm too weak to stand but the knocking continues. It throbs inside of my head, beats in my chest. I can't stand up. I'm so tired. I pull myself to all fours and crawl towards the front door as the pounding continues. Finally, I reach the door and pull myself up to look out the peephole. My legs shake, and my hands tremble. I look outside where Jonas stands with his arm raised, ready to knock again.

"Go away! Go away! Go away!" I scream over and over again. He shouts my name, but I drown him out with my voice. Eventually noise from the other side of the door stops. I continue to scream as I look through the peephole again and see him walking away, shrinking off into the distance. I continue screaming when what I want to do is chase after him, have him hold me in his arms until all this madness subsides. Until I feel safe again.

I collapse into a heap in front of the door as I realize there's no longer safety anywhere for me. I'm lost within the mind of a madman. The person I want to keep me safe may be the most dangerous of all.

Time passes. I cry. I research. I paint. I vomit. I cry. I research. I paint. I vomit. Time passes. I cry. I research. I paint. I vomit. Through all of it, I become less of me and more of him. I am no longer coherent enough to make sense of my research. Bits of information float around in my jumbled mind. Names, places, pain, fear, memories. I no longer know what is a memory and what is a fact. It all swirls around and around and around.

Olivia Stephens, the girl with the blond hair. Left to rot in a ditch by the side of the road. Eaten by the vultures so that nothing was left of her but her bones. Hazel eyes.

She begs for her life. "My mommy needs me. She needs me." She cries over and over while I rape her. It gives me such a feeling of power to hear her beg. I laugh in her face when I finish. She says she will do anything to have her life spared. She takes me in her mouth to prove it. She continues through her gagging and tears. I grab her by the hair and press harder and harder and harder. I want to smother her with myself. After she finishes, she collapses onto the ground, sobbing. "Please. Just let me go. I won't tell." I wrap my hands around her thin neck, feeling her racing heartbeat beneath my fingertips. I squeeze until her hazel eyes bulge, and it beats no more. I take her floral panties with me when I leave.

Vomit. Paint. Research. Night. Day. Cry. Vomit. Paint. Research. Night. Day.

The girl with the auburn hair. Alexis Montgomery. Green eyes. I'd seen her somewhere before...I knew of her death before he invaded me. A flash from her, a glimpse into her future. Her body was found next to an abandoned barn outside of town two weeks after she went missing.

She won't cry. She doesn't scream. She refuses to plead. It is as if she knows her fate and just wants to get it over with. I prolong it, needing to hear her fear. Needing her cries to give me power. I cut her over and over. Her face. Her legs. Her arms. She is covered in blood and still won't cry. I rape her over and over, her blood smearing all over me. Covering her. She won't look at me. I need her to see me, but she keeps turning away. Refusing to make eye contact even when I scream at her to look in my damn eyes. I hurt her until she looks at me. Her right arm twists in my hand until it breaks. Her nose shatters with my punch. I pound both of her legs over and over with a hammer I find in the barn. Finally, when I put that same hammer inside of her, she looks at me. Finally, it can end. With the hammer inside of her, I move my hands to her throat and give her the ending she is waiting for. I take the hammer covered in her blood home with me.

Vomit. Paint. Research. Cry. Vomit. Paint. Research. Cry.

I find articles on the first missing woman, the one Jonas loved. I can't bring myself to read the ones about Mallory because each time I begin, my heart breaks a little more. I study Mal's picture. My mind fractures as I look at her. Going back and forth between love and rage. Caressing and hitting. Making love and raping. Her eyes stare at me as we make love; she says she loves me. Those same eyes stare at me in horror. I run my hands lovingly through her brown hair as she leans into my embrace. I grab her hair, whipping her head back, as she tries to run from me. Sobbing as I see her in the casket. Holding her hand in mine. Kissing her cold cheek. Those same cheeks that were drenched with her tears as I raped her.

I am too many people now. I am all the murdered women. I am him. I am no longer Tessa.

Tessa has been devoured by this madman. *Is it Jonas?*

I love. I hate. I hurt. I kill. I cry. I rape.

My heart breaks.

My mind shatters.

My world goes dark.

CHAPTER 13

Someone is talking but I can't force my eyes open to see who it is. They feel glued shut. I have seen too much. I can't bear to see anymore.

A man is talking. It's a voice I know. Is it Jonas? Has he come to kill me? A woman's voice. It's also familiar. I want to see who it is, but I don't have enough strength to pry my eyes open.

Other voices surround me. Someone strokes my hand. I try to pull it away but can't. My arm is stuck. Panic fills me. I am trapped. I can't move my legs.

"Let me go. Let me go. Let me go!" I scream as I pull against whatever or whoever is holding me and try to force my eyes open.

"Tess!" The man's voice shouts. "Open your eyes, Tess! It's alright; it's me."

Jonas? Who has me? "It's Cyle, Tess! You're okay. Just open your eyes."

Someone strokes my other hand. The woman speaks. "Tess, honey. It's Ophelia. I'm here. It's okay. Deep breaths."

Ophelia and Cyle. Ophelia and Cyle. I'm safe. I'm safe. I chant inside my head to calm myself enough to try again. Finally, with all my strength, I pry my eyelids open. The light assaults me, too bright to see anything. It feels like I haven't seen light for weeks. Someone must sense my discomfort as the lights dim.

I'm lying in bed in a room I don't recognize. A hospital bed, I realize as I see the rails, the IV pump next to me, the TV hanging in the corner. Cyle stands on my right, Ophelia on my left. Each of them is holding my hand even though my arms and legs have restraints. I start to panic, thinking I'm in a psychiatric ward again. I pull against the restraints as hard as I can but they won't loosen.

"Tessa, you're okay. Just relax," Ophelia speaks calmly.

"Where am I?" My voice comes out in a raspy whisper that hurts my throat.

"Here. Have a drink." Ophelia holds a straw to my mouth. I take a long drink despite the sting from the coldness.

I can finally speak again in a more normal voice. "Where am I?" My voice shakes.

"You're in the hospital. You're dehydrated so they're pumping fluids into you. They've been keeping you sedated because you've been quite agitated," Ophelia answers.

"Psych ward?" I manage to ask.

Ophelia shakes her head.

"No. Just a regular old hospital room. We both know how you feel about psych wards and wouldn't do that to you," Cyle answers. "You're restrained because you kept flailing and trying to pull out your IV. Now that you're awake, and if you promise to behave, we can call someone to remove them."

"Yes, please. What...? How...?" I can't seem to form a full question.

"Let's get these restraints off you and then we'll talk, okay?" Ophelia says.

A nurse comes in and removes the bindings on my arms and legs as Ophelia gives me another drink. Finally, I'm free and I elevate my bed to sit up. My whole body aches like I have the flu.

Cyle sits in a chair next to the bed and Ophelia takes a seat on the other side as she asks, "You sure you wanna talk about this right now?"

I nod.

"Okay. Just tell me if it's too much," Ophelia says.

I nod again. "You're in Chandlersville Memorial Hospital and have been for three days. They've been keeping you sedated and trying to get you re-hydrated," Ophelia explains.

"How did I get here?" My voice comes out in a squeak.

"You didn't show last week for your appointment, and I tried to call you. When you didn't call back, I assumed you'd just show for this Monday's appointment. You didn't, so I contacted the police to do a wellness check," Ophelia says.

"I was worried because I'd been trying all week to get in touch with you and you didn't get back to me, so I came down to check on you. You didn't answer so I let myself in. I found you collapsed on the floor in your studio," Cyle says. "Thankfully, Ophelia had already called the police and they arrived shortly after I found you, before I even had the chance to call 911."

"What happened, Tessa? What's going on?" Ophelia asks.

I can't form complete sentences. "A flash...different than before... like lightning. Murdered women...I hurt them...Hailey...in water... don't know who..." Tears flow down my cheeks as it all comes rushing back.

"Shhh...it's okay, Tessa. Let's take this slowly, okay?" Ophelia asks.

"Okay. Cyle, don't leave me, please," I say and grab his hand.

"I found some of the notes you've been making at your apartment. I've also seen your paintings. Some pretty disturbing things," Ophelia says. "So, let's back up. You had a flash, right?"

"Yes. Much different than the others. It was like lightning through my body." I answer, my voice weak, feeling the jolt even now as I mention it.

"When was this?"

"I don't remember. I don't even know what today is." I think for a moment. "After the search. The search for Hailey. Jonas..."

"Okay, so you went on the search for Hailey?" Ophelia asks, and I nod. "With Jonas?" I nod again. "You had the flash during the search?"

"No, after. I was holding Jonas' hand. There were people everywhere, bumping into us. It could've been from Jonas." I break down into a sob. Cyle pulls me into a hug.

I cry in his arms for a few minutes and then push away. "I'm a killer now."

"Whoa…what?" Cyle says sitting back, seeming to brace himself for whatever I'm about to say.

"I have memories of the murders. Killing them, raping them. It's inside of me," I say in a whisper.

"Tessa, that doesn't make you a killer," Cyle says.

"I went out one day to get food. I can't remember when it was. I saw a woman. I followed her, and…wanted to hurt her," I can hardly finish my sentence.

"But you didn't, right?" Ophelia asks.

"No. But my mind…it was hard to walk away."

"Can we back up again? Are you okay to keep going?"

I nod even though I want to beg them to have me sedated again, to protect me from myself.

"So, after the search, you were with Jonas in a crowd and you got a flash that was different than the others, like lightning, right? Then what?" Ophelia asks.

"I remember trying to run away and Jonas grabbing me. I screamed for him to let me go. Everyone was staring. Finally, I broke free and ran home."

"I'm assuming from the things found in your apartment, your flash was of the murdered girls in the area?" Ophelia asks.

"Yes. It's the same person. The same person killed them all. Tortured them, raped them. I did those things. I remember." My sobs take over and I can't go on.

"*You* did not do those things, even though the memories are in you. You know this, right?" Ophelia says.

"I don't know anything anymore. My mind…it's a mess. I'm not me anymore." I cover my face with my hands. "I can't…I need to stop, to sleep."

I push the nurse's button on the remote lying next to me.

"Tessa, you'll get through this. You're still you…my annoying little sister," Cyle tries to joke but his smile is hollow. "We'll help you get through this."

"I don't know Cyle. This one is different. I'm scared."

The nurse walks in and I beg for her to give me something to knock me out so I can forget who and what I have become. The nurse looks to Ophelia as if for consent. Ophelia gives a slight nod and, within moments, I'm given a shot that takes me back to the oblivion that sleep provides.

~

SLEEP DOES NOT PROVIDE the respite I need. My dreams are plagued with memories, with fear, with terror.

Lost in a kiss with Jonas. His hands move to my neck, tightening until I can no longer breathe. Gasping for air.

Eyes stare at me. Blue, green, hazel. They're everywhere and they see me. I try to hide from the eyes but there's no escaping their knowing gaze.

Raping Amber. I take her life, still inside of her. The ecstasy and power radiate through me as the life leaves her body.

Mallory. I hold her in my arms. Kiss her soft cheek as she sleeps next to me. She tells me she loves me. My hands close around her throat.

I wake up screaming with tears streaming down my cheeks. Cyle rushes to my side. It's dark again. *How long have I been asleep this time?*

"You're okay. I'm here," he speaks quietly.

When I can find my voice, I say, "I don't think so. Not this time. Maybe never again."

"I wish there was something I could do to take it away. I'm sorry," he says as tears fill his eyes.

"Remember that time you told me that there was some purpose in all this? That God made me this way for a reason? Why? What's the reason?"

"I don't know, but I still believe that. We just need to get you through this. Maybe we'll understand once we get to the other side," he says, but his voice betrays him. He doesn't even believe himself.

"Don't you need to go home? You can't just sit here and wait for my sanity to return…you've got kids, a wife," I ask, even though I don't want him to leave me.

"I've got a sister that needs me right now. This is exactly where I need and want to be. I'm not going anywhere, okay? Unless you'd prefer Mom and Dad come stay with you," he jokes.

I laugh despite my pain. "Ummm, no. You can stay. Speaking of Dad, how is he?"

"Mean as ever, but physically, he's healing. He's home now and in physical and occupational therapy three times a week. Cory and Michelle are practically living there, helping out. Cory's always been such a brown-noser."

"Yes, he has. I'm glad he's home. I was worried…well, when I wasn't psychotic, I was worried," I laugh.

"So, you gave into that smoking flash, huh? I found an empty pack of cigarettes and a coffee mug full of butts."

"Apparently. Speaking of which, one may be helpful right now."

"Not a chance, sis. That's one that should've gone straight into the box."

"Well…they did, but somehow they kept coming back out and finding their way into my mouth," I smile. "I've got so much to tell you. It's been a wild ride lately."

"There's time. I want to hear it all but seeing as how I don't think you slept for about a week, that's probably what you need to do."

"I know you're right, but the dreams are awful," I say as I push the call button again. "I was falling in love. Falling hard."

"I'm happy for you…nothing like that feeling is there?"

"Nothing except then realizing he may be a serial killer," I try to laugh to keep it light, but tears spill onto my cheeks instead.

Just then the nurse comes in and I plead for something stronger. Something to make the dreams go away. She administers a shot into my IV line and within minutes I am no longer in this world.

WHEN I AWAKEN AGAIN, it's dark and I think I'm alone. I have no idea how long I've been out this time, but the medicine must've been stronger because I don't remember any dreams. I hear soft snores coming from the corner and realize that Cyle has dozed off in the chair. I'm so thankful he's here. Without him, I have no idea where I'd be. Actually, I know exactly where I'd be—a few floors up in the psych unit, locked up like an animal. I don't know if I can even trust Ophelia not to put me up there. Cyle's the only one that understands and knows. All the times my parents sent me away to be caged because they didn't know what to do with me. All the medicines pumped into me throughout the years with the hopes of "curing" me of whatever diagnosis they slapped on me at the time. How much of life I missed being locked away, out of sight, out of mind. He also knows that the motives behind my parents' decisions weren't always so noble. Rather than saving me, it was often to save them the embarrassment of me. Their philosophy has always been, if you can't explain it, then hide it, bury it, and never, ever discuss it. I'm unexplainable, so therefore hidden, buried, and non-existent to them.

I fear now may be the one time I can't snap back. Maybe this time I really do need to be locked away. I remember the girl from Lenny's Bagels...how badly I wanted to hurt her. How can I be trusted to be around people now that the killer instinct has invaded me, permeated my mind, devoured my being? Like the cravings for nicotine instantly overtook me, now, lying right next to it is the craving to kill. I didn't do so well fighting the nicotine urges; how will I ever fight this thing that's so much more?

When Cyle wakes up, I need to convince him to lock me away and throw away the key. Behind closed, locked doors is exactly where I need to be. To keep everyone safe. But before he does that, there is one thing I need him to do. I need him to finish the work I started before I shattered—my research. The one person I never got around to looking up was the most important one of all, Mallory. Of course, I know the details of her actual death but nothing more. Before Cyle walks away and forgets I was ever born, I need him to get me the information on her to help piece together the puzzle that's now my mind. There are only two pieces left to complete the picture—information on Mallory and knowing who the killer is.

I lay there for hours staring at the ceiling, listening to the beeps of the monitors attached to me, the drip of the IV, and Cyle's soft snores. Like my identity, the past week comes to me only in bits and pieces. I remember a few of the paintings I did and some of the research. There are also huge holes in the time, ones I don't know if I want filled in. Mostly, I remember the rapes, the murders, the women's eyes…these are the things that haunt me. I wonder if they've medicated me as my mind feels calmer than it should. Or maybe, just having some sleep and being re-hydrated has helped with that.

A nurse comes in to take my vitals as the first hints of daylight appear, which makes Cyle stir. It takes him a moment to catch his bearings but when he does, he looks to me and smiles. "Hey, you're awake," he says, heading to my bedside after a stretch. "How are ya?"

"Now that's a loaded question," I laugh.

The nurse asks if I need anything as she finishes up. "Coffee and lots of it," I say.

"Now, there's my Tessa," Cyle laughs.

"No problem. I'll be right back with some in a few minutes," the nurse says and pulls the door closed behind her.

As soon as she's gone, Cyle says, "Let me tell you, that chair sucks." He points to it as though it's an evil beast lurking in the corner. "I've got a kink in my neck that will probably be with me for a long time."

"You don't have to stay, Cyle. Well, actually, there's a couple of things I need from you but then you can go home to the kids and Tasha. But in the meantime, sleep at my place or get a hotel or something. You're an old man, you shouldn't be sleeping in that thing."

"I didn't mean to come across like I don't want to be here. I do. But I may need to start sleeping at your place. I could get it cleaned up for you; it's a wreck," he pauses. "Now, what do you need?"

"You saw my research on the women, right?" He nods. "There's one more person I need you to look up. I don't know that they've linked her to the others based on the articles I saw. But it's the same guy."

"Are you sure this is a good idea? I don't think you can take much more."

We spend the next several hours talking about Jonas, the red flashes, the heartbreak, the dreams, the painting, Mallory's murder. When Ophelia comes in around noon, he leaves with the information I have, promising to return with what he can find. The name Mallory along with her description. I give him minimal details on her death, trying to spare him of the horrors inside of me, but tell him she was found by the side of a road, in high weeds. Ophelia gives me a raised eyebrow when she catches the tail-end of our conversation. Neither of us elaborate. Cyle kisses me on the cheek and promises to return as soon as he can.

"You've been talking to Cyle, I assume? You up to talking a bit more now?" Ophelia asks, pulling up a chair. Her hair is more untamed than usual, the curls twisting in every direction.

"I think so," I say. "I've been awake most of the night replaying everything in my head.

I had a long talk with Cyle this morning and lots of coffee, which helped."

"What would be easiest for you? Just talking, or me asking questions?"

"Maybe you should ask questions because I'm afraid of letting my mind wander without some kind of focus right now. But first, do they have me on something? Medicine, I mean?"

"I don't want you to panic, but yes, they do. I debated about what you would want to allow consent for because of your past, but you were a mess. You needed something to get you stabilized."

"I figured. I do feel an unusual calmness despite the situation. What's my cocktail this time?" I'm surprised that I'm not upset at this news, but maybe the meds are keeping me from getting too emotional. Perhaps I will be pissed later.

"Pretty heavy doses of Seroquel, Ativan, and we upped the dosage of Zoloft a bit, plus whatever they're giving you to help you sleep, which I'm sure is some kind of sedative."

"So, anti-psychotic, anti-anxiety and anti-depressant. No wonder I feel calm. I'm surprised I'm not a zombie," I laugh, but I want to cry. I've been on all of these meds numerous times. I'd hoped I was past all of this. I was, until I became a psychopathic killer.

"I think your calmness is a good thing right now. It will help us process all that you've experienced," Ophelia says. "You ready?"

"No. Not really," I say. I close my eyes and take a few deep breaths which does nothing to calm my raging storm. "But I don't know that I ever will be, so let's try."

"Okay, tell me if and when you need a break. I will start with some questions. If you feel like you are ready to just talk, then go for it. Okay?" I nod.

"You said you wanted to hurt someone, a woman, after the flash. Can you tell me more about that?"

Once I start talking, I don't stop, except to pause to blow my nose and dry my tears every couple of minutes. I describe the woman at the deli and the battle that ensued in my mind over wanting to hurt her. I share my memories of the rapes and murders, including the feelings of power, control, and excitement that came with them. The high that coursed through me as each woman took their final breath while looking into my eyes. It all comes pouring out of me, like water spilling over a broken dam drowning everything in its path. I do not pause long enough to filter what I'm saying or process what any of it means. The meds are definitely helping me detach from some of it.

Ophelia furiously takes notes as I talk; the sound of her pen provides a comforting melody as it scratches out my story. I finally reach the end of my memories and lay back against the bed exhausted. I glance at the clock and realize I have been talking for two hours straight.

"That's a lot to take in, Tess," says Ophelia, her pen finally quieting.

"I know. Try having it slam into you all at once. One minute you're a certain person, the next you're someone completely different."

"I can't imagine. It's hard even to hear what you've been through." Ophelia's awe is apparent in her widened eyes and her rigid posture. Before now, nothing I've ever told Ophelia has shocked her, surprisingly. But this...this is different even for her.

I don't say anything. Now that I've stopped talking, the feelings are catching up with me. I have no words left, only the reality of who and what I've become hanging around my neck like the weight of the world, pulling me under the raging waters I've let free.

"We need to take this one step at a time and come up with some kind of a plan for working through it, sorting everything out," Ophelia says.

For the first time ever, I feel like she doesn't get it. She's not understanding the gravity of everything I've said, the reality of the new me. "I don't think there's any working through this one. I'm no longer me. This has..." I choke back a sob. "This has made me someone completely different. I think that ..." I can't go on. I cannot say the words that are stuck in my throat, choking me. Ophelia sits quietly and waits for me to continue. "I think this time I need to be put somewhere for a long, long time. Maybe forever."

Ophelia knows how hard these words are for me. She knows my fear of institutions, medications, and psychiatrists. She's tread lightly with me for years because of these anxieties and helped me heal the still-bleeding wounds that lingered because of all of the failed attempts to "cure" me. Those wounds had finally started to heal, deep scars were the only thing remaining for some.

"I think it's too soon for either of us to make that call. We need some time for you to work through all of this before any long-term decisions are made." I can tell from the formalities she's using that this thought has already crossed her mind. "Let's take everything a day at a time right now, okay? You are in a safe place right now. The medicines are helping, and you said Cyle is here for support."

My voice shakes as I ask the question looming all around us. "So, how will we know if that's what needs to happen? How will you know?"

"I think *we* will both just know," she says sounding surer of herself than she can possibly be. She must be able to see in my eyes the questions still lingering because she continues. "If we can't figure out how to make the cravings to kill go away, then we'll know it's time."

The weight of her words crushes me. Hopefully, we'll know before it's too late. Before I've had time to act on my impulses and satisfy my cravings. Before someone else dies.

CHAPTER 14

After Ophelia leaves, I am mentally, emotionally, and physically drained. Sharing the horrors in my mind leaves me depleted. I try to sleep but to no avail. I want a cigarette. I can't stop thinking of the women. One moment I'm full of sadness and empathy for them, their suffering, their families. The next moment my thoughts become *his* and a flood of pleasure at their suffering, their pain, their deaths wash over me. It truly feels like I have a devil on one shoulder, an angel on the other, both whispering into my ear to sway my thoughts and actions. I am both the angel and the devil. I resist asking for something to knock me out as long as I can, because I want to be fully alert when Cyle returns so that I can take in everything he found out about Mallory. When I can no longer handle the feeling of having multiple personality disorder, I finally give in and beg the nurse to take me out of my misery, at least for a little while.

I wake up and realize the daylight is gone. I immediately look to the chair in the corner to see if Cyle's back yet. It's empty. I start to panic because I don't want to be alone with him inside of me. I pick up the phone and dial Cyle's number. He answers on the first ring.

"You okay?" he asks.

"Yeah. Just wondering if you're coming back tonight or if you already did and I missed you."

"I'm actually heading back that way in a few minutes...trying to get a few more things done at your place before I do. I plan on staying with you tonight...that dreadful chair is calling my name," he laughs. "Do you need me to bring anything?"

My voice shakes and my eyes burn from trying to hold back my tears. "No. I don't like being alone. It helps knowing you'll be back soon."

"Aww, sis. Don't cry. I'm hurrying. Give me a half hour tops, okay?"

"Take your time. I'll be okay. I'm not crying...yet. I'm okay." I ramble.

We hang up after one more assurance that he will be here soon. I turn on the TV and start flipping through the channels, trying to find something to distract me. *Criminal Minds*...nope. *Law and Order SVU* is on the screen long enough for me to see a woman bound and gagged with tears pouring down her bloodied cheeks. I quickly change the channel, but my thoughts spiral out of control. *Amber covered in mud. Hailey's blood covering me as I take her virginity. Cutting Alexis over and over again, trying to make her look into my eyes.*

No! Stop! I scream inside of my head. *This isn't me. I did not do this. I did not hurt them. I am Tessa! I am not a killer. I don't want to hurt anyone. This is not me. Someone else did these things, not me.*

I continue my chant even though the images continue to batter me. I break down in sobs loud enough to make a nurse come running from down the hallway.

"Are you okay?" The nurse asks as she takes my hand. A blue flash shocks me back to my senses. I tell her I'm okay, thankful a good memory will come as a result of her touch. Maybe it will erase some of the bad that now consumes me.

"Do you need another shot?" She asks, concern heavy in her eyes. I'm sure these people have no clue what they're dealing with or what to do with me.

"No, my brother..." I start to say.

As if on cue, Cyle walks in the room. "Hi honey! I'm ho-oooome," he announces with his best Jack Nicholson impersonation.

"I'll be okay now," I assure the nurse. She smiles slightly and pats my hand again before leaving the room.

"Thanks for hurrying back," I say as he takes a seat in his favorite chair.

"No problem-o," he says as he sits. "So, how'd everything go with Ophelia? You look pretty rough again."

I fill him in on my meeting with her minus the gory details, trying to rush through it all. I want to get to the information he found about Mallory.

"So, were you able to figure out anything more?" I ask.

"I did find some things out. I started with the notes you had and kinda worked to fill in the blanks. You're right, they're now looking at whether there's a link between the four girls that have been murdered in recent years. It seems that Cardell has tried to repress any information to that end because it would look bad for the university to have a serial killer on the loose. But now, with all the student protests and some parental involvement, their cover-up is no longer working so well. News stations are now calling him the Cardell Killer," Cyle pulls a notebook out of his overnight bag. "So, it looks like the first girl to be killed in this area was Alexis Montgomery, in September 2011. Next was Olivia Stephens, killed in October 2012—so about a year apart. Then a year and a half went by with no murder, until April 2014 when Amber Martin was killed. And now, of course, only six months later, Hailey Garrison is missing. They still haven't found her."

"She's in water," I whisper, remembering her sinking out of my sight. The beauty of it.

"I'm not sure where, though."

"I don't know that they've done a lot of water searches at this point. They have done bi-weekly group searches and then daily police searches, some even using drones. They've gotten thousands of tips, all seeming to lead nowhere."

"What about...what about Mallory? Did you find anything on her?"

"Now, she was a bit harder to get information on. I did find some things, though, I think. There was a Mallory Kasler who was raped and murdered at Pinkerton University in Georgia in September 2010. From what I could find, she was in town planning her wedding and visited with some friends that attended Pinkerton that evening. A group of them went out to dinner and then Mallory headed back to her parents' house, but never showed. They found her car broken down by the side of the road the next day and her body two days later, not too far from the car, in…"

"In high weeds," I finish the sentence for him. "She was naked. I remember taking all of her clothes with me, everything but her shoes. Purple silk blouse, black tight pants, lacey black thong and matching bra." I remember making her remove each item of clothing while I watched, the moonlight making it all more seductive. I remember the feel of the silk in my hands, breathing in the scent of her perfume when I held it to my face. Binding her hands with the black pants once they were removed.

Cyle interrupts my memories as my heart races with the thrill of them. "What are you thinking?"

"Just remembering," I say, breathless. "She was the first kill. She was the one that showed him what a release it was, that started his cravings for more." What I don't say is how I prolonged her death, wanting to watch her die over and over again. I would choke her until she lost consciousness, then let up, slapping her back to awareness. Then, I would do it again, loving the look in her eyes right before she lost too much oxygen. Each time her eyes would go wide with fear. I did this a total of five times before I could no longer contain myself and had to squeeze tighter and tighter until I felt the crush of her windpipe beneath my fingers, her brown eyes bulging from the growing pressure. The way her eyes sunk back once I released my hands. I remember untying her hands and caressing her body, those brown eyes peering into my soul, seeing me.

"Tess, you're worrying me. What's going on?" Cyle snaps me back to the present. I am panting with excitement at the memories; a slight sweat has worked its way across my brow. Now that I'm back in my mind, I'm horrified at the pleasure coursing through me.

"This is awful Cyle. I remember it all. When I get stuck there, in those memories, I am him and I enjoy remembering. It is sick. *I'm sick!*"

"You can't help the memories he gave you. *You* are not sick. *He* is the sick one. You're just the unlucky woman who happened to cross the path of the wrong person, kind of like the rest of these women."

Tears spill down my cheeks. If only they could wash away this ugliness inside of me. "It feels like me," I whisper.

"We can stop for now if you want. Seems like you may need a break."

"No, I want to know. I'm confused about how Mallory is linked to this same guy since she was murdered in Georgia, but there's no doubt she is." Then it hits me as hard as the lightning bolt flash did. "Did it say who she was engaged to or anything about her upcoming wedding?"

"Yes. I'm not sure you want to know all of this right now, though."

"I do. Please just tell me," I say, already knowing what he's about to say.

"Her fiancé was also in Georgia at the time, although not with her that night, according to her friends." He leans forward and puts his hand on top of mine. "It was Jonas."

"Oh my god. It *is* him, isn't it? Just like me to start to fall in love with a crazy serial killer, huh?" It feels like an elephant is sitting on my chest, crushing me. "But he loved her. I know he did. I remember loving her and the heartbreak after her death. It's as real to me as the murders."

"The police did question him extensively then since most of the time, murders are committed by someone close to the victim. It seems he checked out, though."

"It has to be him. He is the only one that's connected to all the victims. I was holding his hand when I had the flash. There's no doubt he loved her, but maybe his desire to kill took over and was stronger than the love he felt."

"From everything you have said about him, he seems like a good guy, Tess. I can't imagine it'd be him."

"Don't most serial killers seem like normal guys? Ted Bundy. The

BTK killer. Think about it. They blend in. They get people to trust them so that nobody suspects their hidden demons. What a better place for a serial killer who likes to rape and torture young, beautiful women than a college campus! You should see his students with him. The women all seem to adore him." I stop before I can say the words, *just like I did.*

My head swirls in a whirlwind of conflicting thoughts and memories. My feelings for Jonas—how quickly and deeply I was starting to fall. Those dreamy eyes. Those lips. The way he seems to connect with his students. The trust they obviously have in him. Five women dead.

Five women that all have at least one thing in common...Jonas. The heartbreak over Mallory's death coupled with the memories of killing her are unbearable. As the assault on my brain and heart continue, I struggle to breathe. I am being trampled by these parts of me that make no sense. I'm no longer in the room with Cyle, rather lost within the prison of my mind, my memories. Maybe I'm stuck here forever. This time I may not come back.

A NURSE MUST HAVE GIVEN me another shot because I wake up in what I think is the dead of night with Cyle sitting right next to me, watching me sleep. I try to speak but my mouth is too dry, feeling full of cotton.

"Why don't you take a drink?" Cyle says and points to a hospital mug full of ice water on the tray next to my bed.

I take a long drink, feeling like I've been stranded in a desert without water for weeks. The meds they are giving me are working to knock me out and calm me down, but they are taking their toll in other ways, like this unquenchable thirst.

"Feel any better?"

"Yeah. I had a good dream—I think it was from a flash I got with the nurse earlier, a blue one. I remembered having a baby, a beautiful baby girl named Isabella. I remember the feel of her in my arms, the smell of her, the love that overtook me the instant I saw her sweet little face. Quite a relief, actually, to have something like that instead of what I've been having the past couple of weeks."

"Good. You deserve to have a few good moments. These last few weeks have been awful," Cyle pauses. "You scared the hell out of me earlier."

"What happened?" I ask.

"You weren't here. I mean physically, you were sitting there trembling and unable to breathe, but you had some rapid eye movement going on, almost like you were in a dream state. You were talking between gasps for breath, but I couldn't understand what you were saying. I tried to get you to come back to the room with me, but the nurse had to sedate you."

"I remember my thoughts but you're right, I was nowhere near this room." Tears well in my eyes, threatening to spill as I say the words I need to. "Which leads me to what I need to talk to you about. I think this time…I think there's no coming back from this. This isn't something I can stick in my memory box and hope it goes away. It's consuming me."

Worry and confusion fills his eyes. "What are you saying?"

"I'm saying, I think you need to figure out a facility where I can go for a long, long time." The words taste bitter as I spit them out.

"Somewhere like…?"

"A psychiatric facility." A shudder works its way through me.

Cyle crosses his arms and sits back in the chair. "No way Tessa. You've been there, done that and it didn't do a damn bit of good. I'm not Mom and Dad. I'm not locking you away somewhere just to get you out of my hair," Cyle responds, on the verge of shouting. "Psychiatric facilities are for people that are mentally ill, which is not what you are."

The tears flow freely now. I love how Cyle always defends me. I wish that what he says were true, though.

"You're right. When Mom and Dad locked me up, I wasn't mentally ill. I don't think I can say the same thing, now. That flash…I think I now have whatever illness he has. Kind of like I'm addicted to nicotine, now, thanks to a stupid flash. Or when I learned to speak

French through one touch. Same thing...only this time, I inherited a mental illness and a craving to kill."

"Damn it, Tess! It's not the same," Cyle shouts. "I don't want to talk about this with you. You are *not* going away. Period. End. Of. Discussion."

"I already mentioned it to Ophelia."

"I need some air. I'm going for a walk," Cyle says and rises, pushing his chair out of the way and stomping out the door.

I can't remember a time before now that he has ever gotten angry at me. He's definitely never raised his voice with me. I don't really understand where it's coming from. I know he wants to protect me and has always taken on that role, but he must know that I am desperate to even suggest this as an option. He does not understand the war raging within my mind, doesn't comprehend that there's someone evil invading my soul.

I am that someone evil.

CYLE DOESN'T RETURN until morning, and he's accompanied by Ophelia. It can't be good that one, he's stayed away so long, and two, that he felt the need to bring in Ophelia for his return.

"Good morning?" I say more as a question than a statement.

"Good morning," Ophelia says in return. Cyle will not even look at me.

For the first time in days, I'm sitting up in a chair with my hair brushed instead of lying in bed, hair a matted mess of tangles. Ophelia pulls a chair up next to me and Cyle sits on the edge of the bed.

"To what do I owe the pleasure of *both* of you coming today?"

"I called this morning to check on you. The nurses said you had a rough night. I figured it'd be best if we talked about a few things," Ophelia says.

"Okay," I say with raised eyebrows. Are they getting ready to tell me they agree with me? That I'm now officially nuts-o and need to be committed somewhere?

"First, I want to let you know before it hits the news that Hailey's body was found in Lake Minerva," Ophelia says.

I gasp at the memories of her floating on the surface of the water, her hair billowing around her like a crown. Floating and slowly sinking. The beauty of her final moments as she drifted away. The torture of her last moments left on earth.

"Are you okay?" Ophelia asks.

"Yes. Just remembering," I say. "I'm glad they found her, for her poor parent's sake. This past couple of weeks must have been torture for them. Any news of possible suspects?"

"They've got quite a few people that they're questioning but haven't released any names. At least the school and the local police are now admitting that there is possibly some connection between the four murdered women. Student groups have made sure to raise their voices loud enough to national media that they really had no choice."

"Good. They need to tie Mallory to the others, too. That's probably the missing link needed to be able to find the killer," I say, my brain thrown back into overdrive, battling between my mind, the killer's mind, thoughts of Jonas, memories of Mallory.

"Also, I wanted to tell you the doctor is releasing you today. You're physically stable and therefore there's no reason for them to keep you," Ophelia says.

Cyle raises his eyes slightly, anticipating my reaction.

"They can't. I cannot go home. You have to make them keep me or send me somewhere else…" I say, the tightness in my chest feeling like I've swallowed a fist.

"Just hear me out, Tessa. If you get all worked up, you're not going to be able to process what we need to talk about. Can you take some deep breaths and calm down?" Ophelia says slowly. Sometimes her ability to stay so cool and collected just pisses me off.

I breathe deeply like she's taught me to…breathe in to a count of four, hold my breath for seven seconds, breathe out to a count of eight. It takes five times for my racing heart and mind to calm enough to continue. "Okay, I'm good," I say.

"I understand that you don't feel safe being alone right now and don't trust yourself. You think you need to be in a psychiatric facility," Ophelia says, and I nod. "There are a couple of problems with that. One, the waiting list for a bed in a psych facility is longer than my arm. Two, I'm not comfortable with that step at this point and wanted to present an alternative."

Tears fill my eyes. I'm not sure whether they're from relief or panic.

Cyle finally looks at me and speaks. "You know I've always said that I think of your flashes like a gift. And I know that a lot of times, you've felt like they're more of a curse. But I still believe one hundred percent that God gave you this ability for a reason. Maybe helping find the guy who's killing these women is that reason. You can help save anyone else from being hurt if you can figure this out."

"I can't...I've tried, but I don't know how," I'm crying now. Again. I wish I could see this like Cyle does, as a *gift* that I can use to help the world in some way. How can I help save other women from the killer when he's already devoured me?

"I think you can. No, I *know* you can. Just listen to Ophelia's plan and consider it," Cyle says. "Okay?"

I nod through my tears.

"I'm going to stay at your place with you for a while, to make sure you're safe and to ease your concerns about the possibility of you hurting someone else," Cyle says.

"You can't," I sob. "You have a job, a family. You can't drop everything to take care of me."

"I can, and I will."

"I'm a grown woman. I hate that I need a babysitter. If you guys agree that it's not safe for me to be alone then obviously you see my point. Lock me up."

"Tessa, Cyle can't be your *babysitter*, as you're implying. If he says he'll stay, his purpose would be to help you until you feel safe on your own. He would be there as a support system, which anyone would need if they'd been through what you just went through," Ophelia says.

"And what if I never feel safe again. Then what?" I say.

"You will. Just listen to the plan," Cyle says. "Now, can we continue without you shooting it down before you've heard the whole thing?"

I run my fingers across my lips to signal they are zipped, cross my arms, and wait for them to continue discussing their plan to save me.

"First, we'll get you home and let you get settled. I want you to paint as much as you can, and I'll meet with you as often as you need over the next couple of weeks. The goal is to get as many of these memories out of you as we can, whether through talking or painting," Ophelia says. "And I would also like you to meet with a colleague of mine who is experienced in hypnosis. I'm hoping that he'll be able to tap into more of your memories about the day of the flash and possibly even be able to get some of the killer's memories that you inherited that day."

I want to scream but I keep my mouth shut. *Hypnosis*? That's scary on many levels. It is hard enough for me to reveal parts of myself knowingly to Cyle and Ophelia, whom I trust. But, to uncover parts of my subconscious mind, parts that I am not even aware of, to some stranger scares the hell out of me.

"I would like to help you continue your research on the women. Maybe we can even go to the police, I don't know. I think the only way you're truly going to be able to heal from any of this is if the guy is caught," Cyle says.

I can't keep my mouth shut any longer. "Go to the police? Really, Cyle? Why? So they can laugh in my face? Or worse yet, think I am the one who committed these murders. Maybe that's the way to keep everyone safe, make the cops think I did it. Then they'll lock me up."

"I said I don't know. It was just an idea. I wish they'd listen because I think you have a lot of important details that they need to hear. We are trying to help here. Call me selfish, but I can't lock you away like Mom and Dad did," Cyle says, wiping a tear before it has a chance to fall. "I *won't*."

Seeing Cyle on the verge of tears puts cracks in the walls I've put up. "I know, Cyle. I know you guys are trying to help and I appreciate it. I do. I'm just scared and overwhelmed and lost."

"You have every reason to be. Anyone in your position would feel the same," Ophelia says. "Do you trust me... or us, rather?" I nod. "Then will you give the plan a try?" She asks.

I barely get a yes out before Cyle has me wrapped in his arms telling me that everything will be okay. What I don't say is that their plan has one crucial piece missing. I'll wait to tell them my addition to the plan later, after I'm home and settled.

I must see Jonas. I must find out if he is the killer.

CHAPTER 15

I leave the hospital with Cyle to a day that's damp, chilly, and gray with trees that are nearly barren. The only green remaining is in the evergreens. Everything looks and feels dead. *Dead. Like those women. Their eyes, staring at me...*

"We need to stop and pick up your prescriptions on the way home," Cyle says, snapping me back to the present.

I say okay even though I want to scream no. Being back in the world, in the safety of this car, is already assault enough on my senses. I can't be around other people, especially women.

Before I know it, as though I'm on autopilot, we've pulled into the Walgreen's parking lot and Cyle sits staring at me, not budging from his seat.

"Yes?" I ask with raised eyebrows.

"Ummm...I thought we could go in together," he says sheepishly.

"Can I just sit in the car and you run in?"

"Part of our plan is that you aren't alone right now, so it would probably be best if you come in with me."

I unsnap my seatbelt and grab my purse with all the dramatic flair I can muster.

"Seriously? I can't sit in the car by myself for five freaking minutes while you run in and get my meds? This is ridiculous." I get out of the car and slam the door shut before he has the chance to respond.

I march towards the door and his footsteps follow behind. Once inside, he catches up to me. We head back to the pharmacy counter and as always, there is a line. I grab a celebrity magazine to leaf through while we wait, hoping it will provide a distraction from the lights, the chatter, my frustration.

Without a conscious thought, I know that there's a young woman with auburn hair standing alone in aisle three, perusing the lipstick. Another woman with a blonde pixie cut is alone in aisle seven, grabbing cold medicine. I try to focus on the magazine and the pictures of the celebrities all decked out for their latest red-carpet awards ceremony, but instead my attention keeps drifting back to the two women, aware of their every move.

I give my name and ask for four prescriptions that the hospital called in. The woman in aisle three moves towards the eye shadow. The woman in aisle seven heads back towards the pharmacy line.

"Tess?" Cyle says sharply.

I jerk my attention to him. "Yeah? Sorry."

"They need your insurance card," I quickly get it out of my wallet and hand it to the man behind the counter. Cyle turns to me and whispers. "What's going on? You okay?"

"Yeah, I'm fine," I say although my heart races now that the blonde is within such proximity, only two people behind us in line. So close I can smell her perfume—something fruity.

I look back to my magazine and occasionally glance up to watch her. She's on her cell phone. She sends a text and then smiles. I wonder how that same mouth would look wrenched in pain. How would those eyes look with no life left in them? She glances up at me and must notice me staring as she quickly looks away, as if I'm unimportant, insignificant. I could make her see me. I could show her my importance. She's just like the rest of them, looking right past me.

Cyle grabs me by the elbow and steers me away. We quickly walk back through the store towards the front door, Cyle guiding me, forcing me along. I turn back once to see the blonde who now stands at the pharmacy counter. The woman with the auburn hair is at the checkout counter at the front of the store, laughing with the clerk. An ache fills me now that I can see her in full view…those long legs, those rounded breasts, that ass. We no sooner make it out the door than I vomit on the sidewalk.

"Are you okay?" Cyle asks, compassion heavy in his voice.

"No. I tried to tell you and Ophelia that I'm not okay, but you won't listen. No one ever listens! Those women…the things that I wanted to do…"

"Let's get you in the car," he says as he guides me towards it. I again insist on driving and slip into the driver's seat despite Cyle's raised eyebrows. As soon as he's in, he turns to me.

"What women? What are you talking about?"

"Two women in the store. Alone. A blonde and a tall one with auburn hair," I say feeling like I may throw up again. "I just want to get home."

"I don't know that you're okay to drive," he says.

To prove him wrong, I pull out and hit the accelerator, going faster than I probably should. Thank God we're only a few minutes from my apartment.

"I didn't even notice them. You've got to talk about what happened back there. Part of the plan, remember?"

I hate this stupid plan already and I've only been out of the hospital for about a half an hour. "It's crazy. It's like I have this radar now that makes me hyper-aware and sensitive to any young women that are alone. I was simply standing there, pissed at you for making me go in, and trying to look at a magazine. Then my radar goes off alerting me to any *possibilities*," I pause, choking back the bile that's risen in my throat. "The woman at the front counter when we left, with the auburn hair?"

Cyle shakes his head to tell me he has no idea who I'm talking about.

"You want me to share? You guys think talking about this will fix me? Okay…here goes. My thoughts were how I'd love to touch her long legs, her breasts, her ass. The blonde in the pharmacy line…I wanted her to *see* me like I made the other girls see me. I wondered how her face would look distorted with pain," I pause and wipe the tears from my cheeks. "And now you know why I need to be locked away."

Once we've pulled in the parking lot and I've shut off the car, I look at Cyle. All the color is drained from his face and tears glisten in his eyes. "I'm so sorry Tess. This is more awful than I can ever begin to imagine. But you made it. You made it through without acting on anything. You're home now. Safe."

I take a deep breath trying to absorb what he's saying. He is right. No one got hurt. I also have no doubt that it would've been a different scenario had he left me alone in the car. I will never admit to him that he was right in making me go in but thank God he did.

I cannot remember the exact state my place was left in, but from what I do recall, it was a mess. Now it's sparkling clean, and a fresh bouquet of flowers sits on the kitchen table. Cyle has obviously spent lots of time getting everything in order. It's such a relief to be back home.

"The place looks great. Thank you, Cyle."

"Don't tell Tasha how well I clean, or she'll expect this all the time, okay? Our little secret," he smiles. "So, a few things. Ophelia stocked the kitchen, so lots of food choices. I dug the inflatable mattress out of your closet so, if it's okay with you, I'll camp out on your floor. And it's probably best if we wait a bit to go into your studio."

I glance down the hallway at the mention of it and notice the door is closed. "Okay...but why?"

"Seeing all of the paintings you did over that couple of weeks may be pretty rough. Ophelia needs to be here when you go in if that's okay, which...she's coming tomorrow morning. If you want to paint in the meantime, I can bring things out here for you."

I breathe a sigh of relief, knowing I'm not ready to see the images that came straight from the depths of my darkness.

"So, nap or food?" Cyle asks, one hand pointed towards the kitchen, one towards the bedroom.

"Food. I'm starving."

~

WE MAKE SANDWICHES FOR LUNCH, dubbed by him as *Cyle's Classic...* ham and turkey on toasted bread with mayo, spicy mustard, avocado, cucumber, and bean sprouts. They are so good, and I am so hungry, that I have two. The tension leaves my neck as we spend time in the kitchen prepping the sandwiches and chatting away like old times. He catches me up on everything going on with the family.

Cory and Michelle had been staying with Mom and Dad to help out since he was released from the hospital. Cyle says that for whatever reason, they trusted that Chloe, their sixteen-year-old daughter, could effectively look after her younger brothers, Cameron, who's fourteen, and Curt, who's ten. That great plan lasted about a week before Chloe threw a huge party for about a hundred of her "closest" friends that included loads of alcohol the first Friday they were gone. The cops were called, which in turn meant Cory and Michelle were called. It appears Cameron had agreed to go along with it as long as he could invite his friends, too. Ten hormone ravaged fourteen-year-old boys showed up to gawk at all the scantily clad teenage girls. Poor Curt got loaded down with bowls of candy and chips and sent to his parent's room to watch TV until one of them came and let him out. Instead of one of his siblings doing the honor, though, a police officer interrupted his movie marathon and candy binge to have him ride along to the station to await the arrival of their parents. Cyle can't keep a straight face while telling the story, saying that with the stunts Cory pulled when he was younger, he deserved every ounce of this payback. Now Cory and Michelle are taking turns helping with Mom and Dad so that someone can guard their children twenty-four hours a day.

Chris breezed into town two days after Dad got home for a quick appearance before heading off with another group of buddies to do the Rim-to-Rim hike at the Grand Canyon. I'm sure that Mom acted like she'd been graced with the presence of God Himself since Chris has always been her favorite. It's a good thing Chris is brilliant and writes computer programs that earn him boatloads of money so that he can spend most of his life travelling. We've decided that Chris is probably gay, but it'll be a cold day in hell before he tells our very Catholic parents and loses his favorite child status with Mom. Cyle said that he point-blank asked Chris once, after they both had consumed a few drinks, and instead of answering the question, he simply said that our parents would drop dead if anyone ever told them that. Cyle never brought it up again. I must admit, the thought of our parents finding out he's gay gives me a little thrill because for once I wouldn't be the only "outcast", in their eyes. Of course, the rest of us would be fine with it and happy to find out that he had someone special in his life...well, maybe everyone but Cory, who acts more like our parents every day, according to Cyle.

Cyle says Dad is doing well but fights his therapists and Mom like crazy over doing his exercises. Mom, of course, has hired a whole slew of in-house "helpers" to tend to him so that she can continue her routine of shopping, pedicures, manicures, tennis dates, bridge playing, and "girl time" with her friends. Cyle says she runs more now than before since Dad's mood has deteriorated even further since his stroke. *Ahhh...good old Mom.* Does best at taking care of numero uno... herself. Of course, Cyle tries to always spin a positive light on Mom, saying that this has all been really hard on her and that Dad is being so ungrateful and mean that it's no wonder she can't stand to be around him. Cyle, with his middle child syndrome, always acts as her defender.

His stories make me laugh so hard my sides hurt. They also leave me filled with longing. Longing to live in the same family that Cyle does. Longing to know my brothers, my niece and nephews. Longing to be included.

"Do any of them know about what's going on with me?" I finally work up the nerve to ask.

"Ophelia talked with Tasha and encouraged her to tell Mom and Cory that you were hospitalized with some health issues. Do you want them to know more?"

"No. They wouldn't get it, so there's no point. I'm sure it'd just be further evidence to them that I'm a crazy freak," I say. "Did they ask any questions, express any concern?"

"Mom of course cried and ripped up about twenty tissues. She said that if Dad weren't so ill, she'd come down to help take care of you."

"Yeah. Right," I say.

"We both know the likelihood of that ever happening is pretty slim, but she did seem legitimately concerned. Tasha assured her that you were okay and that someone would let her know if she is needed."

I guess her concern is something. It'd be nice if she'd express it to me but at least she feels something other than hatred, disgust, and embarrassment.

"Oh, I forgot to tell you," Cyle says, pointing to a box on the coffee table. "Ophelia arranged for a new phone to be delivered. Yours was kind of in pieces on the floor over there." He points to the wall that I remember throwing it against. "Your number is the same so that everyone will have your contact information."

"Thanks, Cyle. Now my whole slew of friends will be able to reach me," I laugh, but want to cry. "I freaked out when Jonas called after I ran away from him at the search. My poor phone was the casualty of my freak out."

"I see that. Which is why Ophelia and I couldn't reach you. Now, you're accessible," Cyle says clearing our plates and loading them in the dishwasher. "I don't know about you, but I think a nap is in order. You up for that?"

"Sure am. I've got a full belly and lots of meds pumping through me. A nap sounds great."

"Speaking of meds…sorry, but it's time to load up," Cyle tosses the prescription bags to me.

I pull each bottle from their paper bags and inspect them. They still have me on pretty heavy doses of Seroquel, Zoloft, Ativan and now Trazodone (to help me sleep, I assume). It says to take the Trazodone at bedtime, but one now won't hurt; nap time could be considered bedtime. I down my pills and collapse onto my bed, pulling the comforter snuggly around me. The last thing I remember thinking is how nice it is to have Cyle here, keeping me safe, as I drift off to my sleep escape.

∾

I JOLT awake after an hour and a half with dreams of Jonas still swarming around my mind. I lay in bed trying to piece together my dreams, with Cyle still sleeping soundly on the air mattress next to my bed.

I was kissing Jonas, lost in his arms and the warmth of his lips. Then, without breaking our kiss, his hands were around my throat, choking me. I tried to force my eyes open to look at him but couldn't. As I'm about to lose all of my air, his lips still working their magic on mine, I open them. Instead of Jonas' face, I am looking into my own eyes. Then, my perspective in the dream changes and I become the one with my hands around Mallory's throat, kissing her and choking her at the same time. She opens her eyes to plead for me to stop and that's when I woke up. I don't have to be a dream analyst to figure out the meaning behind this one. I have to know if Jonas is the killer. If he is, I've got to figure out a way to let the police know, to help them figure it out. Cyle's right, yet again. I cannot just sit by and idly do nothing while more women are at risk of getting killed.

As quietly as possible, I get up and tiptoe towards the kitchen. I grab my phone, knowing I need to send this text before Cyle wakes up and stops me.

> *Hi! Long time, no talk. I'm truly sorry about everything. I've been ill and staying with friends. I'm back now and feeling much better. Would you let me buy you a cup of coffee or glass of wine to make up for my awful behavior?*

I pause a few seconds before hitting send, wondering if I'm making a huge mistake. Despite my racing heart, I hit the send button. This is the only way to know. I get up to make a pot of coffee when my phone pings, indicating a new text.

It's good to hear from you. I have been SO worried about you. I'm glad to hear you're better. And yes, you were awful to me (but I might forgive you) and you owe me a cup of coffee AND a glass of wine for that!

I chuckle. He is the same old Jonas, the one I was starting to fall in love with before the insanity took over. As I dump coffee grounds in the filter, I pretend that we are the same people as before. Tessa, the artist, falling in love with Jonas, the professor. I push start on the coffee maker and respond.

I'm glad you're such a forgiving person. I probably owe you dinner too if it's payback for my awfulness.

Gosh, I miss this playful banter with him and the person I thought he was. The person I was allowing myself to become—more open, more carefree, willing to risk a few flashes to be with him. My phone pings.

Well, now that you mention it… lol. Seriously, now. Whatever you're up for is fine. I can even come by and bring dinner, coffee, wine, whatever. Sooner rather than later would be good. I've missed you.

My heart melts a little. He's so sweet. Or, he has me targeted as his next victim and wants to get on with it. No way a guy that can be so thoughtful and romantic could torture, rape, and kill these women. But my flash, my memories, his connection to all of them…

How about coffee tomorrow afternoon? Monticello's around two?

I have no idea what time Ophelia is stopping by tomorrow but assume it'll be early as she's one of those dreadful morning people. Figuring out how to sneak away from Cyle or convince him this is okay is another story altogether. I will think on that one later.

Sounds perfect…counting the minutes. Let me know if you need ANYTHING. So glad to hear from you.

He's so caring and romantic…so perfect. Except for that one little part where he may be a serial killer.

I can't wait. See you then.

I just hit send when Cyle walks out of the bedroom, yawning and stretching.

"Do I smell coffee?" He says, stumbling towards the kitchen.

"Sure do. Come sit and I'll get you a cup," I say as I rise.

He plops onto the couch. "I would object but I'm exhausted. Did you sleep?"

"Yeah…just woke up about fifteen minutes ago. I was trying to let you sleep. You were out."

I pour our coffee, putting lots of sugar and cream in Cyle's.

"That wonderful smell of heaven woke me. I was out, but you could've gotten me up. I'm supposed to be here to help you, not catch up on my sleep," he says and takes a drink of his coffee. "Perfect."

"I would've woken you if I needed you, but I'm okay. I was thinking maybe I would do a bit of research."

"If you give me a few minutes to wake up, I'll help. Or, if you want, you can just relax and not do anything today," he says.

"That's an oxymoron…me relax. Impossible right now. Relaxation allows way too much time for my thoughts to run rampant."

"Okay, but I don't want you doing too much. Researching is likely to do the same to your thoughts."

"You're right but to quote someone very insightful, *I was given this gift for a reason and maybe that reason is to help find the killer.* I can't do that if I just sit here and try to avoid it," I say.

"Touché."

We chat as we finish our first cup of coffee. After re-filling our mugs, I grab my laptop and ponder where to begin. I really have no choice but to continue the search where Cyle left off, with Mallory.

WE SPEND the rest of the evening researching and talking through everything. The only breaks I take are those I need for meltdowns or psychotic breaks, whatever they are. Cyle helps pull me back whenever he senses I'm spacing out, going to a different time and place in my mind, carried away by my memories. Ophelia must've given him some counseling techniques training. He's really good at forcing me to talk instead of internalizing. Either that, or he's missed his calling in life.

I join Facebook pages for all the women. *Justice for Alexis, Help find Olivia Stephens' Killer, Help find Hailey Garrison, Memories of Mallory* and *Save our Girls*, a page that links together all the women from Cardell that have gone missing or been killed. Mallory's page is the hardest to look at. Her sister, Janine, started the page right after her murder and posted almost daily at that time. She's kept it up for five years and vows to do so until her killer is brought to justice.

In the beginning, Janine posted a new picture of Mallory every day, but it's slowed to once a week, some from right before she was killed, others back to infancy. My heart shatters as I fill with memories of loving her, of *still* loving her. There are many pictures of her and Jonas together. The most devastating are their engagement photos...their love for each other is apparent. The most touching is of them standing in a field, Mallory facing the camera, eyes downcast and a slight smile on her face with Jonas' arms wrapped around her. He is gently kissing the side of her head, his eyes closed, seeming to savor the feel of her in his arms, the scent of her, the beauty of their merging hearts. That photo shows their love—the strength of it.

I decide again that there is *no way* he could have killed her. Then memories of her murder attack me. With each memory, my heart breaks again over losing her. My thoughts spiral out of control. Jonas loved her. Jonas may be her killer. I can't make the two thoughts mesh in my mind. Even in my confusion, my heart quickens with elation at the memories of the horrors she endured. Cyle notices me drifting away and pulls me back each time, making me talk it through. It is absolute hell.

We both spend time reading through comments on anything we can find via social media, news reports, blogs, trying to see what ideas others had about who the murderer could be. There are so many people trying to play detective, but we thought that maybe if we see some similarities in folks' suspicions it would give us a good starting point. The only common thread is that people speculate it is someone who works for the university in some capacity. Several psychics have even reported their visions to the police, and that a Cardell University employee is responsible for the murders. Chaundra Raines, one of the same psychics that claims this, was also the one to report her vision to police of Hailey in water and Amber covered in mud. I'm not one to go with whatever a psychic says because a lot of them have simply mastered the art of BS in exchange for large sums of money. I do believe some are born with a gift (or curse), like mine, though. From Chaundra's comments, she seems to truly want to help find the killer and stop this madness. Even though it scares me almost as much as hypnosis, Cyle and I decide that I need to go see her, too, see what she can get from me. I call and leave her a message asking her to please return my call as soon as possible.

Before we head to bed, we come up with a solid plan for tomorrow. Ophelia is coming at nine. *Ughh...I hate morning people.* Then, since this psychic may be onto something, we plan to spend as much time on campus as we can. I'll take the risk of touching as many people as possible, hoping to get a flash that leads us back to him. I am still fragile from my fractured mind, so this is a risk, but Cyle promises to be with me every step of the way to make sure I'm safe and call it quits when I need to. He will also act as my "reporter". If I have any flashes, I will let him know the color and the person so he can write down a description. That way, if the flash doesn't manifest itself until later, hopefully we can look back and piece it all together. I will wait until morning, after my appointment with Ophelia, to tell him the last stop of our day which will probably give me the biggest revelations of all. My meeting with Jonas.

CHAPTER 16

I wake up to the smell of coffee and noises coming from the kitchen, followed by a woman's cough. I glance at the clock. Eight thirty-five. I should've known Ophelia would be early. I scramble to throw on some clothes and head out to join the early morning soiree, hoping Ophelia waits to start pressuring me to talk until I've had at least one whole cup of coffee.

I work myself into a tizzy before I head out. *What was Cyle thinking? Was he going to wait until five 'til nine to wake me up?* He knows I don't function well without my coffee. Maybe I should crawl back under the covers and let him and Ophelia have a session. I am sure Cyle has boatloads of childhood issues to work through, too.

I walk out with a scowl on my face, hoping Cyle sees how pissed I am. I stomp into the kitchen and find a steaming mug of coffee, in my favorite cup I might add, and a smile spread across Cyle's face.

"Good morning, I was just coming to get you. Ophelia's here," he says as I pick up my mug of precious goods.

"Yeah. I heard," I say, still trying to be irritated. But it is hard to stay mad at anyone who greets me with a fresh cup of coffee and a big smile. I head into the living room and sit on the couch, next to Ophelia.

"Good morning, Tessa," she says with a smile. *How does anyone smile this early in the morning?* "I know it's best that we wait to converse until you finish that cup of coffee, so no pressure."

"You know me too well," I chuckle.

I savor my coffee as Ophelia shuffles through the piles of research from yesterday. She also reads about my *meltdown* in my journal. I drink slower, giving her time to do all the work for me and look at everything. If she does it, then it's less work I must do. Ophelia must have an internal clock because even though I'm not completely finished with my first cup, she turns to me exactly at nine and asks if I'm ready to get started. Sometimes, I don't like this woman.

"Do you have anything to add to the things I've seen here?" Ophelia asks, spreading out her hand towards the coffee table littered with information I printed off.

"No, not really. I think you've got it all covered. As hard as it's been, I've been trying to share everything with Cyle," I say. "And of course, he notices whenever I zone out and pulls me back, which is helpful."

Cyle laughs. "That's probably the closest thing I'm gonna get to *You were right about staying with me, Cyle.* So, I'll take it."

"And how was your sleep last night?" Ophelia inquires.

"Actually, very restful. I think it's the best I've slept since the flash."

"There could be several reasons for that. One, you're back in your bed, which must help. Two, you are actively processing everything with Cyle as memories hit you. By dealing with it as it occurs, you're not carrying it over to deal with in your subconscious mind as you sleep."

"Makes sense. Okay, I'll say it...you guys were right about Cyle staying to help me out," I say with a smile and look to Cyle. "You happy now?"

"Very," he says with a wink.

"So, today I wanted to go over some of your paintings. If you feel ready."

"I don't know that I'll ever be ready, so we might as well start today."

"We can do this one of two ways. We can bring out one painting at a time, which may be less overwhelming. Or we can go into the studio together and see all of them at once."

The tightness in my chest instantly builds. Looking at my paintings will be like staring at my madness straight in the face. "Give me a minute." I say and then take a few deep breaths to calm myself. "Let's just go in there. I do not want to drag this out any longer than necessary. It'll be just as torturous to look at them one by one I think."

"Okay. The goal is for you to describe to me what you see and feel when you look at all of the work you've done. Just let it free flow. We'll process it all later," Ophelia says. "I'm going to set a time limit of an hour so that you don't get too overwhelmed."

"Okay. Can Cyle come with us?" I ask, my voice shaking.

"Of course," they say in unison.

"Okay, let's do this," I stand, my knees trembling.

When we reach the door, Ophelia opens it and stands back, allowing me to go in first. I take three steps into the room before my knees buckle and I fall to the floor sobbing, bile rising in my throat. Cyle instantly drops down next to me and puts his arms around me.

"You're okay, just breathe," he says.

I close my eyes to block out all the paintings, trying desperately to catch my breath, to calm my racing heart. They are everywhere. On easels, leaned against the walls, covering every inch of space, and some even haphazardly thrown on the floor. I did more paintings in my delusional state than I've done in my entire life. Typically, I'm sure to clean up well after myself, not leaving any paint to go to waste or splatters on anything. In my frenzy, I left paint to dry on several palettes in the room; my brushes are crusty and hard; and, paint is splattered everywhere—the walls, the floor, even some splashed on the ceiling.

"Tessa, talk me through this. What are you seeing, thinking, and feeling?" Ophelia says.

I try to gulp down the lump in my throat. I open my eyes again to take it all in. "I see my madness. All these paintings. I don't remember doing them. Parts, yes, but not all of them. It feels like chaos, craziness."

"You're doing good. Look around and spout off what comes into your mind."

I do not want to do this. I want to run from the room, close the door and forget all these haunting faces. "I really don't want to do this. I don't think I can."

"You have to. If not now, sometime soon," Ophelia says.

I may as well confront these demons now since she is apparently not going to let me off the hook. I look around the room, studying them closer and letting the words flow as quickly as they pop into my mind. "Chaos. Pain. *Beauty*. Eyes, lots of eyes. *They see me. They finally see me.* Peace. Anger. Rage. Punishment. Insanity. Death. Exploding. Relief. Blood. Screaming. Fear. Craziness. Craving for more. Becoming him." I stop and pull the trash can over so I can throw up.

My heart races, and a cold sweat works its way across my brow. A tremor overtakes my body.

"You're doing great. Can we slow it down for a bit and talk through some of the things you listed?" Ophelia asks.

"My studio is in a state of chaos. Not only has the killer invaded my soul with these memories, these women, he's also intruded on my home. Look at all of these. They're everywhere. The women, the paintings, the memories. They've taken over my life, my being," I sob.

"Are there any paintings in particular which make you feel more chaos than the others?"

I scan them all, stopping to point out several along the way. The one with varying colors and line widths snaking together to form a woman's face, the colors weaving in and out, mixing in places, all coming together to highlight the eyes.

In another I combined the facial features of all the women into one. Individually the women were beautiful. My rendition, with them all merged into one, is horrific. Hailey's eyes, Amber's mouth, Olivia's nose, Alexis' facial structure, Mallory's hair. In this painting, like in my mind, they've become one. They're no longer individuals. I point out several others as Ophelia furiously takes notes, trying to keep up.

"You okay?" She asks.

"Not really, no," I say and take a gulp of the water bottle sitting next to me.

"Do you want to quit for the day?"

"Yes, but no. I can do a bit more, I think," I say, wrapping my arms around myself.

"Okay, next thing you said was pain." Ophelia poises her pen above her notepad, waiting for my response.

"When I am me and able to detach from his memories, that's all I see and feel…their pain. How badly he hurt them. In each painting, I see their pain, I *feel* it. But I see the beauty, too—in the paintings at least. Not in my memories. There is no beauty there. If I were someone looking at my work, who didn't know the horrors behind them, I would find them beautiful," I say and start pointing out different paintings. "That one, there, is of Mallory. All the colors come together beautifully, like they're dancing across the page. It's lovely. But then, I remember my hands around her throat, her eyes begging for mercy and any loveliness in the paintings is erased."

"You really have done some amazing things here, Tess. I hope someday you can see how beautiful they actually are. Most of them are breathtaking," Cyle says.

"Thanks. I hope so, too," I lean into him, and he kisses me on top of the head.

"You talked about the pain and the beauty. Do you have anything to add about either of those before we move on?" Ophelia asks.

"Their screams haunt me. They're constantly echoing in my head. Mostly it repulses me but sometimes," I pause, trying to spit out the words lodged in my throat. "But sometimes, their screams excite me. Like a sexual excitement, almost. I can feel them work their way through my entire body. It's sick."

I rest my head on my knees and cover it with my arms. I want to block all of this out. Now that I've mentioned the screams, they're taunting me, echoing louder and louder inside my mind. I can't distinguish one from the other. They all merge together, like in my painting

combining all their features, into one hideous sound. I want the
screaming to stop.

"I think that he keeps killing because it's the only way to make the
screaming go away, at least temporarily. Because, right now, the
screaming is so loud in my head. I would do *anything* to make it go
away. But the one thing my mind keeps returning to over and over is
that I know how to make it stop. And I do know. By killing," I say,
vomiting a second time, and then burying my head again, rocking back
and forth, back and forth.

"One more for today if you're able," Ophelia says.

I let out a weak, "I'll try." God, I just want to stop. I want out of
here. Why won't she just let me leave this room?

"*Eyes. They see me. They finally see me.* Talk about that for a bit,"
Ophelia says.

"When I remember their murders, I remember the relief I felt
knowing that they finally saw me. Kind of like I was invisible to them
in everyday life and raping them, taking their lives, was the only way I
could get them to truly see me. The rapes were a release of sorts, and
they gave me feelings of power and control. But the only moment of
true relief, like a weight being lifted off me, was when their dead eyes
stared up at me," I pause and look around the room. "In all the paintings, that's what stands out to me the most…their eyes. In that one,
look at the fear reflected in her eyes, the sadness, the knowledge her
life is about to end. There, that one has her face entirely blotted out
with swirls of color, with the only discernible feature being her eyes."

"Do you know which person each picture represents?" Ophelia
asks.

"In some of them, yes. It's obvious to me based on my memories
and what I've put on the canvas. In others, no. Those seem to be a
combination of all of them. The most haunting one of all is that one…
with nothing but their eyes. Most of the women…I found ways to
cover their entire bodies with something…leaves, mud, weeds, blood,
every part except their eyes. I wanted them to be forced to have their
eyes wide open to their fate, to me, even after I was long gone."

"I hate to interrupt, but again, you are talking as if you committed the rapes, the murders...as if you are the killer. You are not. It may help if you could change the way you talk about it, which in turn could help change the way you think about it," Ophelia says. "An example... compare the two statements. *I wanted them to be forced to have their eyes wide open to their fate, to me, even after I was long gone.* Versus the truth. *He wanted them to be forced to have their eyes wide open to their fate, to him, even after he was long gone.* Do you see my point?"

"I do. I agree that changing my perspective, my words, whatever, could be helpful. It is so hard because it feels like me. I have *his* thoughts, *his* memories, *his* feelings inside of me, tearing me apart. It's hard to believe that they are separate from me or to pretend they are, because they're not. They're in here and here, taking over everything else," I say placing one hand on my chest and one on my head.

"I get that. I do. I'm just saying one way to distance yourself from his thoughts, feelings, and memories is to give them back to him. Since you have no physical way to do that, the best step you can take in that direction—right now, at least—is to verbally place it where it belongs...*on him*. Don't take on anymore from him than you have to."

"I'll try. You guys will have to point it out to me. Sometimes I'm not even aware that I'm doing it," I say.

Ophelia finally says she thinks we have done enough today, and relief washes over me because I'm physically and emotionally drained. She asks if I have anything else to add before we leave the studio.

I look around at all my paintings.

"Thank you for finding me and to both of you for getting me help. It is apparent to me just how crazy I was, now that I see all of this. I must have worked around the clock for weeks to do all this work. I don't think I could've gone on much longer if you guys hadn't gotten me help. I think the madness would've completely taken over and convinced me to kill...either myself or someone else."

"I'm glad, too. I can't do life without my little sis," he says and pulls me into a hug. I brace for a flash, but none comes.

It's been a long time since I've gotten a flash from Cyle. I long for a blue flash from him filled with happy memories. Even a yellow flash to show me a future without all this madness.

We leave the studio, shutting the door tightly behind us. As Ophelia packs up, she compliments me on all the hard, emotional work I did and suggests that I spend the rest of the day relaxing, trying to give my mind a break. She also suggests that I stay out of the studio for now until we have time to talk through the rest of the paintings, the feelings. I couldn't agree more. I have no desire to step foot in there again any time soon. At least that's my plan until she announces she'll call later to check in. If all is okay, she will be back in two days to continue our work, unless I need her sooner. I'll take whatever break I can get though—a day's reprieve is welcome.

I'm exhausted after Ophelia leaves. Our original plan to spend time on campus needs altered to allow for a nap. Cyle stays up to do research. I load up on my meds, head to bed, and bury myself under my covers, blocking out the memories, the screams, the paintings, the eyes.

MY PHONE RINGING rouses me a little after one. I answer with sleep heavy in my voice. It is Chaundra, the psychic, returning my call. She tells me that she has some time this afternoon at three if I'd like to meet. After agreeing, I send a quick text to Jonas to let him know that something has come up and I'll have to reschedule our get together. His response is quick with just a frowny face and telling me to let him know when I can meet up. Not his usual joking self...my last-minute cancellation must have him a little ticked off. I don't know whether to feel bad that I've possibly hurt his feelings or scared that I've made a potential serial killer feel slighted.

Cyle and I eat lunch together, another one of his famous combinations—peanut butter and pickle sandwiches. He's been making them for me since I was little and even though they sound disgusting, they're one of my favorites. They always taste so much better when Cyle makes them, probably because it reminds me of home, feelings of love, and being cared for.

At two-thirty we head to Chaundra's house across town. I'm not really sure what to expect...a smoky room with a crystal ball and a beaded curtain? We're both pleasantly surprised to pull up in front of a small two-story house with a nicely manicured yard and a scattering of children's toys, bicycles, and balls left in the driveway. It looks like every other house in the neighborhood, which confirms my earlier inclination that she's not a whack job.

A boy with shaggy blond hair who looks about five opens the front door. "Are you Tessa?" He asks, peeking out from beneath his bangs that are way too long.

"Sure am," I say. "And this is my brother Cyle."

"You can come in and wait on the couch for Mommy. She'll be just a minute."

We follow him into the house, which is clean, but lived in. The little guy leads us to the living room and then patters off up the stairs. We have to move several toys off the couch to make a place to sit. I hear a woman's voice and what sounds like several children coming from upstairs. From the photos on the wall, it looks like she has another son a bit older than the one who answered the door and a daughter who is still a toddler. So far, no crystal ball, no beaded curtain, no smoke, no tarot cards. It's as if Cyle can read my mind because he smiles at me, then we both breathe deeply and sink back against the sofa at the same time.

After a couple of minutes, the whole gang plods noisily down the steps, the toddler and older boy bickering and their mom telling them to play nicely. She finally comes into view, carrying her daughter in her arms. She looks exactly like any other young mother who has her hands full with children. She blows her also too shaggy blond bangs out of her eyes and holds up a finger to us, stopping the boys in the hallway.

"Okay. You can go play on the Wii while I have my meeting. Behave, alright?" She cups the chin of the older boy, forcing him to look at her, while the little girl wraps her mother's hair round and round her small wrist. The boy who answered the door nods. "Did you hear me? No interruptions, please. We shouldn't be too long."

Finally, the older boy nods in agreement and the two of them run off, their feet beating down the basement stairs.

"I'm sorry about that and this mess," she says and picks up toys off the chair across from us, throwing them into the toy box in the corner. "When I told you I'd have an opening at three, what I meant was I thought I'd have things a bit more *together* by then. But, with these kids…impossible. I'm lucky to be out of my pj's. Anyway, sorry. Is it okay if Lily stays? I can't trust him to watch her."

Lily has already pulled the toys back out of the toy box, plus a few extras.

"That's fine," I say. "She's adorable."

"Thanks," she says as she takes a deep breath and sinks back into her chair, curling her feet under her. Chaundra seems to be around the same age as me. I can't imagine having three kids so young.

For the first time, she really makes eye contact with me as I'm introducing Cyle and she freezes. After a moment, she breaks her gaze away from mine and is visibly shaking. "Okay. Sorry. Wow!" She says, making me so nervous I don't know what to say.

"Is everything okay? Did you see something?" I ask, not sure if I really want an answer.

"Give me just a minute," she says and grabs a water bottle off the end table, taking a long drink. "Sorry about that. I've never met anyone like you."

"I'm sure that's true but why do you say that?" I ask, letting out a nervous chuckle.

"You have a gift. I can see it. I hate to describe it this way because I sound like a nut job, but it's the easiest way for me to explain what I just saw." I like her already. "I'm sure you've heard of some people being able to see auras, right?"

We both nod. *Uh-oh. She's right, starting to sound quacky.*

"I refer to it as being able to see people's colors. With most people, I look at them and I see one color, like blue for instance. Blue would indicate to me that someone is very intuitive, stays calm in crisis, and loves helping others."

"Sounds like she's describing you, Cyle," I say.

"I sometimes also see a bit of another color, but there's always a primary one that stands out," Chaundra continues and then takes another drink of water.

"Makes sense," I say again. I'm starting to be convinced that there's something to this. Anyone who talks and sees in colors is my kind of person.

"You, on the other hand are an anomaly. Something I've never seen before, or even heard about," she says. *Like I have never heard that one before.* "You're every color and its variation. The first time I looked at you, you were so covered in colors that I couldn't even see your face. Normally, the colors just kind of outline a person, like a glow. But with you, Tessa, they completely take over your entire body. And at the end there, when I had to take a break, there was what appeared to be a flash of lightning that washed over all the other colors, practically blinding me for a second. Like right now, I have to really force myself to focus to be able to see past your colors."

I'm stunned speechless. This woman has just defined my entire life so simply. She may not understand it, but I do. I am so surrounded and intruded upon by other people and the flashes, that I'm practically invisible. A tear slides down my cheek. I'm not sure if it's from feeling understood or realizing how little there is of the real me left for someone to see.

Cyle puts his arm around me but I scoot away. I can't bear to have a flash right now.

"I'm sorry. Are you okay? Lily put that down," Chaundra says. "Sorry."

I nod, unable to speak.

"You have no idea how well you just described my sister. I think she needs to process it for a minute," Cyle speaks for me. "What does it mean that you saw all that? Did you see anything else?"

Chaundra stays silent, seemingly pondering the question. After a moment, I finally say, "Well, what does it all mean?"

"I don't think I can say with one hundred percent certainty what it means because, like I said, I've never seen something like this before. I've seen people with rainbow auras surrounding them which usually means they are healers or trained to work with people's energy fields. But those are more like a sunburst around a person. Yours completely block you out."

Lily sits on the floor at Cyle's feet, staring up at me. "Pretty, mama. Pretty," she says pointing at me.

Chaundra turns her attention to Lily. "What do you see, honey?"

"Pretty colors. All over," she says and giggles, pulling herself up on Cyle's leg.

"Very pretty, aren't they?" Chaundra replies. "Sorry, but she was born with my gifts, plus a few, I'm afraid. But instead of trying to squelch it and convince her she's a liar or crazy, I'm trying to nurture it in her. Hopefully that way she'll learn that she's special, not a freak. Sorry, letting a few of my childhood issues come out there." She laughs as Lily toddles over and climbs onto her lap. Lily plucks her thumb into her mouth and sits back against her mom, seemingly mesmerized by my colors.

The more Chaundra talks, the more I trust her. We seem to have a lot in common.

"Here's my best interpretation of what I'm, wait, what we're seeing. If you know anything about auras, you'll know that each color indicates a character trait. From all of the colors I see consuming you, here is what I gather. You have a gift of the strongest kind, although your gift feels as though it's consuming you, which is why I can't see past the colors. Your gift also manifests itself in color. I can't see how, though. Perhaps you can tell me. You have a bit of everything in you... a healer, a student, an artist. You've experienced great loss—the biggest being loss of self. You're on a journey right now, perhaps a spiritual one, to discover the truth about something. You're self-sufficient but long for understanding, love. You've recently fallen in love but feel betrayed. You're fearful of the future. You're honest, trustworthy and dependable. You have angels protecting you. I see newness and purity. A reinvention," she pauses. Lily is still staring at me, but her eyes are heavy as if her mom just read her a bedtime story and I'm the picture to go along with it.

"That lightning I saw at the end. That's why you're here. You've also seen it. You're hoping I can help explain it," she says.

She has completely won my trust so finally I tell her all of the ways she is absolutely spot on in her interpretations, giving her the shortest possible description of my life, my gift, leading up to the lightning flash. I purposefully don't tell her about all that has come as a result of it, to see what she picks up on instead. Lily has drifted off on Chaundra's shoulder, with an occasional suck on the thumb still in her mouth.

"Do you mind if I take your hand for a moment? I think it'll help me get a little further in my visions," she asks.

Cyle looks anxiously at me, I'm sure questioning what my response will be considering I wouldn't even let him put his arm around me earlier.

I hesitate for only a moment before I say yes and rise to walk to her so that she doesn't have to jostle Lily. I take a seat on the ottoman in front of her chair and lean forward with my hands outstretched. It's only then, when I look into her eyes, that I see she's as nervous about this as I am. I've finally found another person that finds touch to be as anxiety provoking, scary, and life-altering as I do. Most people find comfort in affection. Not people like Chaundra and I.

"You ready?" She asks.

Instead of answering, I grab her hands. An incredible energy surges between us and I'm bombarded with an onslaught of flashes, all blending into one another. I'm not sure how long we maintain contact, but it feels like an eternity before she drops my hands. Whatever has passed between us has also impacted Lily, who is awake and crying. She no longer looks at me in awe, but rather she hides her face in her mother's chest like she wants to get as far away from me as possible.

"I need a moment," Chaundra says and walks into the kitchen with Lily, still crying.

I move back to the couch with Cyle. "Well, how was that?" He whispers.

"Lots of flashes but no immediate connection to anything," I reply. "She looks pretty shaken up. Lily, too. Wonder what she saw?"

"We'll find out soon enough. Hopefully something that can help."

We sit in silence, waiting for Chaundra's return. She's talking quietly to Lily. Finally, Lily's cries calm to an occasional whimper. After a trip to the basement, Chaundra finally returns sans Lily.

"Sorry about that. That was intense. Obviously for Lily, too," Chaundra clears her throat. "I took her to the basement to hang out because she's pretty shaken up."

"I'm sorry for scaring her," I say.

"It's not your fault. I should've been smart enough to put her down first, knowing how easily she picks up on things. Don't feel bad."

"What did you pick up?" Cyle asks the question I'm afraid to.

"I saw women...dead. Their eyes. I could see them being raped, murdered. I've had visions of all of them before...all but one." Chaundra shudders.

"So, how does your ability work? Like mine where you absorb it all, but in real time?" I ask.

"Mine is more like bursts of pictures. Sometimes they make sense, sometimes they don't. Like the times I've helped the police, those were visions I got out of nowhere before I'd even heard of the missing girls. One day, I was doing the dishes and *bam*! I saw a girl covered in mud, with only her eyes visible. I could tell in the brief second her face filled my mind that she was in a field. Then the next thing I know, I'm staring at the sink full of soapy water again. It wasn't until later that night, after the kids went to bed, that I turned on the news and saw the report about the ongoing searches for Amber Martin. As soon as her picture flashed across the screen, I knew it was her in my vision. Sometimes, they never make sense...at least not yet, anyway. I just carry them around inside of me, hoping someday they'll be useful to someone." Chaundra says.

"Did you...did you see anything else with me?" I say, even though I don't think I really want to know.

"Yes. So much that I don't even know if I can explain it all. I've never had the visions hit me so quickly before," she says.

"Yeah...there's no one quite like me out there, so that's not surpris-ing." I try to sound light-hearted but instead it comes out as a complaint. "I had quite a few flashes from you, too. We'll have to wait to see what comes of those."

"Hopefully, you get good things from me instead of some of the crap I've been through," she chuckles but there's pain in her eyes. It feels like looking in a mirror.

Besides Ophelia and Cyle, she is the only other person that's just accepted me and my story at face value, with no need to diagnose, explain, rationalize, or even fully understand it. She believes me without question. This revelation brings tears to my eyes.

"So, a few other things I saw, maybe they'll make sense to you… paintings, lots of them. A casket, white, with flowers all around and you are standing next to it crying. Blood curdling, ear piercing screams —I've never had an auditory type response with someone, so that was new," Chaundra pauses as feet pound up the basement stairs. Lily cries out for her mother. "Oh great. Sorry, I've got to…"

She meets the children in the hallway and scoops Lily up into her arms.

"Sorry, Mommy, she wouldn't stop crying," the older boy says.

"That's okay, sweetie. C'mere Lily. Shhh…it's okay. I'll take her back in the room with me. I'll just be a bit longer. You okay?" Chaundra asks the boys.

"Yes, now that she's gone," the older boy's voice rings out.

"That was mean," the younger boy says, nudging his brother. Surprisingly there's no shove in return.

Feet pound back down the basement stairs. Chaundra returns after a few moments with a calm Lily who has a sippy cup, her face still reddened from crying.

"I'm sorry about that. I should've known that wouldn't last long," Chaundra says sitting back down. Lily instantly turns to watch me again, this time with hesitation as though she only sees my ugliness instead of the pretty colors that mesmerized her earlier.

"That's okay. We can wrap things up here today. You look like you have your hands full. Can I ask one question though before we go?" I say.

"Sure. And we can schedule another time to meet, hopefully on a day when school's in session and this one has a babysitter." she says tousling Lily's hair. "I can tell we have lots more to talk about."

"You were quoted in some of the articles I read as saying that the killer was someone who works at Cardell. How do you know?"

"Again, it's like putting together a puzzle that's only given to you a few pieces at a time. But each time I get a vision involving one of the murdered girls, I get another one later, usually within minutes. It is always of the same person, in the same place. I can only ever see the back of them, so I can never get a full picture. He has dark brown hair. He is always walking down a low-lit hallway filled with plants and a marbled floor. There are columns every twenty feet or so. It's a huge, unique looking building. My curiosity, and my desire to help, got the best of me so I went to Cardell and started walking through the buildings trying to find the hallway from my vision. I finally found it, without a doubt. It's the atrium hallway connecting Lindley Hall and Bradley Hall. Exact match."

I ask the question I already know the answer to. "What department's classes are held in those buildings?"

"Lindley is the English Department and Bradley is the Journalism School," she says.

The air escapes me as though I have been punched. I manage to ask another question despite having no breath left in my lungs. "Anything else you can describe about the man?"

"No. I've tried. Just the dark brown hair. I can't even tell if he's white or black, how tall he is…nothing. It's always dark in my visions, the lights are dimmed or it's night or something. He's almost like a shadow."

Lily pulls on her mother's shirt trying to get her attention. "Mama. Mama!"

"Yes Lily…sorry," she looks to her daughter.

"Bad," she says and points at me. "She hurt Mommy."

My brain swirls with the words Lily keeps saying over and over again. What does she see? What I—he—did to those women? Something I am going to do to her mother? I can no longer hear her. I manage to rise despite my light-headedness and make it onto the porch before I throw up.

As I heave, the truth also comes up, burning my throat and searing my eyes as tears fall, stabbing me right through the heart. I know what Lily saw. I wasn't even aware of it, until she spoke the words. I am bad. She could see what I couldn't. The whole time we have been here, a part of me, the part that *he* owns, the part I thought I was burying, made itself clear to her. I kept imagining my hands around Chaundra's throat. Her screams. Her eyes.

CHAPTER 17

We somehow managed to make it back to the apartment and I immediately took my meds. I slept for eighteen hours straight. It wasn't a restful sleep because dreams plagued me—some pleasant, many nightmares. Cyle checked on me many times throughout because I kept crying out in pain or horror, or maybe a bit of both.

Now that I'm awake, Cyle seems to be treading lightly with me. I must've been more of a mess yesterday than I remember.

After my first cup of coffee, I break the formalities hanging in the air between us. "So, what's up? Why are you being so careful with me today?"

He laughs. "I see your caffeine kicked in. You had a bad day yesterday and an awful night's sleep. Figured you could use a break."

"You wanna tell me about what happened yesterday? I remember vomiting, getting in the car, and walking in the apartment. Everything else is a blur."

He talks me through the holes in my memory. He and Chaundra came to the porch to check on me when I ran from the room. I screamed at Chaundra to get back, stay away from me. I explained to Cyle on the way home that I wanted to hurt her. He said I sobbed and cried the entire way, switching back and forth between talking about wanting to hurt her and being sad because I'd actually felt a connection, and the possibility of a friendship, with Chaundra.

He said that a lot of the things I shared didn't make much sense and wondered if they were from flashes. I kept referring to my daughter. I explain the flash from the nurse in the hospital. I kept asking him how Adam could do this to me. As soon as Cyle mentions him, I feel the heartbreak. It was indeed a flash from Chaundra—the memories of the day her husband walked out on her and the kids. Lily was only ten days old. His excuse was that he just didn't love her anymore and didn't think he could do the whole *fatherhood thing*. I absorbed Chaundra's shock, betrayal, loss, disgust, heartbreak, fear, and devastation over this. I feel her frustration over the plaguing question: why didn't she pick up on something so important when she gets visions of strangers' fates all the time?

The most intriguing things I told him were to tell Chaundra not to let Aiden ride his bike on the street in front of their house, only in the alley, and to keep the older boy (whose name I suddenly know is Liam, somehow) away from the stove. Cyle said I kept repeating this over and over. Finally, after numerous attempts at him asking for an explanation, I finally uttered something about Aiden being hit by a car backing out of the driveway and terrible burns to Liam's arms and legs from something on the stove. I have no idea how I picked this up; I didn't touch either of the boys.

Once he got me home, Cyle gave me my meds and then sat with me until I drifted off, talking about stories from our childhood which broke up some of the madness enough for me to relax.

We decide to take the rest of the day to chill out, watch movies, journal if I remember anything from my dreams or flashes, read. No research. No investigating. No searching for the killer. A break I desperately need.

CYLE and I watch a few light-hearted movies together which is a nice distraction, but my dark thoughts keep creeping in. I keep my journal next to me and jot down phrases to remind me to come back to them later, to help me get it out of my brain by putting it on paper.

Want to smoke
Miss my daughter
Worried about Aiden
Eyes
Want to be seen
Feel of skin
Cravings
Adam
Sadness
Heartbreak
Mallory
Insecurity

Cyle and I have just finished our dinner of grilled chicken, sautéed asparagus, baked potatoes, and a salad when my phone rings. It's Chaundra. I'm afraid to answer it after knowing how I left things with her yesterday.

"Hello?" I say hesitantly, half expecting her to demand that I stay the hell away from her.

"Hi Tessa! I wanted to call and check on you. You okay?"

I let out a sigh of relief. No yelling, yet. "I'm okay. I'm sorry about everything. I don't seem to be in control of myself very well lately."

"I get it, trust me. I got a little more out of Lily. Not a lot but as much as I'm going to get out of a two-and-a-half-year-old..."

I interrupt before she can finish. "I wanted to hurt you. I wasn't even aware of it until Lily said something. That's what made me act so crazy."

"Yeah. That's what I gathered from her. But I don't think it was you that wanted to hurt me. It was him, wasn't it? The same guy who killed these women?"

"Yes. The lightning flash was from him, the killer. That's why I came to you. I hoped you could help me figure out who it is."

"That explains a couple of things in my visions. One of the times when he was walking down the hall, I saw a woman who at first was walking next to him, but then merged *into* him. That was the one time I was able to see a face...he turned, and it was a woman's face I saw. I now know that woman was you. Also, when we touched, I felt like you had been there when they died," she pauses for a breath. "Wow! So, does any of that make sense to you?"

"Unfortunately, it all does," I say without elaborating.

"If you're feeling up to it, would you like to get together again later this week? We have so much more to talk about."

"Definitely. I feel better now. I slept for almost a whole day! Let me know what works for you since your hands are pretty full," I pause, not sure if what I'm about to say is okay or not but feel like it needs put out there. "One of the things I got from you is memories of Adam leaving. I know how hard it was for you. I felt it. I know you were plagued with doubts about whether you could do the single parenthood thing or not. I just want to say I'm sorry that he was such an asshole and from what I can see, you're doing a great job with the kids."

Chaundra sniffles. "What a great thing for you to get! Sorry about that. And I do appreciate it. God knows I try, but it's hard. Damn hard. It's a good thing he never comes around, because I'm still so angry. Anyway, thank you."

"Speaking of kids. This may sound weird, but does Aiden have a bike that he rides in the street in front of your house?"

After a brief pause, she says, "Ummm...yes."

"I don't know that I understand why I'm about to say this but, here goes... Don't let him ride in the street for a while, only the alley. I saw him get hit by a car backing out of a driveway."

There's a moment of silence on the other end and I think I've scared her off. Then, she says, in a voice heavy with sadness, "Yeah, I'll tell him. No riding in the street. Just the alley."

"One more weird thing. Sorry, please bear with me. Keep Liam away from the stove. I saw burns on his arms and legs from something he dumped off the stove."

Again, the line goes silent until I hear her yelling Liam's name in the background. A few moments pass and all I can hear are muffled voices. Then, Chaundra returns to the line breathless. "Thank God you said that. I have a huge pot of chili on the stove right now and he was just getting ready to stir it. I wonder if that's what you saw. Anyway, he's sitting next to me, now."

My eyes fill with tears. For the second time, she believed me. *No questions asked.* No explanations needed. No hesitation. *She just believed me.*

"Tessa? You still there?"

"Yeah. Sorry. Good. Like I said, don't know where that came from but just want them to be safe," I say.

"Sounds to me like maybe you picked up more from me than just memories of Adam," she says.

"What do you mean?"

"Well, seeing as how you didn't touch Liam, but you did touch me…looks like you picked up a new gift. Welcome to the world of a psychic."

Shit.

CHAPTER 18

Ophelia, once again, arrives bright and early for our nine o'clock appointment. I got up in time to shower and have two cups of coffee before her arrival, hoping to be more alert for today's session. There's so much to talk about.

Once we're both seated, she dives right in.

"How have things been going?" She asks with her pen poised and ready to go.

"Loaded question for sure. Well, where to begin?" I take a drink of coffee and sit back. "I can't remember a lot of what I told you in our last session, but did I mention seeing the name of a local psychic in several of the articles I read during my research?"

Ophelia shakes her head.

"Well, one name kept coming up in some of the cases for the missing women, Chaundra Raines. I decided to reach out to her to see if we could possibly meet. I heard from her the same day of our last session and Cyle and I went to see her. Let me just say, that meeting was intense."

"How so?"

"First off, she could instantly see all of my colors. She explained it like an aura but instead of one color, I was surrounded by them. Her two-year old daughter also has some psychic abilities and was able to see the same. She was spot-on in her description of what she saw about me in my colors. Then, she suggested we join hands so that she could try to get a clearer picture of what was going on with me." I pause and chuckle at Ophelia whose raised eyebrows show her surprise.

"And did you touch her?"

"Try not to die of shock but yes, I did. And man, let me tell you. It was powerful. Through that touch she was able to see the women, their eyes and knew about their rapes and murders. She'd seen all of the women in her visions before, except for one. Mallory. She also said that she knows beyond the shadow of a doubt that someone on staff at Cardell is responsible for the killings."

"How does she know?"

"She's had visions of the killer in a unique space on campus and can only see a few details about him each time, but knows he has dark hair. She did some research to see where this place from her visions was and it's an area located between Lindley Hall and Bradley Hall." I pause to see if that information resonates with Ophelia at all.

"The English Building and Journalism School," Ophelia says still writing in her notebook.

"Yep. Someone with dark hair, on Cardell staff, that frequents the area. Makes it seem that my feeling that it may be Jonas could be right," I say and am instantly overwhelmed by a wave of nausea. "And that's not all. It seems I gained a few things from her as well."

"Like?" She stops writing and looks at me, waiting for my newest revelation.

"Well, I had lots of flashes with her and got her heartbreak and loss over the split with her ex-husband which sucks. But the worst of it is, I've gotten some psychic abilities. Which I am not happy about. At all."

"How do you know that you've gotten these psychic abilities?"

"Well, first off, I didn't even formally get introduced to her sons but somehow know their names are Aiden and Liam. I know that Aiden rides his bike on the street and that if it continues, he'll be hit by a car. I also knew that Liam was going to be badly burned by something on the stove and mentioned it to Chaundra during our call yesterday. Right at that very moment, Liam was climbing onto a chair to help stir the pot of chili she had cooking. Chaundra stopped him just in time."

"Wow! This is definitely a new one!" Ophelia says as she scribbles in her notebook.

"Yes, it is. And like I said, not an ability I want or need. Don't need another thing to add to the list of ways I'm abnormal."

"I wouldn't get too wound up just yet about this, Tessa. It sounds like you've had only those two visions so far, so maybe that was some type of anomaly from the powerful connection between you and Chaundra. I think it's best to give it some time to see if it manifests in the future."

"God, I hope that's the case. I already can't tell who I am versus who others have made me from my flashes. Add psychic visions in there and woah! That'd be crazy-making for sure." I laugh. "But, in all seriousness, I really liked Chaundra. She's someone I could see actually developing a friendship with. Because of her ability, she seems to understand me like few people have. And she just believes what I'm saying without questions or labels."

"I'm happy for you Tessa. You need a friend. It sounds like this could be the start of something beneficial for you." A smile spreads across her face.

I know she's right; I really do need a friend. I hope I don't scare her away with all of the madness.

"So, how about we head to the studio to process more of your work?"

I agree even though I would literally prefer to do anything else.

It feels like a punch in the gut as soon as the door opens, and I catch a glimpse of my work. It physically hurts to see myself poured out like that. Ophelia places her hand on my back to gently nudge me along since I can't seem to force myself through the doorway.

"Talk to me, Tessa. What's going on? What are you thinking, feeling?"

It takes a moment to find my voice. "This is overwhelming. Since the flash, I feel like he's invaded me but talking with Cyle, journaling, etcetera has helped keep him at bay a bit. When I come in here it's like he wakes up in me, if that makes sense. The battle intensifies and it's like we're duking it out for control of my mind."

"That was a great explanation," Ophelia says. "Can we continue with where we left off on Monday or would you like to just talk for a while?"

"I think a focus would be helpful so let's continue from then," I say, my eyes roaming from one painting to the next.

"Okay. Let me see," she says, looking to her notepad and getting her pen ready. "Peace. What do you see here that makes you feel peace?"

"The two showing Hailey in water. Those are peaceful to me. Her face is distorted by the constantly moving liquid; the way the colors meander and intertwine with her body makes it look like she's at peace. As if she and the water are one," I say. "Besides, I think that the part of me that's still *me* knows that their deaths offered them peace from the torture he subjected them to. The part of me that's *him* sees peace in that the only way to quiet the itch inside is to kill. So, their deaths meant peace for him as well."

Even though my emotions are still a jumbled mess, today, I can recognize the beauty in my paintings. I did some amazing work during my madness.

"Let's lump together the next two since they seem to be so closely linked. Anger and rage." Ophelia lets her arms relax at her sides, her notebook out of sight while she waits patiently for me to respond.

I look around at the colors that indicate anger. Red. Orange. Black. "I see a lot of that. Feel it, too. Remember him filled with it. That one," I say pointing. "With all the eyes, surrounded in red swirls. That's their anger. Their anger at being forced to see me."

My eyes scan the room and point out each painting that represents anger and rage, which seems to be about half of them. Lots of reds, blacks, and grays. Harsh strokes across the canvases. Lots of images of eyes. A couple that are women in profile, mouths open, screaming out their rage, their pain.

"Whose anger do you think is represented in most of these Tessa?"

Ophelia says, with her pen poised above her notebook ready to write whatever I say.

"His. He's filled with rage. I feel it. Part of the reason he kills and rapes them is because it's an outlet for all his rage. To quiet his storm," I pause and scan the canvases. "Theirs, too. The women. Anger at their lives being stolen. The unfairness. The injustice."

"Anyone else's?" She asks with raised eyebrows.

Yes, of course. "Mine. I'm pissed. I'm angry that this guy has invaded me and taken over or is trying to. I'm mad that I feel pleasure at remembering what he did to them. I'm pissed that I'm another one of his victims, even though he hasn't killed me yet. I'm furious that I bumped into him. I'm disgusted that it could be Jonas. I hate that I'm cursed with this, whatever it is…*ability*. Why? Why me? I just want to be normal."

I break down sobbing and Ophelia sits down on the floor next to me. "Can I touch you?" She asks with her arms held out for me to lean into. I nod and fall into her embrace.

I don't let myself get onto the pity train very often, wondering *why me*, but I'm on it right now, a one-way ticket barreling full speed ahead. My jaw clenches and my hands clamp into fists. I would rather have a disease like cancer or multiple sclerosis than have to deal with this for the rest of my life. At least with a physical illness, there's a *chance* for a cure. There are meds and treatments to try to remedy it or at least quiet the symptoms. For me, there's no hope of a cure. There is no quieting of symptoms unless I stay completely alone for the rest of my life. Even then, *he's* still with me, *in me*. I want to die. I want this all to end.

After what feels like forever, Ophelia breaks our embrace and looks at me, asking if I'm okay.

"No. I'm not. I want to disappear. I wish I was one of the women he killed. I don't want to live like this anymore. Not just him, *all of it*. I'm tired. Just so tired of it all."

She nods. "I get it. I do. We've been through this before. It sucks. I wish there was something we could do to help you take it all away. There's not. The best we can do is what we're doing right here, right now. Talk about it. Paint it away. Try to live life despite it."

"What if I don't want to anymore?" I say in a whisper.

"Giving up is not an option. You know that."

Do I? I don't know. It seems like the best option right now. It was hard enough when it was just the flashes, questioning who I am, avoiding others. But now I have to worry about hurting other people, taking someone's life because of this. I can't live with that for the rest of my life. Even if I can, I don't want to.

I'm about to tell her this when I get a vision. This is different from a flash. It doesn't feel like it's a part of me, rather it's something I'm observing, like a movie. It is a woman, no one I recognize, running down an alley. A man chases her. His hand grabs her green shirt. It's him. I know it. I've just seen his next victim.

Without speaking, I get up and grab a fresh canvas. I need to get this down as soon as I can. I don't even bother with a smock. Ophelia sits back and watches me work. I'm lost in it and have no idea how much time has passed. When I'm done, I look and it's a perfect match to my vision: a man's hand, a woman's green shirt. Her face, broken into a scream. Her brown hair blowing in the wind. The alley, clear to me now, is the one behind *Coffman's Music* and *The Chocaholic*.

The vision has given me a new resolve to live. If for no other reason than to save this next girl; to find him before it's too late.

AFTER OPHELIA LEAVES, I message Jonas asking if he can get together today for coffee. After about an hour, he answers saying he can meet with me at two at *Monticello's* between his afternoon classes. His text is all formalities with no playful banter back and forth. Obviously, he's still angry that I blew off our plans before.

At about one, I finally tell Cyle my plan. He's pissed. "Like one of the more stupid ideas you've ever had," were his exact words. He insists on coming with me, agreeing to sit across the restaurant. He'll be there in case I need him. I put up a fight about him coming, but I am a bit relieved he will be close in case something goes wrong.

We leave forty-five minutes early and stroll across campus, hoping I'll pick up on something along the way. Cyle noticed the extra care I took today in getting dressed, fixing my hair, and actually wearing make up for the first time in weeks. As much as I hate to admit it, considering he could be a sick and twisted serial killer, I am looking forward to seeing Jonas. I miss him, or at least the idea of him, and the easy relationship we'd started to build.

I take a deep breath of the crisp fall air and watch leaves slowly meander to the ground. A chipmunk with stuffed cheeks runs in front of me, preparing itself for winter. God, I've missed the feel of sunshine and fresh air. The first few minutes of our walk is peaceful and relaxing, until we hit College Green, which is bustling with life; students heading to class, to lunch, to their dorms, to the library. Students everywhere. All of it is overwhelming — the sounds, the hectic pace, the people, the young women. My breathing grows rapid and I grab onto Cyle's hand for support. He pulls me off the pathway and we walk the rest of the way to *Monticello's* by cutting between buildings, down side streets…anywhere but the main thoroughfares. The seclusion helps calm me, but my senses are still on overdrive when we finally walk up to the restaurant.

I peek inside and see that Jonas hasn't arrived yet. Cyle heads to a booth in the back corner. He'll remain hidden there unless I need him. If that happens, he promises to go into ninja mode and kick some butt if need be. Thankfully, the café is empty except for the staff. I order a coffee from the young man (*thank God!*) behind the counter and sit at a table near the window so I can watch for Jonas. Within minutes, I see him crossing the street heading towards the restaurant.

My heart quickens. He looks amazing. His hair has grown a bit, curling nicely around the collar of his sweater. He has the beginnings of a beard, giving him a rugged, sexy look. There's no way this man is a deranged sicko who preys on young women.

He walks determinedly to the door, not showing any expression whatsoever until he steps inside, sees me and his face breaks into a smile. Without even meaning to, I stand as he approaches the table and lean in for a hug. It's brief but it feels so right. No flashes. No psychic visions. No bad feelings. Only longing and comfort.

"Wow! It's good to see you," he says removing his jacket. "Let me grab a cup of coffee before I sit. You good?"

I nod, and he heads to the counter. As he orders, Cyle looks my way with raised eyebrows obviously confused about our embrace. Jonas returns to the table with a cappuccino and two croissants.

"Only two this time, huh?" I say as he puts the plate down.

He laughs. "Yeah, I'm watching my figure," he says as he pats his stomach. His very lean, muscular stomach. "I forgot about that…is that what made you sick? Too many croissants?"

"I wish. Hey, I'm sorry about all of that. Freaking out on you, disappearing for a while. Everything," I say, tears welling in my eyes. "I've been having a rough time."

"That's okay. No need to explain or talk about it until you're ready. I'm just glad you're okay," he says and grabs one of my hands. "You're still beautiful by the way."

Heat rises to my cheeks. "Thanks. You look pretty handsome yourself."

"I know that we haven't known each other for long but I've really missed you," he says.

"Yeah. Me too." I say. And I *have* missed him. Being in his presence makes that all the more clear. But the women. Is he a murderer? Am I sick for missing a potential killer? "Anyway, how have you been?"

"Okay, I guess. I've been kind of having a rough time myself lately," Jonas says.

"What's up? You okay?" I ask. Is he having a hard time because he just killed another woman and is afraid he'll be caught? I'm not getting any weird vibes indicating that he's a sadistic murderer.

"Yeah. I'm okay. Just some emotional rollercoaster type stuff but I'm getting through it," he clears his throat. "Classes, grading, and my own writing has been keeping me plenty busy which helps. How's your dad?"

"Last update, he's doing pretty well. He's home, getting PT and OT and driving everyone crazy," I laugh.

We make small talk for several minutes while I build the nerve to finally pose the question I've been intending to ask. "So…I've been kind of out of it lately and didn't hear. Did they ever find Hailey?" I look into his eyes, trying to gauge his reaction.

He instantly breaks eye contact, takes a drink of his coffee, a bite of his croissant, and then answers. "Yeah. She was murdered. Very sad."

I'm flooded with the memories of her screams, watching her float away into oblivion, the feel of her. "That's awful," I manage to say even though the memories pulse pleasure through me. "Do they have any suspects?"

"Not that I know of," he says and stands. "More coffee?"

I nod. He grabs both of our mugs and heads to the refill station. Quite a strange reaction. So far, it's the only indicator today that anything is off with him. He definitely wants to avoid this line of questioning. Because he's the bad guy? Because it brings up feelings dealing with Mallory? He's taking his sweet time getting our refills, too, probably deciding how best to change the subject when he returns. He's heading back with our steaming mugs when my cell rings. *Who in the world could be calling*? Cyle and Jonas are with me. I just talked to Chaundra last night. I look at the phone — it's Chaundra. My foot taps with anxiety as I answer.

"Hello," I say.

"Okay, so don't think this is weird. Well, it is weird but I'm a psychic so what can you expect?" She says as way of introduction. "Anyway, are you per chance at a café right now?"

"Umm, yes. Why?"

"I don't know the details but it's a feeling that went along with a vision. I could see you sitting in a café drinking coffee. Am I right?"

"Yes. And…"

"I don't know why or who or what, but you're in danger. You need to get out of there," she says with panic heavy in her voice.

I excuse myself from the table and walk out front. I look around the café. There's Cyle, Jonas, the clerk behind the counter and some staff in the kitchen. Her feeling must be because of Jonas.

"Can you tell me anything more? What kind of danger? From a person? What did you see?" Butterflies creep their way from my stomach up to my throat.

"Like I said, I was picking up toys and kind of went into blackout mode. I had a vision of you sitting in a café, drinking coffee. I couldn't see anyone else in my vision but got this overwhelming sense of fear and dread. If you don't leave, I *know* something horrible is going to happen."

"It's a long story, but I'm with someone right now who may be the one," the rest of the sentence gets caught in my throat. "The one that killed the women. I don't want it to be him, but it could be."

"Please get out of there! Make some excuse and leave. It's not safe," her words spill out quickly, full of panic.

"Okay," I promise, hang up and head back in.

Before I try to explain why I need to leave so abruptly, I tell Jonas I have to go to the restroom, hoping it will give me time to think up a good excuse and to signal Cyle. As I walk by Cyle, I mouth the words "*got to go*" hoping he gets my meaning.

Once in the bathroom, I try to take a deep breath. Since the call with Chaundra, my anxiety has spiraled out of control and my breathing is shallow. Finally, I am able to draw a deep breath. So many emotions roil through me, it's hard to make sense of them. It must be Jonas…his strange reaction to my questions, Chaundra's phone call and warnings. I'm sad because I don't want it to be him. Could this handsome, kind, thoughtful gentleman be the same one invading me, giving me these horrible memories, this awful craving to kill? Can someone really hide that type of darkness? Now that I'm ninety-nine percent sure that it is him, what can I do about it? Confront him? Go to the police? How do I stop him from hurting the next girl, the one from my vision? Does he have feelings for me or am I being primed as one of his future victims?

I splash water on my face hoping to quell the nausea that's risen as the questions pummel me. I no longer have to make up an excuse for leaving; I legitimately feel sick now. I dry my hands and open the door to head back out to end our meeting. As I walk down the small hallway back to the table, a girl excuses herself as she squeezes past me. A woman I recognize. One that I painted. The girl from the alley. The next victim.

Part of me thinks I should tell her she's in danger and to avoid going anywhere alone right now, especially that alley. The other part of me wants to follow her to that alley myself, to hear her screams, feel her skin, see her seeing me, watch her die. Chaundra was right, I've got to get out. For that girl's safety. For mine.

On quivering legs, I make my way back to the table and don't bother to sit. "Hey. I'm sorry about this but I've gotta go. I'm not feeling well," I say, feeling like I could vomit all over the table.

Jonas rises. "Are you okay? Can I walk you home? You're not looking so hot."

I don't tell him Cyle is there to help. "No, I'm okay. I just need to lie down for a while. I'll be fine."

He grabs my coat and holds it up for me. As I'm slipping my arms in the sleeves, the bell on the front door rings. A man walks in, his eyes shifting around the room. He has on a burgundy Cardell Polo shirt, khaki work pants, work boots—probably on the maintenance staff. He walks to the counter as I button my coat. Jonas pulls me into a hug as the man at the counter turns and meets my eyes. A chill works its way through my body and the hair on my arms stands up. The women's dead eyes flash through my mind. I choke down my nausea. I need to get away from here. From Jonas. From the man who's trying to consume me with his gaze. From the girl in the green shirt. I don't know where the danger is. But, it is here. Right now. With me. *In me.*

"I've gotta go," Breaking the embrace and the gaze, I run out the door.

I still don't have any concrete answers but one of them is the one. Jonas or the maintenance guy. I'm not certain of much these days. However, there is no doubt I was just in the presence of the killer.

CHAPTER 19

Other than me, I have no idea which one of them wants to hurt her, but I have to get away to save her from *me*, from *my* desires. Cyle follows me out of *Monticello's,* chasing me as I run down the street. He yells for me to wait up, but I can't make myself stop. Finally, I reach a bench and drop onto it, far enough away that everyone is safe but still within sight of the door of the cafe. Cyle finally catches up and sits down heavily next to me. "What the hell, Tess?" He asks, short of breath.

I tell him about the girl from my vision, Chaundra's phone call, being in the presence of the killer. Wanting *to be* the killer. As we talk, my racing heart calms, and we watch the front door. Jonas walks out first and heads left towards central campus. Next, the girl from my vision leaves with a cup in one hand, a bag in the other. My thoughts start to spiral out of control again seeing her walk off by herself, her hands full, distracted, vulnerable. She also walks towards central campus. A few moments later the man in the maintenance uniform walks out. He looks around and pauses when he sees the girl a few yards ahead of him. Instead of following her though, he turns right and saunters away. For now, everyone's safe. We sit a few moments longer to give my heart time to stop trying to beat its way out of my chest, then we head back home.

We meander slowly across campus as I fill Cyle in on the details about my latest freak-out and Chaundra's warning. By the time we reach my apartment, we have decided that I need to see Chaundra again, and soon. There's so much I haven't shared with her yet. Things she may have picked up on already, but if not, ones she definitely needs to know. Information that may help us both figure out who the killer is and how to stop him.

I call and ask if she can come over this evening. I can't risk going out a second time today. She texts a few minutes after we talk to let me know she made arrangements for a sitter to come over at seven and that she'll be to my place at seven thirty. Letting someone new into the sanctuary of my apartment fills me with dread. I quickly dismiss it, though. I've already allowed her into the depths of my crazy mind.

I spend the afternoon doing research to see if anything new has been posted about suspects, the murders, Hailey. The only new information from the police is that they've identified some "persons of interest" from the video recordings of Hailey from around town that night. A detailed map outlining her steps the evening of her disappearance is available, and authorities urge anyone with any information to come forward or call the tip line. Reading through comments on social media has been the most informative, albeit probably not one hundred percent accurate. People claim to have seen Hailey that night with a group of men following her. Others say they saw the moment she was grabbed, yet each has a different account of who the perpetrator is. Balding white male, late thirties, about six feet tall, with a green shirt and jeans. Black man, mid-twenties, well over six feet tall, muscular, with dreads. Short, twenty something, Hispanic man wearing jeans hanging low and a white t-shirt. People claim to have heard screams coming from the alley where she was last seen. Comments point out the similarities between Hailey and Amber's disappearances.

I read through as many comments as I can hoping that something resonates with my memories and points me in the right direction. I finally force myself to shut off the computer and rest for a while. My head feels like it is going to explode with all of the possibilities.

There's a knock on the door promptly at seven-thirty. I take a deep breath and open the door for Chaundra.

"Hi! Thanks for coming over," I say as she walks in.

She scans the room, her eyes settling on the painting behind the sofa. "No problem. Wow! That's amazing. Did you do that?"

I blush. "Yeah. Not too long before my trip to insanity," I laugh. "That one's called *Calm Chaos*. It reminds me a lot of someone who I now think may be involved with all of the murders. I'll have to tell you that story a bit later though."

"It's awesome. I'd love to see more of your stuff at some point, if that's okay. And I can't wait to hear the story behind it."

"I've got a whole room of it. Most I did when I was completely out of my mind so it's a bit disturbing. But some of it isn't half-bad if you don't know the backstory," I say. "Maybe after we talk. Can I get you anything? Water, wine, coffee?"

"Wine would be great. I always limit myself to one glass when I'm on mommy duty since it's just me. But tonight, they're taken care of so bring it on." Chaundra kicks off her shoes and sits on the sofa, her feet curled underneath her. My heart feels full seeing how comfortable she is around me already.

"Chardonnay or Zin? I don't have anything sweet," I call out from the kitchen.

"Whichever. Both."

I pour both of us a glass of Zinfandel and head to the couch. Cyle peeks his head out of the bedroom and says hello but then excuses himself to give us some girl time.

"Holler if you need anything!" he says.

I smile at Cyle and turn back to Chaundra. "So, I wanted to have you over because there's a lot I haven't told you that I think you need to know. Things that may help us figure out who this guy is before he hurts someone else. I know who his next victim is," I say.

We finish the first bottle of wine as I talk, filling her in on as much as I can. Meeting Jonas. The flash. My cravings to kill. My new psychic abilities. Today at *Monticello's*. The girl that brushed by me in the hallway. Jonas' strange reaction to my questions. The man at the counter. *Knowing* that one of them is the killer. She listens intently and chimes in at some points. She had already picked up on some pieces that I share. After hours pass, I finally sit back, take a deep breath, and tell her it's her turn.

"I'm stunned. How hard this must be for you! I just see things or feel them. But, to absorb everything making it change me, become a part of who I am...I can't imagine. I'm so sorry," she says and takes my hand. "Thank you for sharing with me. I know the shit I've had to put up with over the years because of my *gift*. I'm sure you've been through it, too."

I sit back and relax while she tells me a bit about her life and her abilities. Her first memory of having a psychic vision was when she was six years old. Her family was in the car, driving to her grand-mother's house in rural Tennessee. They drove by a farmhouse that sat off to the left of the road, a peeling red barn off in the distance, the whole place surrounded by fields. Chaundra said she awoke instantly from a deep sleep, screaming that her parents needed to stop. They needed to help the little boy. She could see him trapped under a piece of farm equipment in the barn. Her cries were hysterical, so her father finally turned around and pulled into the long drive, heading towards the farmhouse. While her parents went to the door, she ran to the barn and found a young boy trapped underneath the front of a tractor. As the boy's mother answered the door, Chaundra let out an ear-piercing scream and all the adults ran to her. Ten-year-old Jimmy had been chasing one of the cats in the barn. It ran under the tractor that was jacked up on wood for repairs. Jimmy chased the cat under the tractor and his laces caught under the wood. As he pulled to free his foot, the wood came loose, sending the tractor crashing onto him, crushing his bottom half underneath its weight. When Chaundra found him, he was passed out from the pain or shock or both. The four adults were able to get the tractor lifted enough to free him. Jimmy ended up with internal bleeding, a perfo-rated bowel, a crushed pelvis, two shattered femurs and busted kneecaps. The doctors said that had he been found even ten minutes later, he probably wouldn't have survived due to the blood loss and shock. To this day, Chaundra and he stay in touch via social media and phone calls.

Her parents were convinced after this incident that God had placed it on her heart to have this vision and wake up just in time to save him. As the years passed, though, her parents became almost delusional with fear that instead of a gift from God, she was demon-possessed. Her parents asked the Catholic Church to perform an exorcism when she was sixteen. Before the church had the chance to agree, Chaundra ran away from home, straight into the arms of Adam who was three years older than her, done with school, and working full-time. She was with him up until he decided he didn't want her and the kids anymore. Chaundra still sees her parents occasionally, but their relationship has never been a healthy one. She's created a new family for herself with a few close friends and her children. For years she tried to hide her abilities, only talking about them with Adam. When he left, she felt like she had no one to open up to that would truly understand. No one knew of her abilities, other than her kids, until her name was printed in the paper and on websites in connection with tips she'd called into the police.

Listening to her talk is like wrapping myself in a warm, well-worn blanket. It feels like we've known each other forever, and although this is only our second time meeting, I trust her. Completely. It seems like she's telling my story in so many ways. The gift that feels like a curse. The dysfunctional family that's convinced something is horribly wrong. Trying to run from yourself. Wanting to hide from the world. Feeling so alone, like no one really gets it.

Our connection feels so deep that my question comes spilling out before I have time to think about it. "Would you like to see more of my work?" My hands shake as we walk down the hall, because she is about to see firsthand the depths of my madness. Before opening the door, I turn to her, "I've only allowed two other people to see my art. My therapist and my brother. This is a huge step for me."

"I feel honored then." She nods and smiles.

I open the door and allow her to walk in first. "Wow! Amazing."

She walks from painting to painting, studying each intricate detail, kneeling to examine the ones on the floor more closely. She talks to herself in a barely audible whisper as she moves along. I stand back and watch her take it all in. Finally, she makes her way around the entire room.

"This is incredible. You've done amazing work," she pauses. "I'm not sure how you'll take this, but I know who some of these paintings are of."

She points to one. "That's Hailey. In the water. It looks exactly like my vision. It's so weird that you painted what was inside of my head." She points at another. "And that's Amber. I remember her eyes."

My eyes go wide with her declaration. All my work is so abstract that I'm astonished anyone can see the resemblance to the women they represent. But Chaundra isn't just anyone, she's someone whose soul has also been invaded, to an extent, by these women. She's been haunted by their pain and tormented by the killer. Maybe not the same as me, but still enough to know.

"This one," she says walking over to the painting of Mallory, that I completed before the flash. "I've seen her, but I don't know who she is. I've had several visions involving her. Is she one of the victims?"

I tell her about Jonas and the red flashes, my heartbreak over Mallory. I tell her the same killer is responsible for her death, even though her murder happened hundreds of miles away.

"It has to be Jonas then, don't you think?" Chaundra asks. "My visions of the man walking through the atrium make sense…the dark hair, an English Professor, Mallory. It all seems to fit."

"I know," I say sadly. "I don't want it to be the case but it all fits. All of it except for the fact that he seems like a really great guy. The memories I have of killing and raping the women just don't jive with who he seems to be."

"I think we both know that's often the case with serial killers. Haven't you ever heard the wife of a serial killer interviewed, or the neighbors? Hear them say they had no idea? That *he was the nicest man ever.*"

I nod. "I know. But then that other man, the one who walked in *Monticello's*…he also has dark hair and chilling eyes. He obviously works for Cardell. He could be the one, couldn't he? Or do you think I'm so desperate for it not to be Jonas that I'm inventing suspects out of everyone I see?"

"Maybe. Maybe not. How about this? I have some contacts in the Police Department that don't think I'm a total whack job. How about I call them and drop Jonas' name as a possible suspect? I'll say I had a vision. At least that way they will perhaps question the possibility."

"Okay," I say, even though my anxiety goes through the roof at her suggestion. Yes, if he is the killer, I want him caught and locked up with the key thrown away. But, if he's not...what hell will it be for him to be a suspect in the minds of the police and the public?

"You can run this by your therapist, but I think it would also be good if you and I spend some time on campus, specifically in that atrium to see if you spot the other guy. Maybe if we're together, one of us will get a vision or you can run up and touch him...see if anything happens. It might not hurt for me to meet Jonas either."

"I think those are great ideas. Now, how in the world can I arrange a meeting with the two of you since I've once again acted like a maniac by running away from him? He must think I'm psycho."

Chaundra laughs. "You're worrying that a potential serial rapist and murderer thinks you're psycho? C'mon now."

I laugh at the absurdity of it. "You can tell I've had lots of not-so-becoming labels applied to me over the years; it's second nature to assign them to myself."

Chaundra's phone buzzes and she pulls it out of her pocket. "Oh crap. I totally lost track of time. I told the sitter I'd be back at eleven. I'm already a half hour late."

"Wow, time flies when you're lost in the world of psychics, psychosis, and serial killers," I say as we walk back out to the living room for her to gather her things. "Thanks so much for coming over tonight. It's been nice to have someone to talk to that seems to get me," I say.

"I totally understand that," she says. "I'd offer a hug, but I don't think either of us could take it right now."

"You're right...too risky. Sucks doesn't it?"

"Sure does. Something that most people take for granted is such torture for people like us," she says. "So, I'll call one of the detectives at the police station and put the bug in his ear about Jonas. How about you, Lily, and I take a trip to campus sometime soon?"

"Sounds great. Taking Lily is a really good idea; she may pick up on something that we don't. We'll be in touch," I say. "Thanks again."

"No problem. This guy doesn't know what he's in for with the two of us wonder women trying to track him down," she says, on her way out the front door. I watch as she starts her car and then backs away, waving.

I peek in the bedroom and see Cyle already passed out on the floor. I should be tired but instead I'm invigorated. It's nice to feel like I have a friend. For the first time since the lightning flash, I feel like I've actually stayed myself for the entire visit. What a relief to not be subjected to the feeling of being invaded by an alien.

I stay up for several hours, doing more research. I look at the Cardell website and discover that the man I saw at the café with the burgundy shirt is on the maintenance staff. I look through all the staff pictures trying to spot him, but he's not there. He definitely had the maintenance uniform on, though. I find Jonas' picture on the English Department page and let my eyes linger for a moment. I wish I didn't find him so attractive. I wish he didn't seem like such a caring guy. He sent several texts today checking up on me. I finally answered before dinner telling him I still felt lousy and was headed to bed. Now, I've got to figure out a way for him and Chaundra to meet. Perhaps we'll just run into him hanging out in the atrium, that way I'll be spared the trouble of trying to come up with something.

For the first time since I've been home, I head to the studio by myself. My intention is to make sure the light is off, but once I step foot inside, I'm drawn in by the paintings. Sadness and anxiety wash over me. I grab my painting journal and sit down in the middle of the floor. I take a deep breath, hold it, then let it out. It's time to get some of these feelings out and down on paper by myself. What Ophelia normally asks me to write is a title and feelings associated with the painting, so I decide to start there.

The first thought that comes to mind with picture number one is Screaming Eyes. The only thing on the white canvas is a set of blue eyes with thick dark lashes and heavy eyebrows. I can't tell if the eyes belong to Hailey or Amber, or perhaps a combination of the two. I jot down both of their names with question marks. The eyes are intense and reflect horror, pain. They're surrounded in bold swaths of color, a sharp contrast to the white of the canvas. Colors drip like tears down the page. It's haunting, yet beautiful. I jot down my feelings as I study it: *beauty, horror, pain, reflections, sadness, betrayal, knowing.* I try to bring up his memories as well, but can't distinguish what's from him and what's my own.

The next painting, I call *Distorted View*. I move closer to study this one as it's much different than my usual work. For this one I used a variety of mediums...pens, acrylics, markers, and even crayons. It looks as though I started with a simple pen drawing of a face and then added layers of colors with various mediums to distort, contort, and emote. Again, the eyes are the focal point and help to ground the piece, bringing cohesion and helping the brain make sense of it. I can't tell if the face is a man or woman. It's intriguing. I wish I could recall creating it, but my memory is a blank. My feelings with this one are: *lost, hidden, contortion, distortion, masked, unseen, invisible.* I drop my pen and move closer, hoping to make out more of the features. The one thing that becomes clear to me as I write is that this painting is the key.

This one is of the killer.

I pick the pen back up and scribble furiously as I'm bombarded with his thoughts and feelings. *I am no one to them. They walk by me as if I don't exist. As if I'm invisible. Their eyes meet mine, yet they don't see. They don't acknowledge. I'm hidden to them. I am a no one in their minds. They think I'm unimportant, beneath them. They walk by in their short skirts, their breasts hanging out, laughing with their friends, flipping their hair. They talk about sex in earshot of me, sharing their adventures from the night before, not caring that I can hear because I am no one. They don't care that their stories, their clothing feed my desires. I listen to them, and I grow hard, not that they notice. I imagine their skin beneath my fingers, my mouth on their breasts, being inside of them. I imagine their faces contorted in pain, screaming in horror as I slam into them, making them see me, feel me, know that I exist. I imagine their eyes...forcing them to see me. Forcing them to know my power. If only they knew. I will make them see me. I will make them feel my power. I will be known. They will feel me. I will invade them. I will devour them.*

I'm trembling with excitement. The feeling of power courses through me as I finish writing. His cravings have overtaken me; the need for a woman has grown so strong within me that I'm no longer in control. I must feel a woman's skin beneath my fingertips, feel her eyes gazing into my soul, hear her screams of horror, taste the saltiness of her tears as they stream down her face. My body is alive with desire, fueled by my need. Tessa is gone—overpowered and devoured by him.

I turn off the light to the studio and quietly shut the door behind me. I put on my shoes and sneak out the front door, careful not to awaken Cyle. I am on the hunt. I will find someone to satisfy my cravings. I walk towards campus, knowing *exactly* where I'm headed.

I break into a run fueled by my intense desire, my unquenchable need. The only people moving about campus are those just leaving the bars after a night of partying, or the libraries after an evening of studying. Other than occasional voices, the night is quiet; so quiet, I can hear the beating of my heart along with my ragged breathing. I don't bother to slow until I've reached my destination. The alley behind *Coffman's Music* and *The Chocaholic*. The one where the girl in the green shirt should be.

I lean against a wall, darkened by the shadows of a nearby dumpster, and catch my breath. The alley is empty, no signs of life anywhere. I will wait here for her. I know she will come. The vision told me so. I have no guarantees that it will be tonight. I will wait though, hoping my intense desire is enough to call her here. I crouch down into a sitting position while I wait and will her to me. The occasional murmur of voices float to me as they pass by the alley. Each noise piques my interest, and I anxiously await seeing her turn the corner, towards me, her fate, her destiny. Time after time, I'm disappointed when she doesn't appear.

I need her. Like a person that's been walking in a hot desert needs a drink of water, I *need* to touch her. Like a baby craves its mother's breast, I must hear her screams. My brain might explode with yearning. I hunger for her. My body aches with longing.

I hear footsteps; they are heading in my direction. I peek out from behind the dumpster and see a lone figure walking my way. It's too dark to make out any features other than a glimpse of a green shirt. It's her. She's come to me. She felt me call her. She knows that this is her fate, her destiny. She had no other choice but to come.

As she nears me, my heart rate quickens, and my palms grow sweaty. I can see her now. Her long brown hair is blowing in the wind, just like in my vision. I want to wrap my hands in her hair and pull her head back until she has no choice but to look at me. Ten more steps and she'll be within my reach. I catch a whiff of her perfume dancing in the night air and I salivate with hunger. I crouch up so that I can be ready for her when she's within reach. I finally step out from behind the dumpster, and she looks my way.

"Hi," she mumbles, briefly making eye contact and then continuing to move forward, away from me. There's no fear there whatsoever.

It's because she doesn't see you, my brain screams. *You have to make her see you!*

I fall into step a couple of paces behind her, waiting for the best moment to make my move. We are mid-way down the alley, now, deep enough that even if she screams, no one will hear the urgency of it as it echoes against the brick buildings. I reach forward and grab her green shirt, stopping her. She turns to look at me, this time with confusion in her eyes. She opens her mouth to speak as I hear my name being yelled down the alley, breaking my momentum, stealing my purpose. I let go of her shirt. She stands there for a moment until the voice, tells her to go, to get away. Tessa's voice breaks through, screaming louder than *his*, telling her to run.

Cyle runs towards me. "Tessa, what the hell are you doing?"

Seeing his face, hearing his voice... I fully snap back to myself.

Tears pour down my cheeks as I look towards the woman who is turning the corner, out of the alley. "Oh my god, Cyle. Oh my god!" I can't breathe. I'm being crushed.

"C'mon," he says and grabs my arm, forcing me to start the trek back out of the alley.

I can't do anything but cry. I can't even wrap my head around what was just about to happen. I don't have words to explain how he was able to invade me like that, totally burying the real me. Cyle doesn't speak as we make our way back towards the apartment. Once inside, I fall onto the couch and bury my face in my hands, sobbing.

He sits next to me and finally lets loose. "What the hell, Tessa? I wake up and see that you're not in bed and it's almost two in the morning. I think, surely you must be painting or asleep on the couch. But no. I try to call but you don't answer. Then it hits me. I knew where I'd find you."

"I'm sorry. Oh my god, I'm sorry." Sobs wrack my body.

"Sorry doesn't cut it. You could've hurt her, or worse. You had your hands on her. I thought you were doing better," he says, slowly shaking his head.

"Me too," I whisper.

He's so pissed at me his voice shakes and his face reddens with rage. "I don't even know what to say, what to do. How am I supposed to get a moment's break if you can't be trusted?"

I don't have a response to that. I thought I was doing better, too. *He* seemed to be invading me less and less as the days went by. Maybe *he* was saving up for tonight. Because earlier there was none of me left. There wasn't even a war raging in my mind about what was wrong or right. *He* was in complete and utter control. Maybe my mistake was going into the studio by myself. I don't know.

Cyle stomps into the kitchen and starts slamming cupboard doors. Open. Close. Open. Close. "C'mon Tess, come take your meds," he says impatiently as he slams another cupboard door closed.

I get up and wipe the tears from my eyes. I don't say anything until I down the handful of pills set out on the counter next to a glass of water. "I'm sorry, Cyle. I don't know what happened," I manage to stammer out.

"I'm sorry, too. I don't know that this can work. You, me, this whole arrangement...What if you had hurt her?" he says.

"I don't know. Maybe you're right," I say and take another long sip of my water.

"Let's just get some sleep. You need to call Ophelia in the morning. We need a better plan."

I'm pretty sure he's convinced now that I do need locked away somewhere. That the brilliant plan they came up with isn't working. That I am dangerous.

I crawl into bed and pull the covers tightly around me trying to get the chill out that is settled deep within me. Cyle shuts the bedroom door and then moves the air mattress in front of it, blocking the exit. There is no way for me to get out without waking him. I'm in prison. A prison created by a madman who is holding the only key.

CHAPTER 20

I sleep fitfully through the night. My dreams are plagued with memories of the murders and fantasies of the girl in the green shirt. I woke Cyle up several times shouting in my sleep. Finally, at seven, he suggests we go ahead and get up for the day. My eyelids feel covered in sandpaper, and I can barely keep them open.

Things are tense between us as we make coffee and breakfast. There is no small talk, no eye contact...only avoidance. His disgust with me fills the room with banged cupboard doors and deep sighs. I don't know what I can do to make it any better.

When we sit down to eat, he looks up from the computer long enough to speak to me. "Ophelia will probably be stopping by this morning, and you need to tell her everything that happened last night."

"Okay," I say. "Why are you so angry with me?"

He starts to speak several times but seems unable to spit the words out. Finally, he mutters, "I just am. I don't feel like talking about it now...later."

We eat the rest of our breakfast in silence. I study my bowl of cereal and Cyle stares at the computer screen. Does he think I chose to go out and stalk that girl? Does he think I *want* this? I would give anything to make this all go away. *Anything*. Cyle has always understood me. But, not now. It seems his patience and understanding have run out. That well has dried up. Maybe there is so much of *him* in me that Cyle can no longer even see the real me.

I finish eating and place my dishes in the sink, then head back to the bedroom with my phone. Maybe I can fall back to sleep and avoid reality for a while longer. Within a couple of minutes, I get a text from Chaundra. She called in the tip to her contact at the Police Department.

I briefly hesitate then text her back asking her to call me sometime today when she has a free moment. I need to tell her about what happened. I need to see if she thinks I'm as far gone as Cyle apparently does. Within minutes, my phone rings.

"Good morning! What's up?" Chaundra asks, way too cheery for this time of day. The kids' voices fill the background.

"Hey! Thanks for calling." I try to muster up some false cheer but have none in me.

"You sound like crap. Are you okay?"

"No, not really," I say, and the tears begin to fall.

"Talk to me. What's going on?"

"We can talk later. It sounds like you've got your hands full."

"Stop it. My hands are always full. Talk to me."

I let it spill—last night, the studio, the girl in the green shirt, Cyle's anger.

"Whoa. Wow. Okay," Chaundra mumbles, seemingly at a loss for words. "I had a feeling last night that I couldn't put my finger on. That must've been it."

"I really think this is the last straw. I could've hurt her. I think Cyle's ready to commit me somewhere." Saying the words sends a chill throughout my body.

"We can't let that happen. I don't know how or why, but I think we've *gotta* figure out who this is. Not only to save other women, but to save *you*. It's like he's stalking you from the inside out." I wish I felt as sure as she sounds.

"I don't know how that'll help. Even if he's locked up, he's still a part of me. But, I agree that we need to figure out who it is," I say. "Even if it doesn't help me, he's got to be stopped."

"Okay. The bus will be here any minute and then you, Lily, and I are going to take a field trip to that atrium. See what we can figure out."

"Good luck talking Cyle into letting me out of his sight. He blocked my bedroom door last night with his air mattress so I couldn't escape."

"You just need to convince him that you'll be fine hanging out with us for the day. Plus, it will give him a little break," she says.

"He would probably appreciate that. My therapist will probably be stopping by, too. Hopefully, you'll be able to whisk me away before they lock me up in a padded room somewhere." I instinctively start rubbing my wrist remembering how the restraints felt wrapped around them.

She agrees to come by to pick me up at ten, assuming Ophelia and Cyle haven't dumped me somewhere by then. I'm going to wait to talk to Cyle until Ophelia is here or Chaundra shows up, whichever is sooner. I lay back and shut my eyes, deciding a bit of sleep will be helpful before our day of investigating.

I MANAGE to sleep about forty-five minutes before the doorbell rings, announcing Ophelia's arrival. *Great.* Can't wait for this conversation. Thankfully, Chaundra will be here in less than an hour.

Ophelia takes a seat on the couch, and I sit on the floor, leaning against the wall so that I can face her. I don't want to sit next to Cyle for fear of freezing to death from the chill coming off him.

"So, Tessa, I gather you had a rough night? What happened?" She asks.

"Not sure I have anything to add to what Cyle's probably already told you," I say as I cross my arms against my chest and glare in his direction. Cyle sits, shaking his foot and staring at the floor. Ophelia maintains her professional stance of looking at me, straight-faced with her hands folded in her lap.

Finally, Cyle breaks. "Sure you do, Tess. Like what the hell happened? How'd you end up there?"

Okay, so maybe I do owe them that explanation. I go backwards to the visit with Chaundra, going into the studio, my journal, becoming him. I grab my journal from the studio floor so that Ophelia can read the entry; I bring along the painting, the one of him. She reads the entry out loud. Hearing *his* words coming out of her mouth chills me, makes me want to run from the room. Cyle holds his breath the entire time she's reading.

She asks what happened after I wrote the entry with his words. How did I get from the studio to that alley? I only remember bits and pieces, my memories peek through the filter of a killer's mind. I explain that there was nothing left of me when I was in that alley. I was *all* him. I was being completely driven by my need to be seen. I explained that I didn't re-enter my own mind until Cyle's voice snapped me back to reality.

Ophelia listens without interrupting until I've run out of things to add.

"I'm...ummm...we're concerned that you were so close to hurting her, and I believe you would have if he hadn't interrupted you."

"Yeah. Me too," I say as a tear escapes down my cheek, bracing myself for whatever she's about to say next.

"I'm sure Cyle doesn't mind staying here to help you get better. But, it seems like last night was a giant step backwards. We need to decide if this plan is working. If we're doing enough."

Cyle continues to sit silently, staring at the floor, tapping his foot.

"Can you just speak for yourself here, Cyle? Why do we need Ophelia to interpret for you?" I say, anger rising into my throat. Since when can't he openly share with me?

He clears his throat several times and finally looks at me with tears glistening in his eyes.

"This is hard for me, Tessa. Everyone else has given up on you throughout the years. I don't want to be added to that list but I'm at a loss. I don't know if what we're doing is enough," he pauses. "I'm doing the best I can, but I feel like it's not working. You could've hurt that girl. *On my watch.* How could I ever live with it if you did something like that? I don't know what to do. I want to help, but…" His voice trails off as he buries his face in his hands to hide his tears.

My heart breaks for him. He's the one person I care about hurting, about disappointing. I am crushing him. Not only has the killer devoured me, but this whole ordeal is consuming Cyle as well. I go sit next to him and pull him into my arms.

"Tess. I'm sorry. I don't know what to do." I hold him and assure him it's okay. Even though it's not. Nothing is okay. The lightning flash ruined everything.

After a few minutes, Ophelia interrupts. "What do you think needs to happen?"

Neither one of us answers.

"Tessa, what do you think?" She says again.

"I don't know. I just don't know if this is working." My entire body trembles.

A knock on the door interrupts the silence in the room surrounding my proclamation. I quickly rise and open it. Chaundra and Lily are here. Hopefully, she'll be able to convince them to give me at least one more day to try to find him.

I make quick introductions between Ophelia and Chaundra while Lily buries her face in her mother's hair. She's probably still petrified of me, thinking I want to hurt her mommy. I ask Ophelia if it's okay that Chaundra stay for the remainder of our meeting. Ophelia raises her eyebrows at the suggestion but agrees. I don't know if she's more stunned by the fact that I've asked a new person into such a personal discussion or that I actually have a friend *in* my apartment. Ophelia knows that allowing someone, besides her and Cyle, into the sacred ground of my sanctuary is something I've never done before.

Chaundra sits in the chair with Lily still hiding her face from us all. "So, we were discussing what to do with me since my episode last night. Apparently, no one is comfortable with our arrangement, thinking I may hurt someone," I say, bitterness pouring out of me. Even though I know they're right.

Cyle rolls his eyes. "Did you tell her what happened after she left?

That you snuck out of the apartment like a conniving teenager and almost hurt some innocent girl?"

"Yeah. I told her what happened," I say.

Ophelia studies Chaundra closely as she replies. "How scary for everyone, especially Cyle, to see his sister like that."

Her approach cracks Cyle's tough guy façade, softening the lines around his eyes and mouth. He nods. "It was awful. I went into full panic mode when I realized she was gone. Seeing her hands on that girl was terrifying," he pauses. "If I had been just a few minutes longer, who knows..."

My heart softens a bit towards him. That must have been terrible for him. In my current state, I am too much for him to handle. Now that he's not so angry, I can see what's actually there—fear and concern. I can't do this to him again.

"We were just deciding what the best way would be to keep everyone safe. I think they're right...it's not good for me to be out here, with *him* taking over my brain, my actions," I say past the lump in my throat. "But I have one huge favor to ask of you both."

Ophelia and Cyle nod.

"Can I have just a couple of days to spend with Chaundra, trying to figure out who it is?"

"What if—" Cyle begins.

Chaundra interrupts. "I don't know why or how but I think the key to fixing Tessa, getting rid of him from inside of her, is to find him," she says. "Like I said, I have no idea why but it's the only way. Locking her up isn't going to do it."

Both of them sit in stunned silence. No objections. No agreements. Nothing. I'm not sure what to do. Plead on my own behalf. Agree to get committed. The silence is killing me.

Lily raises her head from her mother's shoulder and looks around at each of us. "Make him leave. Make him leave," she says, pointing at me and starting to cry.

"Shhh...honey, it's okay. That's Tessa. She's okay," Chaundra says, trying to calm her. Lily's cries only grow more urgent. "What are you trying to say, honey?"

She continues her chant of *make him leave, make him leave.* I leave the room to see if it helps calm Lily. I step into the hallway, just out of her sight, when Lily finally spits out something more.

"Get him out of her!" Lily screams. I gasp. She can tell he's in me, consuming me. She sees it. She feels it. She's not afraid of me; she's afraid of *him*.

"We're trying to, honey. We're trying," Chaundra says.

I finally understand what I think Lily is trying to say. I walk back in the room and stoop down so that I'm making eye contact with her. "Do I need to find him to get him out of me? Is that what you're saying?" I ask.

Her tears stop, though her bottom lip is still trembling, as she nods. Only a little louder than a whisper, she says, "Get him out of you."

Enough said. Everyone knows now that there's no other choice. Out of the mouths of babes.

We all agree to give it one more week. Chaundra and I will spend a lot of time on campus, trying to figure this all out, which will also give Cyle a break. Chaundra makes it clear that she will not hesitate to knock me flat on my ass if I so much as make a move towards a woman. If there are any more instances, Cyle and Ophelia will take me straight to a facility because they can't risk having someone else get hurt. I understand, but it still hurts. Cyle is going to continue pulling the air mattress in front of the door routine to make sure I don't escape again. And we agree that I absolutely will not go into the studio without someone with me. I think the only thing missing is the ankle monitoring bracelet. Maybe I should suggest it. In reality, perhaps I need it. That, or to be handcuffed to one of them.

I'm relieved to have another week. I still have no idea how finding out who the killer is for sure is going to help me, but I sense the urgency in both Chaundra and Lily. I'm going to have to trust them because I don't have a clue. Thank God I have people I feel like I can trust with all of this.

After we wrap up all the details of my "incarceration", Chaundra, Lily and I head out to see what we can figure out. The first thing I do, much to Chaundra's dismay, is stop at the corner store and buy a pack of cigarettes. Relief floods me with my first drag. So weird.

The air is refreshing; I take several deep breaths and take time to appreciate the birds singing, the blue sky, the light breeze. The day is sunny and warm for November. So much so, that we really don't even need our jackets. I, of course, leave my gloves on anyway. Don't want to chance any flashes right now. We head to the center of College Green and take a seat on a bench overlooking the pond, Shimmer Lake, which rests in the middle of the Green. It's a fairly quiet day considering how nice the weather is. Usually, this area is bustling with students, the air filled with their chatter, if the temperature is anywhere above freezing. Other than the occasional person walking, biking or jogging by, there's no one around.

On the street by the far northwest corner of the Green, several major news station's vehicles are parked along the perimeter. CNN, Fox News, NBC. It's been a while since I've turned on regular TV, obviously there's still a lot of buzz going on about Hailey's death and the connection to the other murdered girls. I ask Chaundra about any recent updates she's seen on the news.

"Most people are now convinced the murders are linked. The FBI has been called in to investigate. It's getting national attention and outrage." She tells me. "Outrage because of the apparent attempts by Cardell at covering up the murders, keeping quiet that its students were in danger. So much has come to light about the extent to which they've gone to keep everything hidden. Everything from allegations that they've paid media outlets to keep the murders out of the news, to paying the police department to keep a lid on the murders' connection. All to keep the students and their large tuition bills coming in. Apparently, Cardell officials knew that a potential serial killer in the area would be enough to make some students go with their second-choice college. It's hard enough to convince parents to send their children to a private college that costs nearly fifty thousand per year when they could go to a reputable public institution for a fraction of the cost, let alone pay that kind of money to a school that has a serial killer on the loose."

Chaundra and I sit to chat while Lily runs around, pausing every once in a while to throw a rock into the pond. She's returned to her happy, playful self now that we all understand what she was trying to say. It's as if she can once again see me, instead of *him* in me. She's mentioned my colors a couple of times today. It's a relief that she can see some beauty in me instead of only the ugliness lurking.

Lily is in the midst of a full-on run when she comes to a dead stop and starts screaming.

Chaundra and I immediately rush to her side. "What's the matter honey? You okay?" Chaundra asks while giving her a once-over. There doesn't appear to be any physical injury anywhere on her.

Lily continues her ear-piercing screams with sobs caught in the middle. Chaundra picks her up, trying to soothe her, but she's inconsolable and fights to be let go. Chaundra eventually gives up and puts her back down. The screeching stops but the sobs continue. She's trying to say something but neither of us can understand her.

She takes off running away from us, across the Green, seemingly on a mission. Chaundra yells at her to stop, but quickly realizes it's fruitless and takes off after her. I grab our bags and the stroller and follow behind. Lily gets about halfway across the Green and stops at a large maple tree, touching its trunk. She's in a daze…she continues to cry but she's nowhere near us, lost in her own vision. Chaundra senses it and just lets her be for a moment. Chaundra touches the tree trunk too to see if she can pick up whatever it is that has Lily so freaked out. She looks at me and shakes her head. I decide to give it a try. I take off my glove and rub my hand around the rough surface of the bark.

At first, nothing. I run my hand along it until I get to the other side of the tree and then it hits me like a bullet straight to the heart. He was here. I feel him. I see him in my mind's eye, watching us from behind his hiding place. More specifically, watching *me. Wanting me. Choosing* me as one of his victims. Nausea fills me as I feel his desire work its way through me, first as his own and then as mine. I'm lightheaded and my skin tingles; my heart races.

I collapse onto the ground, breaking my contact with the tree. It's too much. Almost as intense as the lightning flash. Lily must know I saw the same things she did, that I know what it means. She snaps back to the present and comes to join me on the ground. She curls up on my lap and we cry together for a moment, both of us overwhelmed by the power of the vision.

After a moment, Chaundra interrupts. "What the heck just happened?"

Lily speaks first. "He here, Mommy. Right here," she says as she points at the tree.

"Who?" Her face scrunches with confusion.

"Bad guy," Lily answers and sticks her thumb in her mouth.

"Did you see it, Tessa?"

I nod. "Yeah. He was here. Watching us. Watching me," I swallow past the lump in my throat. "I could feel his desire for me."

"How? Why you? This is just too bizarre." Chaundra paces and runs a hand through her hair.

"I don't know. I get the sense that he's following me. Maybe that guy from the coffee shop…" My voice trails off. "Maybe Jonas."

"Can you see anything about him? His features, his clothing? Anything?" Chaundra asks.

"No, it's so strange. It's like I'm always looking through his eyes but never able to see any part of him. I just wish I could get something…anything to help," I say.

"What about you sweetie? What did the bad guy look like? Could you see?" Chaundra asks Lily.

"Hair like Tessa's. Hair on his face."

Brown hair. Beard or mustache…or goatee. *Like Jonas.*

Chaundra senses my thoughts. "I think he was *just* here. Let's head over to the atrium and see if we can pick up anything. You okay to do that?"

"I've got to be, don't I? We've got to figure this out," I say and don't add the rest of my thought. *I may be the next woman that we're trying to save.*

Chaundra leans down and picks up Lily. "Honey, we're gonna take a walk. Let me know if you see him. The man that was here. Okay, sweetie?"

Lily nods, still sucking her thumb for comfort as Chaundra fastens her into the umbrella stroller. She looks completely worn out from her emotional outburst. It'd be surprising if she's able to hold her heavy eyes open for longer than a minute.

We make our way quickly across campus to Lindley Hall. We enter on the ground floor and weave our way through the nearly empty hallways. I wonder if Jonas is teaching somewhere in this building right now or if he was just watching me, waiting to make his move. If I were alone, I would walk through the whole building trying to see if I could find him standing in front of a room of half-asleep students. Then, I'd know it wasn't him. There's no way Chaundra can make it up three flights of stairs with Lily and her stroller to entertain my curiosity, though. I'd ask to do it myself but there are far too many young, attractive women around to trust myself. It's best if I stick with Chaundra but I look into every doorway we pass by, hoping and praying to see him at the front of the room or hear his voice reading out Shakespeare.

We finally make it to the side door that leads to the atrium between Lindley and Bradley. It's one of the most beautiful spots on campus. Both Lindley and Bradley Hall are part of the original campus, founded in 1904. The atrium was added two years ago with the hope of giving students a calming, natural setting in which they could study, regardless of the outside temperatures. Essentially, it's a large indoor garden with marble pathways and columns. Wrought iron tables and chairs sit scattered throughout the greenery; wisteria climbs the columns, its lovely scent floating through the air. The atrium is enclosed with a glass roof, allowing plenty of sunlight for the plants. The warmth of sunny tendrils can be felt even on the coldest of days. There's a large fountain on the northern side with benches surrounding it. Some students fill them now, chatting quietly. The room has the ambience of a library; no one speaks too loudly for fear of offending the beauty of the space.

We weave our way through the marble pathways which have an almost maze-like quality to them. People are scattered about, studying, reading, talking, relaxing. The acoustics in the room, along with the walls of shrubbery and plants, do a great job of making the space seem empty when it's not. We try to look in each nook and cranny as we pass by. Looking for him. Hoping to see him before he sees me.

We've almost worked our way completely through the winding pathways when Chaundra stops. "That's it. Right there. That's the place I always see him in my visions," she says pointing to one of the last columns along the pathway outside the doorway to Bradley Hall.

There's nothing remarkable to me about the spot. I don't pick up any vibes or anything. There's a bench obscured by some potted plants across the pathway from the area she pointed out, but within perfect line of sight. I suggest we sit for a while and see what happens.

Lily is asleep, as I suspected she would be. We leave her in the stroller and take our seats on the bench. Within moments, people crowd the walkways, coming from all directions, their voices filling the air. Chaundra looks to the right, and I watch to the left, hoping we don't miss anyone. It's hard to keep track of everyone coming and going. There are so many men with dark hair. There are so many women that call for my attention. I have to keep reminding myself to look for *men*. Men with dark hair. *Not women*. I fidget with my gloves and my pulse quickens as I try to force myself to focus. The tight shirts, the long hair, the short skirts pull my attention to them...My mind races but my thoughts are interrupted by a voice that snaps me back to reality, to the present, to Tessa.

"We can get together during my office hours if you have time later today," Jonas says, looking down at the young woman strolling beside him.

My gaze follows them. "Chaundra, that's..."

"Him," she says at the exact moment that Jonas and the man from the café, who's pushing a broom, collide. Jonas was intently talking to his student and the maintenance man was sweeping, neither paying attention to where they were walking.

"Sorry, man," the maintenance man says to Jonas, but his gaze falls on the young woman walking next to him.

"No problem. I wasn't paying attention," Jonas says as his eyes raise and he sees me.

"Tessa!" He starts to walk my way and the maintenance man's eyes follow, watching Jonas, then shifting his attention to me. Jonas turns back to his student. "Catch up with me later if you need some help. Tessa, it's good to see you."

I'm glued to my seat. I'm unsure whether to stand and fall into his outstretched arms for an embrace, or to run. Chaundra helps with the decision by standing and stretching out her hand.

"Hi! I'm Tessa's friend, Chaundra," she says, taking his hand.

"Good to meet you. I'm Jonas, also Tessa's friend," he says.

The delay has given me enough time to compose myself, to act normal. I rise for a quick hug, praying that I don't get a flash. I don't.

"It's good to see you," he says, giving me a once-over which a couple of weeks ago would have flattered me. Now I just feel exposed. "You're looking well."

"Thanks. You too," I say and force a smile.

"Well, I gotta run. Let's get together soon, okay?" he says. "If you feel up to it."

"I'll text you and we'll make a plan," I say. I don't mean it. Or at least I don't think I do.

"Good to meet you Chaundra," he says and walks off, towards Lindley Hall.

My gaze goes back to the column where Jonas and the maintenance man collided. He's still there, leaning against the column with his broom standing upright beside him, staring in my direction. I quickly look away, uncomfortable underneath the weight of his gaze.

"He's staring at me. Over there," I whisper to Chaundra. "Is that him?"

"He is indeed," she says. "I've got an idea. Based on what you said, the killer wants to be seen, right?"

I nod.

"So, if that's him, give him what he wants. Turn around and *see* him," she suggests.

"You said it was him. Is it? Or is it Jonas?" I ask.

"I'm not sure since they were both there at the exact same time. I just know that one of them is *him*."

"Yeah, me too. Why can't we just know?" I say.

"I'd say based on Mr. Creepy Stare over there, that maybe he's the one," she whispers, cocking her head in his direction. "He doesn't seem to care that I notice either."

Finally, I give in to her suggestion and turn around to meet his gaze. He doesn't break it.

A chill works its way up my spine as he lifts one corner of his mouth into a smirk, still staring.

"You could always walk over and touch him. See what you pick up," Chaundra whispers.

There is nothing in this world I want to do less. My sanity cannot chance getting anything else from the maniac that has already invaded me. God knows I'm already about a centimeter from my breaking point. Another flash from the killer would guarantee my plunge over the edge to the point of no return.

"If you won't, I will. We've got to figure this out," she says. "I didn't get any weird vibes from Jonas. Let's see what he's got."

She leaves the stroller next to me and starts to walk in his direction, not that he notices because his eyes are still glued to me. It takes everything in my power to not look away. I want him to know I see him but a part of me knows that even though I am staring right at him, he still doesn't quite feel seen. It's not enough. I can feel that he wants more. Chaundra is within two steps of him when a voice yells out, finally breaking his gaze.

"Matthew. Buddy. How are ya?" A young black man, also in a maintenance uniform, yells out walking quickly towards him, pushing a mop bucket.

The staring man nods in his direction. "Good, what's up?"

"There was a major puke fest in Lindley. One girl got it started and then bam! Domino effect. Sounds like a real mess," he says. "We've been summoned to do the honors of cleaning it up."

Matthew turns away from me finally and starts walking next to the other man, towards Lindley. Chaundra and I sit back on the bench and watch them walk away. I flop back and take a deep breath. Our little staring contest has me rattled.

Right as Matthew and his partner are about to walk out of sight, he turns and looks back at me, his dark eyes boring straight into my soul as the memories of the murders have. His message is loud and clear. *He sees me.* He is going to make me see him. I suddenly feel like a thousand-pound weight has lifted off me as relief washes over me. Matthew is the killer. I know it now.

It's not Jonas.

The comfort is short-lived and is quickly replaced by a terrible sense of foreboding that makes me tremble from head to toe. Matthew is the killer. And he's got his eye on *me.*

CHAPTER 21

Chaundra, Lily and I return to my apartment, confident that Matthew is the one. We turn on Disney Jr. for Lily after lunch and get to work on my laptop to figure out more about Matthew. If he were a professor, it'd be easy. It's not like Cardell has listings with pictures of all their maintenance staff. After much frustration, Chaundra decides to call the Maintenance Department to see if she can get any more information. She dials and puts the phone on speaker so I can listen in. She tells the receptionist that she found a set of keys dropped by one of the maintenance staff in the atrium, thinking the first name was Matthew. Whoever she talks to tries to convince her to bring the keys to their office, ensuring her that they would be returned to the correct person. Chaundra says she will do that only if she can verify his last name with them. *Man, she's good.* The secretary says that it could be one of three people: Matthew Cottrill, Matthew James, or Matthew Hanover. Chaundra gets more assertive in the attempt to find out which one was working in the atrium today, but madam secretary won't budge. Chaundra thanks her for her assistance, with a touch of sarcasm and the promise of dropping off the "keys" later today. We now have three possible names in hand.

We search Facebook first. Matthew Cottrill's profile picture is public, and he definitely isn't our guy. Cotrill is a forty-something black man. Matthew Hanover also has a public profile picture. He isn't our guy, either. He looks old enough to be my father, and I am surprised that he even has a Facebook account. The third guy, Matthew James, we can't find anywhere. While the name is popular and gets lots of hits, none of them are the guy from the stare-down. We search Twitter and Instagram, still nothing. Finally, we get somewhere when we search on Google. A page of hits comes up. Apparently, our Matthew was raised in this area and graduated from the local high school where he was the quarterback for the Chandlersville Cougars football team. In a town that loves sports as much as this one, he was quite the hometown hero. There were several newspaper articles that featured him riding the float in the annual Thanksgiving Day parade. The last article we find says that he accepted a full-ride scholarship to none other than Pinkerton University in Georgia.

"Pinkerton. There it is. There's the connection," I say to Chaundra, amazed that we found it.

"Let's see…he graduated from high school in 2008 so he would've been there in September 2010 when Mallory was killed," Chaundra said. "Oh my god."

My mouth drops open and Chaundra pulls me into a hug. Thankfully, no flash. I can't believe we found the missing link. *Matthew attended Pinkerton. Matthew is our guy. Not Jonas. Not Jonas!* I sigh in relief.

"I feel awful for thinking Jonas did it. This Matthew guy murdered his fiancé and got away with it. No wonder I got so much pain from Jonas. I felt his heartbreak," I say, guilt creeping through me. I knew Jonas couldn't do something so heinous. Relief mingles with my guilt. I fight the urge to pick up my phone and call him right this minute to tell him I know who killed Mallory. There's no way to do that without trying to explain everything, though. Explaining it all right now would not be the best idea.

"So, what do we do?" I ask after a moment.

"I'll call the name in to my contact at the Police Department. He may not follow-up since I just called about Jonas. I'll come up with something convincing, though." There's no doubt that she will – she's quite persistent.

"It's weird that we can't find anything else about him. It's like he left for college and dropped off the face of the earth. Only, he came back. Doesn't seem like he's a hero anymore," I say, looking through the article about his scholarship to Pinkerton. "Maybe he's found a new claim to fame. Killing women."

"Let me call my guy. Do you mind keeping an eye on Lily and I'll step outside?" Chaundra asks.

It's no problem, especially since Lily has been glued to the television from the moment it was turned on. Chaundra limits their TV time at home, so this has been a special treat for her, plus no brothers are around to have to fight with about show choices.

"Lily, honey. Mommy's outside and I have to run to the bathroom. You okay for a minute?" I ask. She nods without breaking her stare at the screen. "Okay. Be right back." I make a beeline for the bathroom in the hallway. All the coffee we've consumed while doing our research suddenly hits me full force.

As I walk out of the bathroom, I notice the door to my studio is open. *Weird. I know it was just closed.* Maybe Cyle or Chaundra opened it? I walk back the hallway to close it and find Lily standing in the middle of the room, looking from picture to picture. Her gaze finally comes to rest on one.

"You," she says, pointing at the picture.

"No, honey. That's not me," I say.

"Yes, you," she says, and I move over to pick her up.

We walk closer to the painting. It's a haunting picture of a face looking into a mirror. Only half of it is discernible, the other half is smears of paint which block out all the features. The eye that I can see, is full of fear, horror, terror. It hits me. She's right, it *is* me. My features, my eye…how did I not notice it before?

"Him!" She says, pointing.

"No, Lily. It's me."

"Him," she says and starts pulling away from me, trying to get down.

I move closer so that she can touch the picture, to show me what she means. She points in the mirror, at a small image appearing behind me. A man, watching me. I know she's right. It's him. He's in my painting.

My mind reels. How can this be? I painted this in my madness right after the flash before I even consciously remember seeing him. When I *was him*.

"There you guys are," Chaundra says, walking into the room. "What's up?"

I fill her in, with Lily's help. She keeps repeating *him*, over and over. I share my confusion over how I painted this picture of him watching me, before I was even aware of what he looks like.

"Oh my god, I get it," Chaundra says after several minutes of talking. She starts pacing the room, a hand raised to her temple. Her words come out in short clips. "He's been watching you. Before everything... the flash, you seeing him at *Monticello's*..."

"There's no way. I would've noticed," I say hoping that's true but somehow knowing it's not. An image of him watching me through a cluster of trees as I jog along a path on the outskirts of town floods my mind. Another of me, stooping to tie my shoe on the sidewalk cutting across College Green. Another of leaving the hospital with Cyle.

I run from the room and barely make it to the toilet to vomit. Chaundra and Lily follow behind and wait in the hallway to give me my space. After I rinse my mouth and splash water on my face, I rejoin them.

"I..." I start to say when Chaundra grabs my arm and leads me to the couch. I can't seem to catch my breath.

I start to talk again and Chaundra holds up a finger, "Just wait a minute. Take some deep breaths." She gets me a glass of water, Lily a glass of juice, and joins me on the couch. "Okay, now you're good to go."

"I don't even know how to describe what just happened. I'm sure what I was seeing were things I got from the flash, but they were too bizarre for me to be able to process until now." I try to swallow the bile rising in my throat so that I can spit this next part out. "I could see him watching me. You were right, he's been doing it for a while. At least a couple of months."

A shiver races through me. He was watching me before he killed Hailey. It easily could've been me instead of her. No, I don't wander around campus late at night inebriated, but I'm alone all the time. Or at least I used to be. I think of all my time running, my hikes through the mountains, just always being here alone. Talk about an easy target. That would definitely be me.

"Wow. Okay. So, maybe that day at *Monticello's*, instead of being there to follow the girl from the alley, he was actually there for you." She's right. Of course he was.

"And today, he was there watching. Probably waiting for me to be alone," I say. "He was there when I left the hospital which means he knows I was there."

"This is creepy. Okay, I'm really scared for you," she says.

"Yeah, me too." Somehow having all of this click into place is more chilling than not knowing who he was and trying to stop the killings. Now, I'm trying to stop him from killing *me* and it's altogether different. I remember the things he did to those other women. The pleasure he took from their pain. The ecstasy he'd feel at doing the same to me.

"Okay, so I called Joe, my police guy. He was a bit skeptical since I just called yesterday. I told him I bumped into Matthew today and got a very clear vision that it was him. I fibbed a bit and filled in some of the blanks that you shared with me from your flash that I'd have no way of knowing," Chaundra says. "I think he's convinced there's something to it and he promised to follow up."

"Hopefully it's soon," I say.

"Do you want to stay with me for a while, under the radar since he wouldn't know where you are?"

I ponder this for a moment. "That might not be a bad idea. Then, maybe Cyle could go home for a while, see his family. I think he needs a break from me anyway."

"It's settled. Why don't you go pack some things and we'll set you up in Lily's room? Heck, half the time she's in my bed anyway."

I breathe a sigh of relief and get up to pack a bag. This plan makes me feel a lot better. I have no doubt he knows where I live, when I come, when I go. We'll have to make sure he's nowhere near when I leave. I wouldn't want to put Chaundra or her kids in any danger. I'm sure that Cyle will greatly appreciate having a break, too. He took full advantage today of Chaundra's "babysitting" services and still hasn't returned.

I take a break from packing to call Ophelia and leave a message to let her know the plan. I text Cyle and ask him to give me a call when he can. He calls back within minutes. I fill him in and tell him to take a break, to go be with his family.

"I just don't know, Tess. This all makes me uncomfortable. I don't think I should leave town when we now *know* he's been watching and following you," he says.

"That's why I thought it'd be good for me to stay with her. We'll be careful when we leave to make sure he's not following. I'll feel safer there than here."

"And what if he does figure out where you are? Then what? You and Chaundra and the three kids are going to fight him off?"

"We both know that's not how he operates. He waits to get his victims alone, something I'm not allowed to be right now. I'd be more likely to appear to be alone here than at her house, even with you here. Three kids make much more of a ruckus than a middle-aged man," I laugh trying to dissuade some of his concerns. "Plus, you need to see your family. God knows I'd take a break from me if I could. So, you take one for the both of us."

Cyle pauses and clears his throat a couple of times. "Okay, you win. I know you…even if I said no, you'd be so persistent, you'd wear me down. Did you tell Ophelia the plan?"

"I just left a message. I'll make sure to keep meeting with her, either at Chaundra's, here, or her office, whichever she prefers," I say. "Let's hope this will only be for a week or two. Just until the police can follow up on Chaundra's call and piece this all together. I'm sure he'll be locked up soon."

"Okay, but then what? It's not like that's going to make him leave you," Cyle says.

"I don't know. We'll take that step when we get there. I just know him getting caught is the first step," I say.

"One step at a time, huh? I suck at that," he says. "Anyway, check in with me every day, okay?"

"I will. If not, you know how to find me at Chaundra's," I say, and tears fill my eyes. "I love you, Cyle. Thank you for everything."

"I love you, kiddo. I'll be back to your place shortly if you can wait to give your big brother a hug before you take off," he says.

"Of course. See you soon."

We hang up and I finish packing my bag, already missing Cyle. I'm glad that he'll get to go home and spend some time with Tasha and the kids. He must be missing them like crazy.

Hopefully, the police will question Matthew and figure out that he is the guy, he'll go to jail, and…Like Cyle said, *then what?* Where will that leave me? I'll still have him in me, his cravings and desires fueling me. He's right. What good is it going to do me to have him locked up, when he can live on and on through me? I sit on the bed, bury my face in my pillow and sob.

I've been there for a while when a hand gently touches my back. Cyle pulls me into an embrace and holds me while I cry on his shoulder.

Finally, I pull away, blow my nose, and look at him. "Sorry. I'm just…I don't know. Overwhelmed, scared, unsure," I say.

"I know. But, as you have beat into my head, one step at a time. Sounds like going to Chaundra's is that next step," he says.

"I guess I'm just worrying about the *then what's*. Best case scenario, he gets caught, everyone's safe and relieved. Then what, like you said, with me?"

"We're going to have to trust that the then what will come right when it's supposed to, and it will make perfect sense," he gives a slight smile. "I have to trust that you'll be okay.

You're a tough chick. You'll get through this."

I give him another hug, wishing I could believe him. Wishing I could know that after all of this is said and done, I can go back to the way I was before the lightning flash. Even though my identity wasn't necessarily my own, at least it wasn't *his*.

I grab my bag and head to the living room where Lily and Chaundra are waiting for me to take that next step.

LIFE AT CHAUNDRA'S is bustling all the time, non-stop, around the clock. She has her hands full with Lily, Aiden, and Liam. Lily is Aiden's little shadow and follows him around everywhere he goes. Liam and Lily bicker non-stop—it must be that oldest/youngest child dichotomy at work, each vying for the most attention. I get a huge kick out of watching Lily antagonize Liam to the point that he finally retaliates by yelling at her, punching her, or telling on her and then he gets in trouble. I'm sure, growing up, I did the exact same thing to my brothers. Aiden is the one I've connected with the most. He's only five but he's such a deep thinker. He could talk for hours, if Lily would let him, that is. Some of his insights are amazing. I often wonder if he has his own form of a psychic gift that presents itself a bit differently than Lily's or Chaundra's.

Chaundra is an accountant and works from home, or at least tries to. It's ironic to me that she makes her living dealing with the black and white world of numbers when the rest of her world is so non-concrete, full of gray. She says she enjoys it, though, and says it's the one area of her life where she feels like everything adds up, makes sense, is exact. She does most of her work after the kids go to bed for the night. I don't know how she still has the energy to do a job—I can barely think straight after they're down and the house is quiet.

As hectic as it's been, it's also nice to be around so much activity, to feel like I'm part of a family. It's a comfort I haven't felt since I was a young child. In the five days that I've been here, we've fallen into a nice routine. I help with the cooking, clean the kitchen, and watch the kids while Chaundra does the other housework and laundry. She works a few hours each night after they go to bed at eight and then we spend a couple of hours talking over a glass of wine before we turn in. She feels like the sister I've always wanted. While I desperately want them to lock Matthew up and have this madness end, I don't want to leave Chaundra's. In some ways it feels more like home than anything I've ever had. Aiden and Lily are both very affectionate, which at first scared the crap out of me, but I've now grown to love it. I never knew a hug from a child could be so healing, so therapeutic. I've had several flashes with Lily (two blues, an orange, and a red) but it's worth it, whatever they end up revealing. Surprisingly, I've had none with Aiden.

I'm doing the dishes after lunch and Chaundra walks in, an ashen expression replacing the cheerful disposition she had only moments ago when we were all at the table.

"What's up?" I ask, my hands buried in soapy water.

"I just talked to Joe at the Chandlersville PD. They brought Matthew in for questioning three days ago. He got belligerent right away and refused to answer questions. They were trying not to push too hard because they didn't want him lawyering up right away. Anyway, he told them to arrest him, or he was leaving. Since they didn't have grounds to make an arrest, they had to let him go. The police got the judge to issue a search warrant of his car and apartment based on a couple of things he said. They went to serve the warrant today, and apparently, he's gone. He took off. The landlord said she saw him loading his car yesterday and his family said he told them he was leaving. They have no idea where he is but said they found some things that confirm that he's their guy," Chaundra says and slumps down into a chair at the table.

"That's good news, right?" I ask.

"Kind of, I guess. Except for the fact that he's missing right now and could be anywhere. And...he had pictures of you in his apartment," she says.

Surely, I didn't hear her correctly. "Wait, what?"

"Joe told me there were pictures of several women that they couldn't identify. I asked if I could send him a picture of you to see if you were one of them. I sent the one I took the other day of you and

Lily reading on the couch. He said it was a definite match to several of the pictures in his place."

The hair on my arms stands at attention despite the warmth of the water. "Wow. Creepy." I don't know what else to say. *Pictures*? How could he get pictures of me without my awareness? "I'm glad, though, that they believe us, or you anyway. They know it's him. Now they just need to find him."

"They've started a search that's going viral since this case has gotten so much national attention. They're confident they'll get him. I worry since we know he's got his eye on you."

"He could be anywhere by now. Hopefully, he's smart enough to stay under the radar, especially since he's got to know they're looking for him."

"I'm just glad you're here."

"Yeah, me too," I say and mean it. Being around Chaundra and the kids has been a lifesaver. The distraction and chaos have kept *him* at bay most of the time. I have moments where he starts to creep forward, but Chaundra picks up on it instantly and calls me out, snapping me back to the present. One of the perks of rooming with a psychic.

Chaundra asks me to keep an eye on the rugrats so she can shower. While they're sitting quietly glued to the TV, I try to call Cyle to give him an update. His voice mail picks up and I give him the latest news on Matthew. "Anyways, you don't have to call me back. I just wanted you to know."

We've talked a couple of times since I've been here. He's been happy to be around his family, but he's been worried about me. I assure him each time that Chaundra and the kids are taking good care of me. A little *too good* in all honesty—I've put on a couple of pounds already just from eating three meals a day. Living alone, my routine was to grab a bite to eat when I felt hungry, not preparing meals for growing children. The extra weight is fine, though. I'm still under where I need to be thanks to my crazy week of no eating.

I check Facebook from my phone and see that many of the pages I follow for the murdered women have updates with Matthew's picture and a note that he's wanted for questioning in connection with the cases. Studying his face sends chills over my entire body. *That was fast*! I don't know how police ever found missing or wanted persons before the age of social media.

I read through the comments trying to get more information about him. Many of the comments are from locals that remember Matthew's glory days as a football star. They know his family, and there's no way such a "smart, gentle young man" could be connected to the murdered women. Apparently, Matthew is currently an assistant coach for one of the local youth boosters football leagues and the children and parents love him. They rave online about his care and concern for the team. Then, on the flip side of the coin, are the claims that he was expelled from both Lincoln University and Pinkerton University for sexual assaults on fellow students. Relief floods me. They *finally* made a connection to Pinkerton. Hopefully now they will dig further and link him to Mallory's case, too. No criminal charges were filed in either sexual assault case from his college days because the women didn't want to go through the brutality of public shaming, a court case, etcetera. After his expulsion from Lincoln, he came back to live with his mother in Chandlersville, at which point he accepted the job at Cardell.

My hands start to shake in outrage and the desire for vengeance on behalf of all the women. How can somebody who was expelled from two different colleges for rape get employed by a university? How can the system allow for such "mistakes"? Letting him roam freely in the midst of young, beautiful women is like setting a child loose in an ice cream shop. He was a ticking time bomb. I know that the women he killed came later in the game for him. His list of rape victims is probably much, much longer than anyone suspects or will ever know. Knowing how strong his cravings and urges are, I have no doubts that he has raped many women. He must be caught. He has to be locked away forever.

The kids' show ends and instantly Lily and Liam start bickering. I'm just getting ready to get off Facebook to intervene when I see a comment that stops me in my tracks. It's Jonas, on the thread mentioning Matthew's time at Pinkerton. It's a simple sentence but carries such weight... *Look up Murder of Mallory Kasler.* Jonas has made the connection. He knows. I've got to reach out to him. I have no doubt he needs someone right now, for support. All of this being dredged back up must be hell for him. As hard as I'll have to fight the images and feelings from Mallory's murder, I need to be there for him in case he needs a listening ear, a shoulder to cry on, or just a distraction. I owe him my support to make up for all the doubt and distrust I've had with him. Not to mention all the crazy ways I've acted lately.

I text him asking if he's available in the next couple of days to get together and then turn my attention to the kids, who are now in full-on tantrum mode.

"Do you guys wanna do a project?" I suggest, having to raise my voice so they can hear over their own ruckus.

"Yeah," they all yell, turning their attention to me.

"Let's do a painting. Sound good?" I suggest, staying in my comfort zone. Plus, I haven't been able to paint for a while so this is a good excuse.

They all run to the table, and I pull the supplies out of the cupboard. I add paint to a makeshift palette for each of the kids on paper plates. I smock us all up and dole out fresh paper. The kids get to work. Aiden uses his fingers; Liam and Lily go back and forth between brushes and their fingers. I sit back for a while and watch them work, complimenting their masterpieces. Maybe when all of this is over, I can teach art classes for kids. I love watching how their little minds and hands work together to create the most interesting pieces. When I can't stand it any longer, I dip my finger in the blue paint and set to work on my own project. A slight smile spreads across my face -- I haven't finger painted since I was a child. The feel of the paint on my fingers and my finger gliding across the paper is so soothing.

I'm in heaven. Paint on my fingers, children's laughter filling the room, and the feeling of freedom that always comes when I create washes over me. I wish this moment could last forever.

CHAPTER 22

J onas replied to my text later that evening saying he'd love to get together. As happy as I was to hear from him, I also was a little heartbroken because his response had none of his usual playful tone. It was all business—schedule a time to meet. Maybe I lost out on a real opportunity for a grown-up relationship. All because of these stupid flashes. Chalk *loss of love* up to another thing they've cost me. Another piece of my life the way it was supposed to be, gone.

Jonas and I made a plan to meet for lunch at noon at *Gatsby's*, a local pub, allowing for a couple of hours before my meeting with Ophelia at my apartment. Having a shorter time for a get together with him may be best since things feel a bit awkward after all my recent antics.

Chaundra wasn't keen on the idea of me being alone—she's filled Cyle's shoes quite nicely. She insisted on going to *Gatsby's* with me and waiting until I am safe with Jonas before leaving, *if* I promise to have Jonas walk me to my apartment afterwards, where Ophelia will meet with me. Chaundra will come to the apartment at three to take me back to her place. Chaundra doesn't want me to have any time out and about by myself so we don't have a repeat of the alley incident. Even though I've been so much better since staying with her, I do see her point. Time alone is probably not the best idea right now although it sounds quite nice, except for the fact that there's a serial killer on the loose who would love to find me. Maybe someday, after Matthew's caught. If *he* ever leaves me.

Chaundra is more excited about my date with Jonas than I am, I think. She helps me decide what to wear, fixes my make-up and styles my hair. When I stand back to examine her handiwork, I'm pleased with the outcome. Much better than I'd do myself. She picked out tight, dark jeans that show off my curves nicely and a form-fitting dark plum shirt which does the same. She curled my hair with a wand, making long ringlets that flow down my back. My make-up looks spectacular. She's done my eyes in hues of brown, green, and some dark purple which make them pop, looking even bigger than usual. I don't know what she used on my lashes, but they look like they've had extensions. Even I have to admit that I look hot. If Jonas wasn't into our getting together, he certainly will be once he sees me now. As Chaundra said, "Those jeans. Those curves. He's not letting you go."

The best part of all of it is laughing and talking while I get ready. The bond I feel with Chaundra reminds me of my relationship with Cyle. Because of the flashes, I always kept my distance from everyone, so I never really had any close friends that would fill that "best friend" role that so many young women have. For the first time in my life, I feel like I've found that person. When I'm with her, my heart feels *full*.

A sitter comes over to hang out with the kids so that Chaundra can escort me to *Gatsby's* and then run some errands while I have my date and meeting with Ophelia. When we get to the pub, I walk in first so that it looks like I'm alone. Chaundra follows a few feet behind. Jonas of course is already there, waiting on me. He rises when I walk in, his eyes scanning me up and down. Chaundra was right. The smile on his face and gleam in his eye tell me he likes what he sees. I turn around and give Chaundra a quick grin over my shoulder. She gives a thumbs up and heads back out the door. I turn my attention back to Jonas and feel my face flushing. He looks pretty hot, too. I quicken my pace towards him and we meet in an embrace. A yellow flash. A nice change from the red flashes I've gotten from his thus far. I wish I knew what this glimpse of the future holds. *Where are my psychic abilities when I need them*? Could getting a yellow flash instead of a red one mean he's ready to move on from his pain, towards the future? Will that future involve me? A smile spreads across my face at the possibility.

The hostess interrupts and leads us to our table. As soon as we're seated, we both start to speak at once. "Sorry," I say. "You first."

"I was just going to say you look beautiful," he says, blushing a bit. "Really beautiful."

The heat rises to my cheeks to match his. "Thank you. You look pretty awesome yourself." There's an awkward pause while we both try to hide our embarrassment and return to our normal colors. "And I was going to start off by saying I'm sorry."

"For what?" Jonas asks.

"For all the weirdness with me the past month or so. Things were going so well with us and then I had to ruin everything," I say.

"Well, I won't lie. There have been some pretty bizarre interactions between us, but I'm trying to chalk it all up to you not feeling well," he says. "I do agree that things were going great. I'd like to see it head back in that direction."

"Yeah, me too," I reach out and grab his hand, interlacing his fingers with mine. Purple flash. Purple's good. I wonder what talent he's just shared with me. God, my small hand feels so good wrapped in his. "I've missed you. A lot. I promise that I will explain everything, in time. I've been going through some strange things. Hopefully, I'm getting back on the track to normal."

Who the hell am I kidding? Back on track to normal? Me? That's laughable. To get anywhere close to normal, I'd have to go back to pre-conception and have the power of God to make me into someone different. To strip me of my "gift".

So I don't feel like a complete fraud, I add, "At least as normal as I get."

The waiter interrupts and we place our orders. A Cobb salad and iced tea for me; a Reuben, fries and a Dos Equis for Jonas. "I should have ordered for both of us so that you'd actually eat some real food and put some meat back on your bones," he says. I pause, and smile, unsure what to say. "Not that you need it or anything because you look amazing exactly as you are," he adds, red creeping into his cheeks again.

While we wait on our food, he catches me up on what has been going on in his life. I get lost in his voice, listening to his funny stories about students from this semester, their papers, their excuses for late assignments or missed classes. He has the best smile. The best laugh. The best everything. We hold hands the entire time, until our food arrives. I would be content to just sit and hold his hand, listen to him talk, but he probably wants to eat, so I finally let go.

I take a couple of bites of my salad and then I can't hold back anymore. "I really hope you're okay with me asking this...I have to, though. Tell me about Mallory."

His reaction is physical. His eyes instantly well with tears. He puts his sandwich down, mid-bite and wipes his hands on his napkin. He clears his throat several times, trying to compose himself. "How do you know...?"

I interrupt, not making him finish his sentence. "Remember that weirdness I have going on with me, and saying I'd explain it all later... Let's just say that knowing about Mallory is part of it."

"Okay. Are you like...are you like psychic or something?" He asks. I'm grateful that he doesn't obviously recoil when he asks that. Like he might be open to the possibility of people having abilities, gifts that aren't easily accepted or understood.

I'm not sure of the best, honest way to answer his question without going into everything. I finally settle on, "Yes, something like that. I promise I'll explain it all. Someday. But I really want to know about her."

"Okay, just give me a minute. You totally caught me off guard here." He signals for the waiter to bring him another beer. Probably a good idea. After a fresh one arrives, he begins.

"I'm not sure what you know, but I loved her. God, it still feels so weird sometimes to say that in the past tense. Anyway, we were engaged. She was murdered in Georgia in September 2010. We were there visiting family and friends, planning our wedding. She met with some friends at Pinkerton University and then she vanished. She was found in high weeds by the side of the road," he pauses to take a drink of his beer. "She'd been brutally raped, then murdered. They never caught the guy."

Images of her naked body fill my mind. First, remembrances from Jonas' viewpoint; loving her. Then, from Matthew's twisted mind...*needing* her. Those brown eyes watching me, seeing me. My hands wrapping around her slender throat. I force myself back to the table, to now. I must be emotionally present for Jonas as he shares this part of himself with me. I wonder how many of the details he knows of her death or if they spared him of the grim, terrible realities.

"I'm so sorry. How horrible for you. I don't know how you ever recover from something like that...a loss so deep and tragic." I place my hand on his.

"Yeah, me neither. I don't know that you ever really do. At least, I haven't reached that stage yet and it's been five years," he pauses. "But I'm finally to the point where I could see myself moving on, of having a future."

Hopefully with me.

"I have to ask, and I hope this is okay. Do you think there's a connection between the murdered girls here at Cardell and Mallory's murder?"

His mouth drops open. "Do I ever! Once I learned this Matthew guy, that the police are looking for, got expelled from Pinkerton around the same time as Mallory's murder, I knew. I have no doubt it's the same guy. I've reported it to the police. I'm praying that they find evidence to link it all together. Instead of assuming I'm the link, like they've tried to for years."

"That must've been hell," I say.

"Total hell. Not only did I lose the woman I love in such a horrendous way but then they questioned me about it. Then, with Hailey missing, for some reason, they got a burr up their asses and started hounding me all over, even though I was already cleared years ago."

Now, my appetite is completely gone and my chest tightens with guilt. I know exactly why they started hounding him again. Because of Chaundra's tip; because of my awful assumptions about him.

"As frustrating as it is, I do get it, though," he continues. "The police are desperate to figure out who is killing these women and they have to look at all angles. Hopefully, this Matthew guy is the right one and they're not just chasing false leads again."

It slips out before I have the chance to filter it. "He is."

"Is what? The right guy?"

It's too late to take it back. "Yes, without a doubt."

"How do you…?" He leans forward and starts to ask.

"I promise to explain later. I just know," I say and fidget with the napkin in my lap.

His eyes go wide. "Wow. Okay. I hope they find him."

"Yeah, me too," I say and don't add the ending I want to…*before he kills me, too.*

He tells me more about Mallory while we finish lunch. More accurately, while *he* finishes lunch and I push my salad around the plate. I want to know all about the woman that held such a special place in his heart. I need to know more about her than the brutal way her life ended. Hopefully having images of the whole person will take away the memories I have of her disgusting final moments. Jonas seems happy to oblige. The more he talks it's as though a blanket of grief lifts off him. Like sharing about her lightens his load. He laughs through some of the memories and sheds some tears through others. We both get so lost in the conversation that we lose track of time. I finally glance at my phone and see it's one forty-five.

"I hate to do this, but I have to cut this short," I say and reach for his hand. "I have an appointment at two."

"Already? I don't want you to leave," he says and sticks out his bottom lip. "Just tormenting you. I have office hours soon anyway."

"Feeling is mutual, trust me. If it wasn't necessary, I'd stay. Promise," I say. "If you have the time, would you mind walking me to my apartment?"

"Of course I wouldn't," he says and pulls my hand up to kiss it. "It gives me a few extra moments with you. I'll never refuse that."

We walk quickly to the apartment, hand in hand, chatting the entire way. The more positive memories he gives me of Mallory, the more I can focus on who she was to Jonas and let go of some of Matthew's memories. Not that *his* are gone but they are now intertwined with layers of happy ones.

At the door to my apartment, Jonas pulls me into an embrace and tenderly kisses me, sending electric shocks throughout my body. Not from flashes but from desire, excitement. I would love to invite him in. Forget my appointment with Ophelia. Some time alone with Jonas could probably do me more good than a therapy session. I could be easily convinced to blow her off, but he is the one to pull away.

"I would love to continue this right here, but I have office hours that start in, oh, about two minutes, so I've got to run," he says looking at his watch.

"I was going to invite you in for a while," I say playfully. "Are you sure you can't stay?"

"You aren't making it easy," he says and leans to kiss me again, more deeply this time. Again, he pulls away. "But I've got to go, and you have an appointment, remember?"

Before I have the chance to protest, he starts to walk away. "Raincheck, okay?"

I'm all but begging for him to come back. "Soon?" I say.

"As soon as possible. I gotta go," he says and takes off in a half sprint towards campus.

I have an ache in me that I've never experienced firsthand before. I put my key in the lock. I need to calm myself a bit before Ophelia comes. I open the door to my home and instead of peace and comfort washing over me, I am met with a blow to the head. The world around me goes black as I fall to the floor.

CHAPTER 23

Unbearable pain radiates through my head. I try to pull myself back to the present, but I'm weighted down, heavy. I try to move but I can't. I'm trapped. I struggle to open my eyes, to see where I am, but my eyelids are so heavy. I'm lying down. I can't get up. I pull and pull, then realization hits me. My hands are bound. I sense movement. I finally force open my eyes to complete darkness. Panic courses through me and bile rises in the back of my throat. It takes a moment for my vision to adjust. It's a small space, with rough carpet underneath me...the little area I'm in is moving. A car. I'm in the trunk of a car. My feet aren't bound so I start kicking. Kicking and screaming. Every ounce of energy I have goes into every kick, every scream. Saliva runs down my cheeks as I scream so loud my ears ring. Finally, the movement of the car stops, and the trunk opens. Bright sunshine floods my vision, blinds me. I know what's coming before I feel it. A blow to my head that sends me back to oblivion.

I start to come to again. I can't remember exactly what's going on, and then...Oh, yeah. I've been taken. There's movement, but it's different than the car. It's rougher. Every inch of my body aches. Someone is carrying me. My eyelids feel so heavy; opening them seems impossible. My head hurts so badly.

I want to drift off and forget about where I am or who has me. But I can't. I must know. I must fight. Finally, I force one eye open. I'm outside. There are trees all around. A forest. My instincts kick in. I use all my strength to kick and flail to get away from whoever has me. My hands are still tied but my feet move freely. I am thrown to the ground and get a moment's glimpse of his face before his foot kicks me in the temple.

I have no way to know how long it's been. When I open my eyes this time it's dark. I can't see him anywhere, but I feel his presence nearby. My feet are now bound, too, and something is lodged in my mouth, choking me. Gagging me. I try to cry out but can make no sound louder than a whimper. That's enough to bring him to my side. It's Matthew. He stands over me with a smirk on his face. I look straight into his eyes, trying to make him aware that I see him. He doesn't have to rape or kill me to get me to see him. If only he knew how much of him I have already seen.

He pulls me to my feet with gloved hands and first rips my shirt off, then my bra, leaving me exposed to him. He takes a step back, looking at me. His desire is growing, emanating from his pores. Chills run down my spine. I know what's coming next. I know how much he is enjoying this–the mental torture he's putting me through. I've lived it with him. It gives him complete control and power. I've felt it. I enjoyed it, too. Bile rises in my throat again. I force myself to swallow it back down.

He grabs a stick from the nearby ground and rubs it over my breasts, my stomach, and then without warning he draws it back and smacks my side. I wince despite my own desperate desire to keep from showing any pain, any emotion. I don't want to give him the pleasure of a reaction or fear. Alexis' face pops into my head. The torture she endured…she refused to satisfy his cravings. I can't go through the hell she did. Again, he moves the stick tenderly up my arms, along my cheeks, down my pants and then, once more, he draws it back and hits me harder with it, this time on the leg. It bites even through my jeans.

He pulls my pants down so they rest against the rope binding my ankles. The stick, up and down my legs, between my legs, over my ass. Then the hardest slap yet, bare against my thigh. My legs tremble from the fear as much as the pain. They're about to give way. The last position in the world I want to be in right now is on the ground naked, waiting for him to rape me. The part of him that's still inside me floods with memories of the other girls. The feelings of power and control. The high I felt from watching them squirm. From the anticipation of raping them, the screams that would follow. The ecstasy that consumed me as I watched them die, *seeing me.*

I try to tune out what he is doing, the movement of the stick. Burning, stinging pain from the hits. I think of finger painting with the kids. Their laughter. Lily's hugs. Jonas' kisses. How do I escape this? Another hit. *Is anyone looking for me?* Will they find me in time? I've failed in my mission to save the next girl, which is me. I will be his next victim. Perhaps I am destined to be his final victim before he's caught. Maybe he'll never get caught.

Another hard hit across the back of my knees. My legs buckle and I fall forward, face first into the dirt. I try to find him, to see where he's standing, to anticipate his next move as I struggle to pull up onto my knees. He kicks me between the shoulder blades then places a foot across my spine, pinning me. *Oh my god, he's going to kill me. I'm going to die.* I gasp for breath. Searing pain races up my back and surrounds my head like a vice. Faces of those I am going to lose flash through my mind. Cyle. Chaundra. Lily. Liam. Aiden. *Jonas.* Poor Jonas is about to lose another woman to this madman. My heart breaks for him. Matthew has tortured me mentally for the past month. Now he's getting the pleasure of torturing me physically. He's going to be the one to watch me take my last breath. I shudder. What a cruel, sick irony this is.

A kick to my side fills me with searing pain, interrupting my thoughts. How will Cyle handle losing me? Will he ever stop blaming himself for leaving me? Will he always think that if he'd just stayed, he could've kept me safe? Cyle is the last person on earth I want to carry this burden, the burden of losing me. Matthew walks around and around me like an animal circling its prey.

Chaundra…her guilt for letting me talk her into leaving me. It will crush her. God, please don't let her blame herself. There was no way either of us could've known he'd be hiding out in my apartment.

He still circles around me. Rubbing the stick. Poking the stick. Back and forth between strokes that could almost be considered tender, to those that are meant to hurt and inflict pain.

Finally, he speaks. "I've been watching you for some time now. But, like everyone else, you didn't even notice, did you? I'm a nobody to you. Just a janitor that's there to clean up after all these rich snobs."

I try to speak but the gag stifles my words. He leans over and unties it, freeing my mouth. Is he interested in what I have to say? Or does he want to make sure he can hear my screams. His foot presses me to the ground, keeping me in place. "Don't bother screaming. No one will hear you, trust me."

My words spill out quickly, frantically. "Actually, I've seen you several times. At *Monticello's* a couple of weeks ago. And then, just a few days ago at the atrium. Your name is Matthew, right?" I hope that if he knows I've seen him, that I know his name, it will change the outcome.

It seems to throw him off for a moment and he starts pacing. "Let me guess. I was cleaning up after somebody and you thought '*I'm so glad I'm not that loser having to clean up other people's shit.*' Well, I," he kicks me in the ribs, "don't," another kick in the ribs, "need," another kick, "your," kick, "sympathy."

Despite the excruciating pain I spit out the only lie I can think of to help my situation. "Actually, I noticed how handsome you are…that's what caught my attention."

Again, I swallow the bile that's risen along with the lie. His eyes are crazed as he continues to pace in and out of my limited range of sight.

Finally, he speaks. "You're just like the rest of them, you know. Regardless of what you say, I'm a nobody to someone like you. I have to do this to show you bitches how important I am. I am like God, holding the power of life and death in my hands." He laughs, a deep, sorrowful, bone-chilling sound. He takes his foot and lifts me with it. "Turn over. You need to see what's coming. See me."

With the help of his foot, I turn to my back, my mind racing. I know what's coming, what his intentions are. First, he'll rape me. Then, he'll kill me. My whole body quivers in fear. I don't want him to touch me. I don't want to die. My life hasn't been easy, but every part of me wants to live. To build a relationship with Jonas. To have a friendship with Chaundra. To paint. To be an aunt to Cyle's kids. To be a mom someday, maybe.

Thoughts race through my mind. He cuts the binding on my hands and feet and removes my pants. This catches me off guard. What's he thinking? Sure, it will be easier to rape me without my feet tied, but my hands? Does he want me to struggle, try to fight him off? Of course he does. He enjoys the fight. It empowers him, makes him feel strong, alive.

He's been wearing gloves up until this point, to ensure he doesn't leave fingerprints anywhere. Now, he carefully removes them, pulling one finger out at a time, staring at me while he does so. Staring isn't exactly the right word…boring a hole into my soul with his eyes is more like it. *Should I get up and try to run*? I'm naked, it's dark and I have no idea where I am. I scan the area around me but can only see the outline of trees against the night sky, the stars, a crescent moon, and Matthew. I try to sit up and he kicks me in the chest, back to the ground. The kick knocks the wind out of me. I clutch my throat and try to catch a breath. Fear pulses through me with each beat of my heart. He presses his foot back on top of me to keep me where he wants me.

A sound slices through the night air and sends chills down my spine. His zipper. I'm frantic, digging the ground, trying to get out from under him. He presses harder. My ribs feel like they are snapping, boring into my lungs making it impossible to breathe.

"You're gonna like this. Me inside of you. Consuming you," another laugh. He removes his foot and lowers himself onto me.

"Please Matthew, don't. You don't have to do this. I see you. I see you. I see you," I chant, forcing myself to look into his eyes as his face lowers towards mine. He's on top of me, his erection resting against my stomach. There's a glimmer in his eye, enjoying my fear as he starts to grind against me. I want to turn away. I don't want to watch the pleasure in his eyes as he takes my virginity. I remember his ecstasy when he realized that Hailey was a virgin. His hands start to close around my throat, and I think of Mallory, choked over and over again, to the brink of death and back. Her face fills my mind with the growing pressure around my neck. All of their faces consume me as my eyes start to lose focus with the lack of oxygen. *Mallory. Hailey. Amber. Olivia. Alexis.* Then, as blackness envelopes me, the people I love fill my mind. *Cyle. Chaundra. Jonas. Ophelia.*

He loosens his grip before I blackout and draws back, ready to penetrate me. He's right there, working against my tightness. Hot tears stream down my cheeks. I brace myself for what's to come.

Colors overtake me—purple flash, yellow flash, red, blue. The colors devour me, along with them, the memories. I reach up my hands and press them against his chest, pushing with all my strength. Another lightning flash, stronger than the first one. It consumes me, him, the woods, the night, the world. A flash so strong and powerful that I feel parts of me leaving with it. Parts of me flow into him, instead of him into me.

The pain of a broken arm as a five-year-old.

The devastation of my parents always seeing me as a freak.

Polly's emotional and physical pain as she was raped by her stepfather. Her same pain as she ended her life.

The horror of having someone else invade your soul.

The heartbreak over losing the person you love most in the world.

The completeness I felt at believing I had a child and then the heartbreak at never being able to touch, hold, and love a real live daughter.

Each woman's pain and terror.

The intense cravings for cigarettes.

Pain, heartbreak, terror, fear—none of it mine, yet all of it parts of me. Faces fill the lightning...my mom, my dad, Polly, Cyle, Mallory, Hailey, Amber, Olivia, Alexis, Aiden, Chaundra, Jonas. The lightning burns, but I can't pull away. I am stuck to him, like a magnet. All of me pours into him. I am losing myself to him, to this flash. Instead of becoming him, he is taking parts of me. Parts that I have acquired from so many others throughout the years.

Finally, I can take no more—I have nothing left to give him. I am drained. Empty. I drop my hands and fall back to the ground, ready to face my fate. The night swallows me, pulling me away from everything I was, I am, and I will be.

As I drift away from consciousness, I hear Matthew screaming out in pain, an inhuman wail fills the night air. Floating in and out of this world, I hear some of what he's saying. I can't make sense of it. Just screams and words, singing me a lullaby.

"Go away. Leave me alone. You're dead! You're dead," he wails. "I killed you. I watched you die." But I'm not dead. I still feel the cold ground underneath my naked body, the rough earth digging into my back, my legs.

I force open one swollen, sore eye enough to see him batting at the air around him, fighting off invisible predators.

"You're not real! I killed you. I watched you die." Another scream from him as though he's being attacked by unseen forces. "I don't want you to see me anymore. I don't want you to see me."

My eyes are too heavy. I no longer try to force them open. I am going to die in this field, I know it. I am no different than the others. This will be my final resting place because I don't have the strength or the will to fight anymore. He stole that from me.

Matthew's screams grow more distant. I'm not sure if I'm slipping away or he's running away. Maybe it's a bit of both.

I say a prayer, hoping that I'm the last one—Matthew's last victim.

CHAPTER 24

I wake up in the hospital covered in tubes and wires. My whole body aches. My eyes are so heavy, it's hard to open them. I finally do and squint against the bright fluorescent lights.

"Let me turn those off," a voice says. As my vision comes into focus, I see Ophelia flipping the lights off.

I try to speak but nothing will come out other than a raspy whisper. "Don't try to talk. You've had some damage to your throat and it's best if you don't strain at all," Ophelia says and hands a notepad and pencil to me. "You can use this, though."

I have so many things I want to ask but don't know where to begin. I'm too tired to write complete sentences...I write five questions. *Where? How? Matthew? Cyle? How long?* Those should cover the burning questions.

"You're back in Chandlersville Memorial. You've been here for four days now. I went to your apartment for our meeting and could tell something was wrong because your front door was open a crack. I let myself in and I could see there had been a struggle. I called Chaundra and we figured out that either Jonas or Matthew had you. Later that night, Lily told Chaundra that you were in the woods and hurt. We got together a small search party and started looking immediately. At

Chaundra's urging the police joined the search the next day. One of the searchers, a man named Carl, found you."

Carl. His fatherly face fills my mind. I point to Matthew's name. "His body was found in the Holcomb River two days after we found you. The police believe he jumped off a bridge. That it was suicide."

I point to Cyle's name.

"Do you see him here?" Ophelia asks.

What a strange question. I look around the room and shake my head. I raise my eyebrows to indicate that I need her to further explain.

"You need to get some rest. We'll talk about Cyle later. He's not here right now, though," she says. "Chaundra and the kids and Jonas have been by to visit. We've been taking shifts to make sure someone's always with you. I called your parents to let them know you're here. I'm not sure if they're coming or not." My mouth falls open in disbelief. *She called my parents?* "Tessa, we weren't sure you were going to pull through or I wouldn't have called them. You were severely dehydrated and have several areas of frostbite. Along with the laryngeal trauma, a couple of broken ribs, and a concussion…you were in bad shape. They did a lot of testing to make sure you didn't have any other internal damage."

My eyes fill with tears. The fact that she called my parents feels like such a betrayal. I hope they don't show up. I can't deal with all of the emotions of seeing them right now. I hand the paper and pen back to her and lay back against the bed. I'm so tired. And I feel so empty. I remember bits and pieces of the struggle with Matthew. The thing that's most ingrained in my memory is the lightning flash, feeling parts of me pour into him. I will figure all of that out later. Right now, I need to sleep.

I WAKE up sometime later to Lily's voice. A smile spreads across my face before I even open my eyes. Chaundra, Liam, and Lily are here.

"Hi there, sleepyhead," Chaundra says. "It's good to see those eyes of yours."

I start to talk…again, a raspy whisper is all I can muster.

"Ahhh…no talking," she says and hands me a notepad. Lily comes over to the side of my bed and stands on her tiptoes to see me. I rub her head and tears fill my eyes. Were it not for her and her vision, I'd be dead.

"Look Mama, colors bye bye," Lily says. "Just shiny."

"I know sweetie. Just silver," Chaundra says.

I scribble *Huh?* across the paper.

"Your aura has changed. It's no longer a rainbow. It's all silver."

What does that mean? I write.

"It means something happened out there in the woods with Matthew to change your colors."

I nod and write *So much happened. Have to tell you.*

"You can tell me later. I don't want to wear you out right now, so we can just entertain you with stories. Can't we kids?"

Liam tells me about his holiday party at school and lists off one by one all of the items he's hoping Santa brings. Lily shows me her princess coloring book and all of the pictures she's colored. Chaundra tells stories, as only she can, about the kids and their antics over the past couple of days. It's all lighthearted and I let out a raspy laugh several times. Finally, I grab the paper and write *Where's Aiden?*

Chaundra looks at me and tears fill her eyes. "You don't see him?" *What is it with these people asking me such stupid questions?* I look around and shake my head.

"He's…he's gone, honey. He died about a year ago. He was hit by a car while riding his bike down the street." Chaundra says in a whisper, as tears fill her eyes.

He's gone? Died a year ago? What the hell? No, he didn't. He was here just a few days ago, painting, cuddling with me, letting Lily follow behind him.

"Right there. Aiden right there," Lily says pointing. "See him?"

I look to where she's pointing and see nothing other than a light gray wall. I shake my head. *What in the world is going on?*

Chaundra must see my confusion. "I know you're confused. How about we pick this discussion back up when you feel better?"

I write *NOW!* on the paper.

Chaundra takes a deep breath, seemingly trying to compose herself. "Since Aiden died, two people have been able to see him. You and Lily. I never said anything because I know that he was very real to both of you, could talk, cuddle, laugh. To be honest, I like that he's still around even if I can't see him. It makes it hurt a little less."

Why can't I see him now? I ask even though there are a million other questions swarming around in my head.

"I'm not sure. Lily, honey. Is Aiden here?" Chaundra says.

"Yes, silly Mommy. Right here," she says and puts her arm out around air. "Aiden loves Lily. And Mommy. And Liam."

I start writing out some of the questions because it feels like my head is going to explode. *What about the day Cyle and I came over? Aiden let us in. We both talked to him, not just me.*

Chaundra clears her throat and takes my hand. "Can we please talk about all of this later? You've been through so much. I don't know that you can take anymore right now. Please."

No NOW! I write.

Her eyes plead with me, and she wraps her arms around herself. She really doesn't want to have this discussion. She turns on the TV to Disney channel and tells both kids to watch so we can talk. She scoots her chair close to the bed and takes my hand again. I brace myself for a flash, but there is none.

"Yes, Cyle could see Aiden, too. You're right. What I saw when I came downstairs, though, is you sitting alone on my couch, talking to yourself or someone I couldn't see. I was a bit bothered by the fact that you let yourself in until Lily said Aiden opened the door. It was then that I knew you shared Lily's gift…you see people that aren't still with us in the physical form."

I need to be able to talk. I can't comprehend what she's saying. She saw me alone on the couch talking to myself? I was talking to Cyle. Why couldn't she see Cyle? And I can see dead people? What the hell? What does that even mean?

I pick up the pencil to write more and then the truth hits me like a barreling freight train cutting straight through me. The truth that I have denied, buried, explained away.

I flash back to a day a little over five years ago, one of the worst days of my life. The day I lost the only person in the world that genuinely believed in me…my brother. The day Cyle died.

I knew ahead of time that he was going to die. A yellow flash, I saw into his future. My dad chartered a fishing boat and took the boys out to the open sea for a day-long expedition. I begged my dad and mom to please change the date of the trip, to not let Cyle go with them. I knew a storm would blow up and catch them off guard. I saw the rough waves, the boat rocking uncontrollably, Cyle going overboard. I knew that trip would kill him. Like always, my parents thought I was being dramatic and crazy so of course they didn't listen. I talked to Cyle about it, too. I pleaded with him to stay home. He said that if it was his time to go, it was his time to go.

I think he knew he couldn't change his destiny. But I believe he would have changed his fate had the trip been cancelled, had he just decided to stay home instead. No one would listen to me. Not Chris, not Cory, not Dad, not Mom. Cyle listened, but didn't alter his choice to go, believing firmly that our time to die is pre-destined. He believed that he would've been hit by a car or something else if he didn't die on the fishing trip. I think he knew that my flash was correct. He left a long letter for Tasha, Hunter, and his unborn daughter, Harper.

My heart breaks anew at the realization that he never got to hold his baby girl. His beautiful daughter. He left a letter for me saying how much he loved me and that he believed in me. Now, I remember his funeral. Me crying, inconsolable, standing next to his white casket with flowers everywhere—the casket that Chaundra referenced in her vision when we touched. I had assumed she was talking about Mallory. But it was Cyle. I remember packing up whatever I could fit in my car and leaving my parent's home as soon as the graveside service was over. I blamed them all for Cyle's death. For not believing me. For not doing everything in their power to make sure the one person I truly loved in this world was safe and protected.

I drove with no destination in mind. I knew this was where I was supposed to be when I drove through the center of town and saw Cyle standing on a sidewalk, leaning against a lamp post, waving at me. He was gone by the time I could park and get to him. That was the first time I saw him after he died. Somehow, my brain convinced me that he was still alive. That I really had some kind of mental breakdown, convincing me that he'd died. I called his cell phone and he answered. I talked to my supposedly dead brother that day and convinced myself that he was alive. Any other possibility was out of the question. It was never considered. I've heard through my years of counseling that DENIAL stands for *Don't Even kNow I Am Lying*. I guess that my denial served me well. Throughout the years, I clung to the truth that I could still see Cyle, talk to him, hear about his family. To me, he was alive. The accident, the funeral, my heartbreak was buried deep within —so deep, I couldn't even see it anymore.

Ophelia always pressed me to talk about why I finally decided to leave my parent's home. I could never pinpoint my exact breaking point, only talking in non-specifics about how my parents never believed me, thought I was a freak, wanted to lock me away…all the usual. Never once did I talk about Cyle's death. I did talk about Cyle as a living, breathing human being that I assumed had met and spoken with Ophelia. Did she know I could still see him, or did she think I was insane with hallucinations of my dead brother?

My head throbs, like it might burst. My heart shatters into a million tiny slivers. *Cyle is dead.* Why can't I see him anymore? Where did he go? I can't take it anymore and shout, in the loudest voice I can muster. "Cyle!" I tremble as tears stream down my cheeks. I am lost in the sea of my memories until I feel Lily crawl into bed with me. She curls up next to me. I wrap my arm around her and pull her close.

"Tessa no sad," she says. "Cyle here."

Chaundra speaks for me. "Where, Lily? Where's Cyle?"

Lily points to the other side of my bed. "There. Holding Tessa's hand. He says no be sad."

I look over to where she's pointing. I only see the bed rail with the cool gray wall behind it. No Cyle. I close my eyes and try to feel his hand holding mine. I feel nothing. I try to muster up the strength to imagine it, to feel his presence but instead all I feel is air. No Cyle. I've lost him somehow. Lost him forever.

CHAPTER 25

Ophelia comes in later in the afternoon to relieve Chaundra from her "shift" with me. Chaundra ended up calling the nurse and having them give me something to calm me down because I was hysterical. My head was swarming with memories of all of the interactions I'd had with Cyle over the past six years. He was alive to me. I *saw* him. I *touched* him. I *talked to* him. He talked to me. Was the ability to see dead people, like Cyle and Aiden, something I picked up in a flash along the way? If so, where did my ability go? Is anyone else in my life not really alive when I thought they are?

I rouse when I hear Ophelia and Chaundra whispering—about my meltdown, I'm sure. Chaundra and the kids give me a hug and tell me they will see me later. Again, all that touching and no flashes. Ophelia takes a seat next to the bed.

"So, I heard you've had a rough couple of hours," she says.

I nod, and tears fill my eyes. I write on the pad of paper *Did you know about Cyle? Why didn't you tell me?*

"It took me a while to figure it out, but yes, I knew. I did some research and found his obituary, so I pieced it all together," she says. "I didn't tell you because he was alive to you. That's all that matters. He was still there for you when you needed him."

Where did he go? Why can't I see him?

"Now that, I'm not sure about. Chaundra said Lily can still see him, so my guess is that he's right here. Why you can no longer see him, I can't explain," Ophelia says.

Another lightning flash with Matthew. I need to tell you about it. I think that's why.

"Maybe we should wait on that until you can talk," she suggests.

I need to know now. I can't wait.

"If you're up to it, you can write it. I know your voice isn't going to hold out long enough to process everything that happened to you with Matthew. That was quite an ordeal with lots to tell, I'm sure."

I'll write. And for the next hour, that is what I do. I press through the cramp in my hand and fill page after page after page of my experience with Matthew in the woods, ending with the lightning flash. I describe to the best of my ability what I felt happening when I touched him—parts of me leaving, going into him. I write about the images that filled my mind, the colors, the memories. As I write, everything clicks into place. I end my writing with my conclusion: *I dumped all the parts of me that I've gained through flashes into Matthew. All of them, including my ability to see Cyle.*

As I write the last sentence, everything that I remember about that night with Matthew, after the flash, makes sense. He wasn't talking to me when he was yelling about me being dead. I gave him my ability to see dead people. The "air" I saw him swatting was *them*. The women he murdered were surrounding him.

I finish and hand the papers to Ophelia, slumping back against the bed and closing my eyes. The exhaustion is almost painful. I know that what I wrote is the truth. Maybe I even dumped the ability to have flashes into him since I've had none since the incident. I don't know how it worked, or why, but for some reason it did. I don't know what any of this means for me, for my identity, for my future. I've wanted to get rid of the flashes my entire life, for as long as I can remember. I've struggled to figure out who I am without all of the pieces I've acquired from others. I've questioned who I really am. I guess, if my theory is correct, I'll have the chance to find out.

I feel so alone, so broken now that I don't have Cyle. It helps to know that Lily still sees him. But as hard as I try to feel his presence, I feel nothing. Just alone and empty. A tear slides past my still closed eyelid down my cheek, leaving a trail of hotness as it falls. I want to disappear. Perhaps, the person I thought I was, already has.

Papers rustle and Ophelia clears her throat. "Tessa?" she says. I open my eyes and look towards her. "There's so much here we need to talk about. First, let me say, I'm so sorry you had to go through all of that. That must have been one of the scariest experiences of your life."

I want to tell her she is wrong. That position would be taken by the way I am feeling now. Losing Cyle…again. Feeling so alone in this world.

She continues. "We'll work through all of this in our sessions, I promise, but I kind of want to jump to the end. To what you think happened. You say you feel like you dumped all the parts into him that you've gained from the flashes over the years. Can we test that theory?"

I nod. The first thing she does is reaches out and grabs my hand, holding it tightly.

"Anything?" She asks.

By anything, I assume she means a flash. I shake my head.

"Have you had any flashes since the incident?" Another shake of my head.

"Okay," she says and hands me the pad of paper and pencil. "I want you to write the following sentence for me in French…*I can't wait to get out of this hospital and be able to sleep in my own bed.*"

I pick up the pencil. I write *Je* but then freeze. This was a task I could've completed with ease before. Now, beyond knowing how to write I, I'm drawing a complete blank. I no longer know French.

I can't, I write instead.

"Interesting. What about smoking? Any desire for a cigarette?"

The thought of a cigarette sounds repulsive to me and actually turns my stomach. I emphatically shake my head.

"Last one. I want you to close your eyes and think about the women as I say their names. First, Mallory," she says and goes silent giving me time to process. She then says the names of the other four with a long pause after each.

When I open my eyes, tears fall freely down my cheeks. I grab the paper and pencil.

I only feel sad. For them. For their families. No heartbreak over losing Mallory. No desire to have them see me. No desire to kill. No pleasure at the memories of their deaths. Those feelings all seem so distant. I write.

Ophelia sits back and smiles. "Well, I'd say this is an answered prayer. I think your theory about what happened is correct. You're fully and only you, for the first time in maybe forever."

I wish I could match her smile, her happiness. Part of me is glad that all of the sick, crazy thoughts and feelings I got from Matthew are gone. But mostly I'm full of questions.

Who am I now? What will be different about me? How do I even figure out who I really am? Will I like the person I find? What will I do without Cyle? How can I go on and figure all of this out without him to help me? The thoughts tumble around, crashing into each other. I'm too tired to talk, write, or think anymore. I just want to sleep.

I grab the pad of paper and write. *Tired. Overwhelmed. Please tell the nurse I need something.* Ophelia pushes the nurse's call button and tells her that I need medicine to help me sleep. Within minutes, they've given me a cocktail to take me away from all of these questions. From the new me.

I WAKE UP LATER—I have no idea how much later—to Jonas sitting in the chair next to the bed watching me sleep. "Hey there, sunshine!" He says as soon as I open my eyes. "That's the first time I've seen those beautiful eyes since you've been here."

I give him a slight smile and hate that he's seeing me here, such a complete and utter mess, with breath so rancid, I'm sure he can smell it from where he's sitting. I attempt a hello and my voice comes out a little closer to its normal tone.

"I've been given strict instructions that you are not to speak. Got it?"

I roll my eyes and nod. I grab the pencil and paper. *Thanks for being here. Sorry about all of this. Sorry you have to see me looking so lovely.*

He reads it and laughs. "You are a sight. But still beautiful to me. And I wouldn't leave your side if your other two bodyguards didn't make me."

I'm pleased to realize that my attraction to Jonas was not acquired from anyone. That one's all me because I still find him incredibly, overwhelmingly, *jump his bones now* kind of attractive. I smile at the thought.

"What's so funny?" He asks and grabs my hand.

I have so much to tell you. To explain to you. Stuff that's best if you hear it straight from the horse's mouth. Not through writing.

He grabs my hand and looks at me, a more serious expression now on his face. "We've got plenty of time. I'm not going anywhere."

Even though I'm no longer psychic, I know he means it. We have plenty of time for me to figure out who I am, and possibly who we can be together. The door to my room opens and Chaundra, Lily, and Liam's laughter breaks our moment. Lily runs over to the bed and kisses my hand.

"Hi Tessa and Jonas," she says in her sing-songy voice and then waves towards the corner. "Hi Cyle!"

Maybe I won't have to be alone after all.

EPILOGUE

The last year has been a roller coaster ride of emotions, trying to figure out my life without the flashes, without Cyle, and without all of the bits and pieces of other people defining who I am. With Ophelia's help, I've made a lot of progress. I'm nowhere near finished with all the hard work I must do, but I'm getting there one day, one step at a time.

It's been quite interesting figuring out who I am and who I'm not. I've discovered that I'm naturally an extrovert. I used to lock myself away from the world to protect myself but really, truly I love people. For the first time in my life, I have a job and earn my own money.

I'm the lead teacher for a class of twenty-two three-year olds at Little Learners pre-school here in Chandlersville. I love feeling like I have a purpose, somewhere to go each day, and the impact that I have over all of these little people, who keep me laughing. I've also joined a book club, signed up for a photography class at Cardell, and have even enrolled in cooking classes with Chaundra. I've joined a gym and go daily to workout. I discovered that I absolutely hate jogging. I swore off it after the first week of trying to get back into the routine and realizing that there was nothing fun or rewarding about it. The only thing it gave me was the inability to breathe. It's also helpful that for the first time since I was in preschool and "broke" my arm, I can lift and workout without pain.

I've also discovered that I'm actually a morning person. The time I feel most alive and productive is from five thirty to eight thirty in the morning. *Ha! Who would've thought?* It's Jonas' favorite thing to tease me about since I'm up before he is now. I make sure to text him often as my form of payback for all of his early morning texts in the beginning of our relationship.

Speaking of Jonas…we're still seeing each other and getting serious. The subject of marriage has come up a couple of times in the past few weeks. We're both going to give it more time, but I can see spending the rest of my life with him and making lots of babies (none of whom will have a name that begins with a 'C'). I tried to explain everything to him, about my flashes and what happened to me. I don't think he really, truly gets it, but he does believe what I tell him, even though most of it sounds completely unbelievable, even to me. He says I'm the most intriguing woman he's ever met. I'm not sure if that's a positive or negative, but I'll take it. It beats so many of the other labels I've had over the years. Intriguing is one I can live with.

Chaundra is the best friend I was never able to have growing up. We laugh together, cry together, and just act plain old goofy together. I'm with her and the kids several times each week, having adventures, laughing, living, loving. On the bleakest days, she and the kids are my lifeline. One hug from Lily is usually all it takes to turn a depressing day into one where I can see a tiny glimmer of hope. I love those kids. Lily said Aiden is still with us everywhere we go, joining right along with our silly antics and adventures. Lily almost always comments on my "colors" when she sees me. I assume she's talking about my aura, although several times she's mentioned that my rainbow will be back. But, she shuts down every time I press her further about it, refusing to give me any more information about what she sees in my future.

I still meet with Ophelia at least twice a month. My life has gotten so busy and full that it seems like all I need. The main point of discussion in most of our sessions now is trying to work through my family issues (*blech*), the loss of Cyle, and figuring out who the new me is. I tried to reach out to my parents several months ago, to re-gain some kind of relationship with them. It became apparent in only two conversations that moving beyond all of the hurtful things in our past may never happen. They can't let go of the old me and their opinions of that person. I can't live with the negativity. So, it seems right now we're at an impasse. I hope that we can mend things before my parents pass away. If not, though, I will be okay.

Last month, I went to stay with Tasha and the kids for a week. It was the closest I've felt to Cyle since he disappeared after I lost the ability to see him. I see him in Harper's face, her smile. I hear his voice come out of Hunter's mouth—he's got his dad's same kind heart and gentle spirit. He's a great big brother to Harper. Not that she fully understood it, but Tasha knew that I was able to still see Cyle. She never had the heart to bust through my denial to tell me he was gone. The kids are coming to stay with me next month. I'm so excited to be able to spoil them rotten and do some of the things with them that Cyle will never have the chance to do. Although, I have a feeling he'll be right there with us, every step of the way.

Sometimes I can still feel Cyle's presence, late at night as I'm trying to drift off to sleep. I can almost hear his voice telling me how proud he is of me for who I've become, for all I've survived. I can almost feel his kiss on my cheek as I drift off. The sadness of losing him is sometimes unbearable. I miss him so much. Some days, I would give anything to have one more day to see him, talk to him, believe he's alive. But then I remind myself that he is here, even though I can't see him. I'm thankful that my flashes gave me six extra years with my brother after his death—that's more than most people would get. I still laugh when I realize how much Cyle was still trying to mend the relationship with my parents and I even from beyond the grave. Just like him, the middle child, always trying to fix everything. He's still my hero. Just my invisible one—my own personal guardian angel.

Some things about me haven't changed. I can still paint, which was a huge relief to discover. My paintings have changed somewhat and become less abstract, more realistic. They're still colorful. I think so much of my being was surrounded by color that it will take decades to get it all out of me through painting. I actually presented some of my work in the Cardell Art Gallery and sold several of my pieces for more money than I ever could've dreamed of making from something that is my coping mechanism, my hobby. Everyone's favorite pieces were those that I did during my week of madness, those of the women who died at Matthew's hand. I plan to stick with my painting and have started a website to sell more pieces. If my work can touch someone's heart, speak to them, give them a moment's solace as they've done for me, then I want them to be available. My main goal in life is to help others as so many have helped me along the way. Painting is my way to do that.

I also still love coffee. And wine. And food. That hasn't changed. Jonas teases me all the time that I'm the one woman who can eat him under the table. Thus, my need for a gym membership.

The memory box Cyle gave me so many years ago sits on the top shelf of my closet. I haven't had to put anything in there for over a year. Someday, I will get it down and look through all of the parts of me that I put in there over the years. I'm not ready to do that yet. Someday, though. And I know Cyle will be right there next to me while I do it.

I am Tessa. I'm still discovering what that means, who I really am. I do believe Cyle was right. For whatever reason, the flashes were a gift, not a curse. They were horrible, life-altering, confusing...but I survived. And, I helped bring a killer to justice. I know that he killed himself because he couldn't take living with all I dumped in him. What I survived with for a lifetime, he couldn't bear for forty-eight hours. It shows me how strong of a person I really am.

I am nowhere near what I'd call normal. But, for the first time in my life, I am me. And, for the most part, I like who I am.

I can't wait to see who I become.

The highly anticipated sequel to *Bits & Pieces*, the psychological thriller that kept readers up at night.

For the past five years, Tessa has lived a normal life, the kind she always dreamed of. One without her gift and the flashes that tormented her for as long as she can remember.

All of that changes on a winter's day when, out of nowhere, the flashes return. Only this *time they're different.*

Along with the flashes, Tessa makes a gruesome discovery on her property. Images haunt her. Voices from beyond the grave plead for her help. She is thrust into a quest to find and stop a murderer. Time is running out.

Tessa scrambles to fit all the pieces and parts of this hideous puzzle together before someone she loves becomes the next victim.

***Pieces & Parts* is a spine-tingling psychological thriller with a touch of the supernatural that will keep you guessing and turning the pages until its chilling end.**

ALSO BY DAWN HOSMER

~

Two families, forever linked by tragedy.

Ruby Dunkin is in an abusive marriage. Her best efforts aren't enough to shield her two children from an abusive father whose cruelty knows no bounds. Their volatile situation ends in tragedy when Ruby's eldest son, Billy is torn away from everything he loves. Consumed by hatred and self-loathing Billy becomes the thing he hates the most— his father.

Chelsea Wyatt, a senior in high school, goes missing after work one night, never to return. Her parents are devastated, only knowing this kind of tragedy from the news. Crimes like this are unheard of in their quiet, midwestern town. Consumed by the tragic fate of their friend, family member and neighbor, their lives and futures are forever altered.

For over eighteen years, no one knows the connection between Ruby Dunkin and Chelsea Wyatt. A journey through time reveals the common thread stitching their heartbreak together. Yesterday echoes throughout each character's life as they decide how, and if, they will break the chains of the past.

Will they continue to leave a legacy of pain and loss for future generations? Will they break the cycles of abuse that have destroyed so many lives?

~

My name is Mackenzie Bartholomew, or at least it was. I'm staring at my dead body, lying in a casket. I was a healthy, thirty-nine-year-old, mother of three.

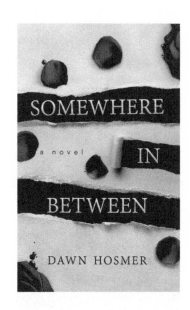

I have so many questions but very few answers. Was I murdered? Did I commit suicide? I don't know if I'm in some sort of purgatory or if I've gone straight to hell.

I'm stuck somewhere in between life and death, forced to travel back in time to relive moments from my past, ones I'd rather forget. I'm desperate to piece together the details surrounding my death. If I don't, I fear my soul will never find rest.

Chock full of family drama, secrets, betrayal, and lies, ***Somewhere in Between*** is a Psychological Thriller with wicked twists that will keep you hooked until the last page.

Mosaic is a collection of very short stories, ranging from scary pieces to those full of hope. Through these stories, I hope to provide glimpses into what it means to be human. Each of us is made up of many different pieces that, when fit together, make a beautiful, messy whole. Those tiny pieces in and of themselves don't mean much and are easily overlooked. But, when we put them all together, a full picture of what it means to be human starts to form.

ACKNOWLEDGMENTS

Writing often feels like a solitary journey. Authors spend many hours in isolation plotting, planning, writing, editing and thinking about their books. However, *Bits & Pieces* would not have been possible without the support of so many people in my life. While space does not allow me to list everyone who has helped me on my path, there are a few that I need to mention.

I would like to start by thanking my husband, Steve. You have believed in me every step of the way on this writing journey, without fail. You have listened to me talk about my characters like they are actual people. You've listened to me cry and scream when I received yet another rejection. You encouraged me to keep writing and trying even when I felt like giving up. Also, thank you for the idea behind Tessa and her abilities—*Bits & Pieces* would not exist without your suggestion, your love, and your support.

A huge thank you to my children—Gabriel, Dominic, Jesi and Krystyna. I am so proud of all of you. You are four of the most wonderful people on this planet. The four of you inspire me daily and motivate me to be the best version of myself. You fill me with love, laughter, and joy every single day. You've made my life complete.

Thank you to my mom. You have always been my biggest cheer-leader in life and have loved me unconditionally. You have shown me what it means to overcome hardship and the value of perseverance. You are not only my mother, but one of my best friends. I am so grateful for you.

Thank you to everyone at Ant Colony Press for initially bringing *Bits & Pieces* into the world. To Sarah Bredeman for believing in my work and for the outstanding job you did with edits—helping *Bits & Pieces* to become the best it could be. Also, thanks to Jordan Belcher for the amazing initial cover design. In addition, I have so much gratitude for Gestalt Media for publishing the 2nd edition of Bits & Pieces, especially Jason and Anna Stokes. You two have been a blessing, and I'm so glad I had the opportunity to partner with you. I'm even more glad to call you both friends.

Also, thank you to everyone who has read *Bits & Pieces* so far. Each of you has helped give me the courage and confidence to take this giant leap into self-publishing. In publishing this 3rd edition, a huge thank you to Rebecca Yelland for your help with formatting, my website, graphics, and for basically jumping in to help me every time I panic (which is often). Also, I'm so grateful to Carol Beth Anderson who has been instrumental in providing guidance for this new journey into self-publishing. You both are godsends.

I have had many friends who have supported me throughout my journey. Thank you to Jen Yan for being a beta reader. I appreciate your willingness to read and provide feedback, as well as your constant words of encouragement and your friendship. Thank you to Kate Minear Sorenson for not only your friendship but for my author photo as well. You are a talented artist, and I am so thankful that you used your skills to help me. You are a true gem. Gratitude to Jan Watts for many decades of friendship. You have always encouraged me and introduced me to many of my favorite things in life. You have always been a mentor to me—my life would not be complete without you in it. Thank you to Rachel Hopmoen for twenty years of friendship and for helping me edit the first part of my novel to improve the flow. Also, many thanks for encouraging me to join Twitter to help with my writing career. I've had lots of big ideas over the years, and you always jump right in with me and help me believe in the possibility of them coming true.

Also, much gratitude to the Writer's Community on Twitter and the Booktok community on Tiktok. I have made some invaluable friendships through both and have learned so much about writing since joining. You have made me laugh, cry, and persevere. Mostly, you made me realize I'm not alone in this crazy writing journey. Your kind comments about my writing have helped give me the courage to keep putting my words out into the world.

My sincere thanks to every friend or family member that has offered words of encouragement, love, and support along the way. I can't list everyone individually but know that your kindness has been what's kept me going.

And most of all, thank you to God, who has provided me with more blessings than I can count.

Indie Authors rely on reviews to help spread the word about our work. Please take a moment of your time to leave a review on Amazon, Bookbub, and/or Goodreads. Thank you!

ABOUT THE AUTHOR

Dawn Hosmer is the author of psychological thrillers and suspense. She is a lifelong Ohioan. She received her degree in Sociology and spent her career in Social Work; however, writing has always been her passion. She is a wife and the mother of four amazing children. In addition to listening to true crime podcasts, drinking coffee, and coloring, Dawn is busy working on her next novel.

For more information, visit www.dawnhosmer.com or follow her on Twitter @dawnhosmer7, Instagram @dawnh71, Tiktok @dawn_hosmer, or Facebook. Dawn can also be found on Goodreads and Bookbub.